THE WOLF BANE

Societas Aenigmatum

Book 1

SADHBH FROST

Fungous Anthropoid Productions

The characters and events portrayed in this book are fictitious. Any similarity to real persons, living or dead, would be really disturbing but coincidental and not intended by the author.

Cover design by Wendi Strang-Frost

ISBN: 979-8-9958186-2-5

First Print Edition: May 2026

For Wendi,
who supports all of my nonsense

Contents

Prologue: Livinia Monroe

She held aloft the hourglass that she'd filled with her life's blood. The ritual was nearly complete. All that she had to do was smash this on the consecrated altar, and her legacy would be assured. The lives of everyone associated with the Society for Preternatural Investigations, in this branch and all the others, had amounted to nothing. Extra-dimensional incursion continued unchallenged. The beings that hid at the edges of human civilization had not been assimilated into society. All she could hope now was that the knowledge they'd accumulated would be useful to future generations.

She would watch over the books and papers. They would grow under her care, and she'd familiarize herself with their contents. This was the only purpose left to her, and she would sacrifice her life to achieve it. She brought her hand down sharply, smashing the hourglass and spilling her blood on the sigil she'd drawn. The force of the spell tore her body apart, but she felt no pain. Her mind had already been ejected into an empty realm.

Livinia Monroe, the person, was no more. She'd expected to become a spirit inhabiting the library, but what remained of her didn't seem to be anywhere. There wasn't even darkness.

Without a body there could be no senses, not as she understood them, and she saw nothing—felt nothing. She wondered how she would interact with the world.

Then the world returned. All of it, all at once. She was lost in a barrage of shifting experiences, none lingering long enough to identify. Images, feelings, thoughts—all coming too quickly to process as more than a constant assault on her mind. Battered by the stream of moments, she careened through centuries without processing anything.

She was outside of time, and thus it was impossible to know how long she spent in this torrent of experiences. Eventually she held onto a scene for a split second. It was not long enough to catch anything identifiable, but it created a noticeable interruption in the chaos. She tried to recreate that brief reprieve but had no idea how it had happened. It was hard to form thoughts in the midst of everything happening all at once. After focusing her thoughts, she realized that everything was the very problem. Her mind was processing hundreds of thousands of years, all of which had occurred in the instant of her spell's conclusion.

The book that had described the ritual had cautioned that spirits could only experience events through recollections, unable to use their memories to apply knowledge out of linear sequence. This sensory torrent must be her future memories expanding too rapidly for her to filter. She wondered when she'd start remembering what had happened and what she'd done. What she'd learned. Who she'd met.

She could not cry, but she felt sad. She'd chosen to risk this, in part, because all who knew her well were gone. Some still lived, though they'd drifted away after the end of the Society. Only one remained in contact, but she was neither dead nor technically alive. Janice Altura wasn't a close friend, but she understood loneliness and lack of purpose. Livinia thought now that it would be nice to see her again.

For a heartbeat she saw Miss Altura, sitting carelessly on

the loveseat in the mansion's parlor. She—no, *it* now—wore a black dress, trimmed in lace, with black lace-up boots and long black velvet gloves. Its face was covered in white foundation, contrasting starkly against the rich red of its lips and the deep black of its heavy eyeshadow and long hair. Silver jewelry glittered from its pale hands, neck, ears, and waist. As ever, its face revealed no emotion.

"Dead gals are the cat's whiskers now," it said.

The moment was gone. Livinia didn't know when that had happened or what Janice had been talking about, but she felt glad that they had met again at least once. Given the nature of Janice's existence, they could have known each other for centuries.

The chaos of her experiences settled into another memory. She sat in the mansion's attic, crowded with disused furniture and boxes whose contents were long forgotten. There was a small candelabrum on a table next to her, and a book lay open in her hands. She knew it was an adventure story from the Noram Empire, which had collapsed over a thousand years earlier. Though her watching mind had never encountered Norashan, her mind at that time knew it well. She was reading the book aloud to Miss Altura, who lay unmoving on a nearby sofa. Though it appeared to simply be asleep, the Livinia of the experience knew it had been in this state for almost four hundred years. Neither quite alive nor fully dead, Miss Altura had always had periods of deep rest, and they'd increased in frequency and duration until it was uncertain whether it would ever wake up again.

The Livinia that read to her friend knew that she could navigate future memories to see how Miss Altura would fare, but she had long ago abandoned such self-indulgent queries. The futures were many, and finding one risked bringing it to fruition, a risk she had decided to stop taking long ago.

This attitude of her remembered self made her curious. Had something happened because of seeing the future? Had she been able to communicate what she'd seen out of historical order?

With a little more practice, she felt that she could navigate her memories. Perhaps she had best focus on finding the moment of the spell's casting and progress through time linearly for a while.

Part One

THE PHANTOM WOLF

CHAPTER ONE

The Package

The moving cell was horrible. The noise hurt my ears, and all the bouncing made me feel sick. My old cell had a bed where I could rest and a window to let in light. This was nothing but a dark metal box with no fresh air. When it finally stopped and the rumbling from the front ended, I was tired and sore. The doors opened, and I could see it was daylight. I didn't know what time of day it was, and everything was gray and cold, and I just wanted to crawl into my new cell and eat something.

The guards dragged me out and walked me up the outside of a long building. I went along quietly. They hadn't had to threaten or punish me since I was much smaller. Long before they'd started keeping my head shaved. They trusted me to do that myself now, and it felt natural to me. I couldn't remember why I'd cried when they'd cut off all my hair.

The air was different here. Less cold than at home, but not by a lot. It felt humid, and I thought it might rain tonight. Some guards said they could tell if rain was coming from the clouds, but I had no idea how. For me it was a smell and a feeling in the air. There was a hint of it now, but it wasn't strong enough to know for sure.

Dry orange and yellow papers skidded along the floor

outside, blown by the breeze. The guards had mentioned leaves falling again, and I wondered if that's what these were. I'd never seen one close up, but the colors seemed to match some of the trees I could see. They were really pretty before they fell.

The steps were a problem for me. There weren't any in my cell, and I'd never left it until they brought me to the moving cell. I did my best to keep up with them so they wouldn't get mad, but I had to watch my feet the whole way up. By the time we reached a flat surface again, I was able to put only one foot on a step like they did. I felt proud of learning it so quickly.

We walked past several doors and windows, and I looked at all of them. Everything else was too much. It scared me. There was no ceiling, and the walls were far away from each other. I didn't recognize most of it. I'd seen similar things in my dream wanderings but had avoided them because I'd smelled people. Doors and windows were familiar. It was nice to think there were cells behind each of them. There were so many next to each other that I wondered if this was a prison. Some of the guards watched shows on the screen at their station, and they liked it when people were put in prison cells. No one had ever told me what I'd done to be put in mine. Maybe someone told me when I was too young to remember it.

We met another guard, who stood outside of a cell. She stuck a card into the door and led us through. Back home, a guard would open my cell from the security desk to let the doctor in. I didn't have time to think about that, because this cell was unlike anything I'd ever seen.

It was large. My old one could fit in it twice. And it was filled with things. The floor was completely covered in a rug that felt a lot better than the cold floors I'd just been on. The cot was so large that I guessed there'd be other people in the cell with me. Probably not the guards. They liked to be on the other side of the door from me. There were a few lamps and small tables, and framed drawings on the wall. A large desk of some kind sat across from the bed. On top of it was a very large screen. I saw a door to another, smaller cell. That was probably for me. The guards would be stationed here.

I went straight to the cell in back as the guards looked over theirs. Mine was dark and small. There wasn't even a window. It had a good toilet and sink, but they took up most of the space. The rest was a strange bed. It looked to me like a large sink, complete with faucet and drain. There was a shower head above it. I didn't like the thought of sleeping there, but at least I could stay clean. There were a lot of towels, too, and I could use them to make it more comfortable.

I heard the guard come in, but I was surprised when a light came on above me. That would help when they shut me in. I turned and watched as he looked over the cell. He took most of the towels, a roll of toilet paper, and a small tool I didn't recognize. I followed to the doorway as he left and saw him go all the way outside. So much for making the bed nicer.

"You good for a while?" he asked the guard outside.

"I'll keep it quiet," she told him.

The other one who brought me in was gone. The one who'd let us in came inside and locked the door behind her. She picked something up from the desk and sat in a chair by the window. After examining the thing, she pointed it at the screen and squeezed it. The screen came on, showing people talking to each other in their own large chairs.

I stared at the screen. I'd heard shows before but never seen one. I couldn't tell where the people were. It seemed like a large empty room at first, but then suddenly the screen was filled with more people than I'd ever seen, sitting so close together that it was hard to make out their chairs. They didn't look as comfortable, but I was standing on a cold hard floor, so I guessed they were okay. Then the screen showed one of the people talking again, but this time all I could see was her head and upper body. What was happening? Guards had talked about filming, acting, and editing, so I knew this had all happened somewhere else and been put together, but I had no idea what to make of it changing so often.

The image shrank into a corner as the rest of the screen filled with long boxes of text. They'd never taught me how to read, so it was just a lot of white figures on a blue background. One line was bigger than the others, and it started moving down the screen. After it moved a few times I realized that the row had stayed put, but the size difference was moving through them all. I saw the guard squeezing the thing in her hand, so it had to be her doing. While I watched her, the sound from the screen changed, and a familiar voice replaced the others. Lieutenant Buster Grimes of the homicide unit. His image filled the whole screen now as he talked to the medical examiner.

I'd heard *Major Indictments* many times from my cell. It was strange seeing Grimes at last. He was older than I'd thought he sounded. The medical examiner was pretty, but what got my attention was the victim's body. I'd never seen a dead body, but the actor looked truly awful. It was honestly amazing.

"Get the fuck out here and sit on the bed where I can see you," the guard ordered.

I came out and crawled onto the bed. There were four pillows, and all of them were thick. I pushed on one, and my hands sank into it. Poking at the others had the same effect. On impulse, I started slapping them, enjoying the soft noise they made as my hands hit.

"Hey!"

I'd forgotten myself. The guard was angry. She'd granted me the privilege to come into her station, and I'd already screwed up. I stopped what I was doing immediately and made myself small. I squished my mouth and widened my eyes, letting her know I was sorry. Some of them didn't like it when I said I was sorry, but they all liked it when I looked "like a whipped puppy."

I quietly stacked the pillows and rested against them, watching *Major Indictments* with the guard. By the end of the second murder case, I'd learned how to follow the story. The images helped more than I'd expected, especially once I started to recognize the different places the actors moved between. The hardest thing to understand was how free they all were to move around. Some parts happened outside, and there were so many people just walking around. Were there really so few of us not allowed to leave our cells?

Would I be let out from my new cell sometimes? I hoped it would be bigger, like this one, with a screen for shows and a lot of soft pillows. I wouldn't even mind sharing it with a guard. The bed was certainly big enough. I thought about what it would be like to sleep next to this one, but like all the guards she didn't like to be near me. It would be awkward.

I'd gotten used to the sounds coming from outside. Even over the noise of the screen, I could hear a lot of what happened out there. Mostly it was people walking and talking loudly to each other, but every now and then there were rumbles that sounded like the moving cell. Other guards were coming or going.

Then there was something new. A cracking sound, followed by something landing on the floor outside. The guard noticed too, and she quickly crouched down. She looked scared, maybe because her gun seemed to be stuck. The last thing she'd said was for me to get on the bed, but I didn't figure she was going to complain if I hid. I rolled off on the side away from the window and slid quietly to the floor.

The window broke, and I saw the guard move toward the door. Something landed on the rug, and my heart shook at the sound it made. While I was still confused by that, someone came in. Everything was quieter now, but I could still kind of hear things. There were a few more cracks and something else fell. I recognized the sound of the door lock, then the door opening. I didn't think these people were my new guards, and I doubted they would be nice to me. The one who came in through the door saw me peeking over the bed. He sent the first one out and came closer to me.

He held a gun pointed at me, and all I could do was shake. I hadn't even done anything. I'd been good for years. Was this because the doctor had said I was getting long teeth? He was very worried about my eggs, which he accused me of losing. I didn't know how I was doing that, but I knew that these were important to my keepers. Maybe I'd lost too many.

The man stopped at the end of the bed, not looking at me.

"When I go into the bathroom, run!" he said. "Don't let anyone find you!"

With that, he went into my cell.

He did seem like a guard, so I followed his order. I hurried across the bed and jumped out the window. Living in a cell hadn't let me learn how to do that kind of thing, and I landed badly, but I got up and ran for the stairs. Shouts came from behind me as I hurried down the steps. My only experience with running had been in dreams, and there I had four legs. I made it down to the ground, but I slipped and fell the last few feet. My left foot hurt when I got back up, but I had to keep moving.

Ignoring the pain, I ran in the direction I faced. Cars almost hit me as I sped across streets. Thanks to Detective Grimes I knew what those looked like now. As I kept going, the pain in my ankle became less important. I felt like I could do this for a while longer if I had to, but I wanted to find a place to stop.

Look for a hole. One you can crawl into.

That seemed like a good idea, but I couldn't see anything likely. There had been boxes and barrels in the shows I'd just watched, and they'd been in the narrow spaces between buildings. Alleys, that was it. I ran a few more blocks before I started to see any of those. From there I ran as much as possible through these smaller streets. There wasn't anything large enough to climb into. I'd expected to find people living in small containers, but they weren't any where I passed through.

At last I saw a large building made of rocks that had large, blocky plants all around it. I thought I might be able to fit in between them, so I ran onto the grass. These boxy plants were very thick, though, and they were very close to each other and to the ground. There wasn't anywhere for me to hide here.

There were square holes next to the building, and there were windows in them. I crept over to take a look. Two of the three had crossed bars over them. One of those and the uncovered one had lights on in the cells behind the windows. I went to the dark window. There were leaves at the bottom of the hole, and it would be deep enough to hide me without my getting stuck down there. If only the bars weren't there.

I reached down to see if I could move them. They were heavy, but I found I could pull them out entirely. I slid them out partway and let myself down. The leaves crunched underneath me, making me afraid of guards hearing. I pulled the bars back in place and buried myself in the leaves. It was damp underneath them, but I was too tired to think much about that. My eyes closed, my breathing slowed, and I fell asleep. In my dreams I explored this new place, favoring my back left leg and searching for a den.

CHAPTER TWO

Elena Arana

Three bodies over two adjoining rooms and the walkway in between. All of them dressed in tactical gear. Not to a military level, she'd seen those guys pass through bases on their way to missions. These were minor contractors. Most of them hadn't even drawn their Glocks. The one who did, the victim in the room with the broken window, hadn't turned off the safety.

Detective Arana didn't like it. She didn't like that they were at the Kersh Inn, she didn't like that they had been amateur soldiers, and she especially didn't like that someone had taken them down so easily. Possibly multiple suspects, better trained and better armed. This one could wreck her close rate. Worse, there was no indication yet whether there was more violence to come.

She looked at the outside victim's identification. Massachusetts. Why the hell were they in Shale, Michigan? Detective Paris called up to her from the parking lot.

"Lena! Found their ride!"

Elena went down the steps, looking for anything that might be useful to the investigation. A few cigarette butts, a shred of paper, and what might be bloodstains. She made a mental note to send their overworked technician to collect those, then walked out to where Paris stood beside a gray Mercedes SUV with a small trailer hitched to it.

"Massachusetts plates?" she asked.

Paris nodded.

"Don't suppose you brought the keys down?"

Elena shook her head.

"Haven't looked for them yet. There's a lot to document up there."

Paris led the way to the back of the trailer.

"Locked. But check this out."

She knocked on the metal door, and the sound echoed.

"Hear it?"

She rapped on it again, and Elena concentrated on the sound.

"I don't hear anything, Charli."

Paris waggled a finger triumphantly.

"Exactly! You find any luggage up there?"

"A few small bags in one room," Elena told her.

"Uh-huh. Three people, one SUV, a couple handguns, a bag or two. What's the trailer for?"

"It's for—" she started, then she realized what her partner was trying to say. "It's for something that's not in the rooms and probably isn't inside it anymore either."

Paris gave her finger guns and followed with a mic drop.

"Boom. Motive."

Elena frowned. "Or they're on their way to pick something up. Or they already dropped it off."

"Spoilsport."

"There's a reason no one wants to work with you, Charli. Ideas aren't facts."

Paris started walking toward the stairs. "No one besides you, chica!"

"I'm going to break those stupid finger guns," Elena called after her.

Paris was impulsive and often insensitive, but just this once Elena hoped the junior detective was on to something.

At the very least, the trailer could go a long way to explaining what they'd been doing several states away from home. It looked like a rental. She took a photo of the license plate, the stenciled number on the door, and the telephone number. After she forwarded them to her work email, her phone alerted her to an incoming message.

She opened her DMs, and there was a picture of Charli gloating while dangling a keychain by her face. Elena put her phone back in her pocket and hoped this case wouldn't be as bad as she'd first feared.

CHAPTER THREE

Dale Alexander

The pharmacist came back with a bag filled with my estradiol and injection supplies. Between this prescription, the antidepressants, and the amphetamines, we'd seen a lot of each other.

"You want me to ring up the pop too, ma'am?"

I nodded and set the cold bottle of Diet Dr. Pepper on the counter. I'd never stuck with voice training, so I tried not to talk in public. I paid and took the bag. There was a woman behind me, glaring. Did she suspect, or was she just mad about my mask? I left quickly.

The wind had picked up while I'd been inside, and I pulled the drawstrings of my hoodie tight. I'd wanted to crack open the bottle on my walk back to the apartment but decided it was just a little too cold. I probably should've taken a break to pick up the prescriptions earlier in the day, before the sky became uniformly gray.

Dried leaves shushed across the sidewalk, scurrying across my path. If the rain actually fell, they'd stop being fun. Passing a lamp, I saw that several leaves had piled around its base, and I allowed myself a few vigorous stomps. The brittle crunches were satisfying, but I felt myself drawing attention.

A grown woman wasn't supposed to enjoy such things anymore.

I'd reached Remembrance Park when I heard the whimper. It was only about twenty square feet of grass and a few concrete benches surrounded by hedges, but there was a small plaque commemorating two local soldiers who'd died in World War I, so it got to be a park. I thought that a small child might have made the noise, so I peeked inside. Thankfully, no kid in sight, but there was a large dog curled up in a shadowy corner of the hedgerow. It was roughly the size of Thea, my former in-laws' German shepherd. Much shorter ears, though, and fur like a pale yellow lab. I immediately loved it, though it was understandably wary of me. I pulled down my mask to look more comforting.

"Hey, there, pup," I said, calling on my voice training to hit a more reassuring register. "Was that you crying? Are you okay?"

The dog whined and crawled toward me a little, dragging one back foot. It seemed ready to trust anyone who showed it attention. My heart broke, and I kind of understood. I was done with people now, too.

I crouched down, steadying myself with my free hand. "Does your paw hurt? Where's your owner?"

The dog pulled its head back and gave me the side-eye. It didn't have a collar. No owner, or one that didn't care.

"Kicked out, huh? Yeah, me too."

I wasn't sure how to help. I'd heard that wounded animals could lash out unexpectedly, and this dog was too large to take chances with. I could call for help, but would that be best? There were lots of dogs that needed homes. Would they bother healing an injured one or just put it down? I vowed to check online once I got home. Maybe post on the city board.

I set down my bag, pulled my phone out, and took a picture of the poor thing. It blinked irritably at the flash, which I'd forgotten to turn off.

I picked up my bag, stood up, and pulled my mask back in place. "Gotta go, fur friend. I'll let people know you're here."

I tried not to think about the sad light blue eyes that followed me as I walked away.

CHAPTER FOUR

Mike Lakeland

He'd called off immediate pursuit of the package, hoping that the extra time would let the young woman escape. There hadn't been a lot of pushback, since they'd had to flee the hotel, swap vehicles, and change clothes before the police could find them. By the time they could safely return to the area, she would have had to be sitting on a bench with a big sign for them to find her.

Mike took a calming breath and called his boss.

"Explain to me about why I heard news reports before I heard from you," she said by way of greeting.

"The package escaped. I wanted to locate it before reporting in."

"And did you? Did you fucking find it?"

He steeled himself.

"Unfortunately, not yet."

"So you fucked up, decided to try to correct it before admitting your failure, couldn't fix it, and finally decided to let me know what was happening. Do I have that right, Lakeland?"

"Ma'am—"

"Find my package. Find it and destroy it. That's the fucking job."

With that, she hung up. Mike rubbed the bridge of his nose. She'd always been testy, but this job had been especially tense from the beginning. Not only did she want them to use deadly force, but she seemed to be much more personally invested. He suspected it had little to do with the business jobs he usually did for her, but he really didn't care. He wasn't going to assassinate a woman who was being ferried like cargo, and he didn't want to know what any of this was about.

He chose a few people to keep searching through the night. They weren't likely to succeed, but it would show they were trying and would run up the expenses. They'd need to mount a more believable search in the morning.

CHAPTER FIVE

Dale Alexander

My pizza was turning in the microwave. I sat on my secondhand couch guzzling the pop. After a thoroughly glamorous belch, I picked up my laptop and opened the browser. The tab for my professional email account showed notifications, so I opened it and looked through them. More project meetings. I marked them as read without RSVPing.

One was interesting: a pipeline alert. The details indicated that it was an infrastructure issue, not the code. I checked the time, and it was after five o'clock. No chance anyone else was going to look into it. I fired up the VPN for my client's network and started poring over the logs for details of the issue.

When my stomach started growling, I glanced at the time again. Nearly half past seven. I kicked off the pipeline for another check and got up to put the cold pizza on a paper plate. I'd forgotten to put more pop cans in the fridge, so I grabbed one out of the box. I sat back on the couch, folded the pizza in half, and ate it like a cold sandwich while watching the job run. It took twenty minutes, which I should probably address at some point, but it worked.

I logged into my timesheet and added the extra hours for

the day. I would hit the forty hour limit sometime on Thursday, as usual. Mandatory meetings would eat a chunk of that, leaving me very little time to do any work the rest of the week. I hated having nothing to do, but I didn't work for free. A few months back they'd offered me a salaried position, but I knew that without a cap on hours I'd put in around seventy a week. The math just didn't work out. Plus, my therapist kept trying to get me to have a social life. Make friends and do things with them.

I wasn't ready yet. It was hard enough smiling through the small talk before every meeting. Meeting people in person, talking, laughing—that just wasn't me anymore. Not since everyone had sided with Liz. I still sometimes thought they'd been right. I'd certainly made it easy to abandon me. Therapy voice intruded on my thoughts to call bullshit on me. It thought I deserved happiness as much as that stray did.

The wounded dog.

I took a look at the picture I'd taken of it. Everything in the background was crisp from the flash, but the dog looked badly superimposed over the image. It seemed almost transparent, especially where the light was most intense. Weird effect, but I figured there was enough there to enhance. I might need to get creative with the middle though.

It took an hour to alter the photo enough to look reasonable. I used a stamp to fill in the missing parts and did my best to smudge it into looking less like that's what I'd done. It wasn't professional, but it just needed to get the pup recognized. I uploaded it to the Shale message board along with a note about where I found the dog, how scared it was, its injury, and how much I wanted to keep it myself.

I deleted that last part and hit post.

It might rain tonight. I should probably just go check on the dog. Maybe get it something to eat. Give it shelter for the night. Take it to the vet in the morning. Shit. I was already getting attached.

But I should still check.

CHAPTER SIX

Janice Altura

It had been monitoring local sites since the incident at the Kersh Inn, looking for a way to pique Livinia's interest. This was admittedly unlikely, but it had felt the need to try. The attack had certainly been strange enough to raise its own curiosity but lacked that touch of the paranormal that might get through to its host. Rather, the *preternatural*. That had always been her obsession.

There was an intriguing wrinkle to the multiple shootings, but it remained unverified for the moment. Witnesses had reported seeing a bald young woman in a simple gray dress flee the inn at the time of the event. There'd been a few sightings, but no one had found her yet. Nobody else staying there had confessed to knowing who she was. She might have come with the victims, but no one had seen her before the trouble started.

Janice used social media scrapers to sift through local chatter, and while nothing definitive had appeared about the events at the Kersh Inn, there had been a rash of phantom animal sightings. Those happened now and then and usually turned out to be a feral cat or a mangy dog. The reports this time started as a mountain lion and quickly changed to a blonde wolf. It had deemed these sightings irrelevant until someone posted an appallingly bad photoshop job that tied in to them. Interestingly, the poster didn't actually seem to be aware of the phantom wolf sightings, unless they were being ironic by suggesting the creature was a lost pet.

The picture was of a blonde wolf in front of a hedge. It had clearly been altered, with an exceedingly clumsy bit of work in the center. There was also an appearance of slight transparency at the edges. Janice downloaded it to run through image analysis software. As it suspected, there was a lot of nonsense in the middle, but the rest surprised her. The wolf had been changed to look denser, but the animal itself was part of the original picture. The creature's outline told the story; it blended perfectly with the background. This was real. Someone had managed to photograph an animal that was an actual phantom and tried to make it look solid for some reason.

It sent the results to a tablet and set up a data scrape for the poster, Dale Alexander, before walking down the hall to knock on the library door. This should get its friend's attention. Several rounds of knocking passed before it heard Livinia approaching the door. One of the strictest house rules was that nobody was to open the library door or enter the room without express permission, which in Janice's experience had never once been granted.

The door opened, and Livinia stood expectantly in the entrance. She was rather short, but Janice still had to look around her to get a peek into the library. As ever, the room looked like a rather ordinary, if old-fashioned, home library.

"Miss Altura. You wished to speak?"

"Peep this, boss."

Livinia took the tablet and read the report, frowning.

"This is authentic?"

"Underneath the phony-baloney, sure."

Livinia handed the device back, looking concerned. Janice smelled victory.

"Have there been any other sightings?"

Janice nodded.

"Loads. This is the only picture that's jake though. How bad is it?"

"A phantom animal may be ignored unless sightings persist. It's typically a simple misidentification. A phantasmal animal, on the other hand—that could be quite dangerous indeed."

Janice waited patiently while Livinia thought over the situation.

"I'm going to research this phenomenon. Please watch for any change in the situation, and send the photographer a discreet message."

She dictated her response, thanked Janice for bringing the matter to her attention, and disappeared back into the library. Janice walked back to the computer room and started testing the security of the Shale message board system. There was no reason why it couldn't have fun while following instructions.

CHAPTER SEVEN

Wolf

She had limped after the woman for a while, but there'd been too many other people around. Too many unfamiliar scents and sounds. She hadn't been able to keep up. Cautiously, she tracked the path that the kind human had taken. Her host needed help. Cold, injured, hungry—and, more dangerously, alone with no protection. If she didn't find the human a safe place it could lead to her death, and then she'd be pulled into another related host. This one was the best she'd ever had, the first one that she'd felt close to, and she didn't want to wind up spending several more lifetimes in ill-suited captive hosts.

This was their chance. They may not find a way to break the cycle, but they could live free together for quite a while. That would be a nice break. She hid in an alleyway as a group of people passed. There was still a little sun filtering through the blanket of clouds, but the streetlights had turned on, and she needed to avoid their glow. It was bad enough to be seen by humans, but to be transparent in front of them... The woman hadn't even noticed. She had treated her as a dog. Insulting, to be sure, but promising.

A familiar scent made her whine, and she saw the woman pass in front of the alley. She was carrying a bag again, but this one smelled really good. Another whine escaped before she could stop herself. The human paused before returning to the alley.

"That you, hurt pup?"

She slunk carefully out of the alley. The woman crouched on the grass by the curb and pulled down her mask again. She dug into her bag, pulling out a small package of grayish meat. Tearing off the plastic, she set the meat on the ground. The wolf leaned in, salivating. It didn't matter whether she ate so long as her host did, but she did enjoy the occasional meal. Her preference was for a fresh kill, but—

"Now don't gulp it down," the friendly human cautioned her. "Chew. I don't want you gagging on it."

She gazed up at her benefactor for a moment, then gingerly took a bite of the offering. She swallowed the cold meat and looked up at the human for her reaction.

"What a good—well, good job, whatever your gender!"

The human retreated and slowly stood up. Seeing her withdraw, the wolf carefully picked up the bulk of the remaining ground beef and choked it down in a few gulps. She felt chastened by the woman's disapproving look, but that didn't stop her from cleaning up the bits that had fallen out of her mouth.

"Well, you didn't choke. That's a win. I posted your picture, so maybe someone will come for you soon."

She didn't want someone to come for her; she wanted this woman to come to help her host. She tried to wag her tail to play up to the human's sympathy.

"Oh, no. No, I can't bring you in. Against the lease. We'd both be on the streets. Then where would you get raw hamburgers?"

She tilted her head to the side and whined.

"You stay there. Or go back to the park. I'll do what I can."

The woman replaced her mask and took a few steps away, and she limped along after. That earned her a stern look.

"I said no. You can't come with me."

She sat on her haunches and looked away, sulking. This wasn't working out.

"Good night."

She grumbled and turned to watch the human flee up a flight of stairs.

CHAPTER EIGHT

Mike Lakeland

The overnight search had turned up nothing, which was fortunate for the package. Now the search area would be wider, and there were fewer people to send out looking. The bad news was that they were all rested and well-fed, which might not be the case for their quarry. He decided to send the morning team out singly. They wouldn't be as sharp alone, but he could claim that they'd compensate by covering more ground.

He sent two to drive down streets starting four blocks away while he and Markham searched more carefully inside that area by foot. It was going to be a long morning, but he hoped to give her enough time to slip away.

CHAPTER NINE

Dale Alexander

I dreamt of serving fast food to talking animals. They'd come to my register and order a gooseberry shake, a squirrel burger, or an abalone sandwich, and I'd merge ingredients together until I had enough to fill the order. Then I'd drag it to the counter and collect the money. Animals started coming in faster, with more complicated orders, and soon there was a line of angry customers as I tried to compose basic ingredients into peep stroganoff and parrot cheesecake.

When too many customers left in a huff, I was sent to the drive-thru. Unfortunately, animals can't drive. I spent the rest of my shift alone, thinking about how I'd do better next time. Something started beeping, and I wandered around checking fryers until I woke up and turned off my phone's alarm.

I walked drowsily to the bathroom, where I deleted my restaurant merge game while I peed. When a game fuels stress dreams, it's past time to stop playing it. After washing up, I ran my hands through my hair. A wolf cut was meant to look messy, but more artfully than the weird clumps mine was in. I didn't want to bother trying to spray or gel it into something more presentable, so that made it a hat day. Thankfully it was autumn, so no one would look twice.

I threw on my tee with the shiny pink rainbow-pooping

unicorn and dug up a knit cap that bore an octopus skeleton design. Popped a pumpkin spice pod in the coffee maker and sprayed whipped cream on top when it was done. Indulgent, yes. Also basic. But why shouldn't I enjoy my hot caffeine?

Armed with my cup of power-up juice, I settled onto the couch and checked my work email. There were a few more alerts, but nothing that needed urgent attention. The worst was badly formed data. That information came from user entry, so there was always a chance for weirdness to creep in. For now, someone would need to fix it in the database and rerun the search indices. We'd need to discuss whether to attempt to prevent this particular form of bad data from entering the system or provide an easier way to fix it. Most likely, we'd put it on a monitor list to determine frequency and severity.

My phone chimed. Time for the morning check-in. I opened the calendar on my laptop and clicked on the meeting link. The video preview showed just my chest, which was a little too unprofessional for my liking. I pushed the screen back until my face showed, then slouched so it wasn't a direct view up my nose. The darkness of the room helped hide my stubble. I looked like I hadn't left my underground bunker in years. Perfect. I put on a pleasant but muted smile and joined the call.

When the audio kicked in, Aparna was talking about her son.

"I swear every half hour he threw up again, poor guy. And I had to go run and rinse out the bucket every time because the stupid cat was trying to jump in to investigate."

There were conflicting choruses of commiserations, sounds of disgust, and laughter. I had no guide for how to react, so I used a default meeting starter.

"Whoa, what did I come in on?"

I've been told that my dry delivery really sells the line. I'm not sure that I believe that, but I have heard people try to imitate it only to be told it's not quite right. I'm the shadowy dev what quips in shadows, it seems.

The important part is that it did what I wanted. Larry, the project manager, got the meeting officially started. I tuned out the updates from the other team members. They rattled off task numbers as though we had all memorized the work they represented and only mentioned how much longer they thought they'd need.

"Dale?"

I described the work I'd done yesterday and then added an explanation of the pipeline issue and how I'd resolved it.

"Do you have something to work on?" Larry asked.

"I'll look for something in the backlog that I can finish before I'm out of hours for the week."

Larry gave the nervous laugh that he did every Thursday morning when my hours came up.

"And, ah, how many do you have left?"

"I have about four, apart from what's been scheduled for meetings."

"We'll see if we can get you out of some of those," he said. He'd only gotten me out of one meeting in the last seven months. I figured this was some sort of managerial ritual more than an action item.

"I'm open to overtime," I reminded him. I always tried to make it sound more helpful than hopeful, but I don't think it mattered. Even under tight deadlines, they never took me up on the offer. Their contractor budget was set at the beginning of the year, and paying extra now would leave them short-staffed later in the year. Still, it was the end of October, and there wasn't much time left to use up that funding. I figured the odds were starting to lean my way.

"I don't think anything is that urgent just now," he said.

Ah, well. I went back to paying half attention as the remaining members of the team gave their updates. Larry eventually closed out the meeting, and I exited with great relief. It was a great team, and I genuinely enjoyed working with them, but these meetings were a waste of time that left me feeling drained. Most mornings, I followed the meeting with a nap, after which a Powerbar and a second cup of coffee readied me for work. This morning I just wanted to check on the dog.

I put a note on the team chat that I'd be out until lunch, implying that this was to ensure some availability for Friday. Then I marked the meeting on my timesheet and turned off the VPN.

My laptop was my own again. I loaded the community board to see if anyone had responded to the dog photo. A few people said they loved the sad pupper and would die for it. More expressed sympathy but regretted that they couldn't help. One responder yelled at me for not immediately taking it home, which irritated me by being so close to my inner critic's thoughts. I sat with the feeling, envisioning my self-recrimination as an English judge in robe and powdered wig. As the accused, I stood behind the railing of an elevated platform. I have a shaky grasp of English courtrooms and procedures, but it's my imagination's justice system, so however I picture it is correct.

"May it please the court, I acknowledge that I could have brought the dog home with me last night!"

"You should have!" the judge bellowed, banging his mallet for emphasis.

"Perhaps I should," I admitted. "I wanted to help it, but I didn't know if someone was already out looking. Also, it could have been rabid or something."

"Tosh!" he cried. I think that means rubbish, at least. "It wasn't foaming at the mouth, and it didn't have a collar! These are flimsy excuses for being an awful human being!"

I hung my head. Part of me still believed it wasn't a good idea to just bring a stray animal into my apartment, but I lacked the will to keep defending myself. The truth was that I wished I had brought it home. I wanted to nurse it to health and struggle with it for space on my single bed. It would need walks, so I'd have to get out of the apartment and get some exercise several times a day. Mostly I wanted that sense of complete acceptance.

"You're right," I said. "I suck."

My video therapy session tomorrow was going to bite. Bastian would not let me get away with beating myself up. I needed to focus on positive action.

Thinking it through, there wasn't much hope of finding the owner through the message board. There'd been maybe four hundred active users in the last month. Even if my message filtered out to someone who knew where the dog belonged, it could take a week or more. Who knew what might happen by then. No other option. I needed to get the dog to the vet this morning before it wandered off and got killed in the road. Then I could try other outlets to look for its owner.

I pulled on jeans and my boots, grabbed my purse and the keys to the Crown Vic, and opened the apartment door. The dog sat just a few feet away, wagging its tail as it saw me. I stepped outside, closed the door, and squatted down.

"Well, good morning! How're you doing today, pup?"

The dog leaned forward and sniffed at my hands. I held them out for proper inspection. It took its time and paid special attention to my purse. Maybe it was a Sailor Moon fan. Then it stared into my face.

"Sorry, pup. No hamburger this time."

It grumbled and turned away from me.

"Yeah, I suck," I admitted. "How's your foot?"

It ignored me. Pointedly. Glanced to make sure I'd noticed and everything.

"Come on, you limped up the stairs. That couldn't have been fun. Let's get you to the vet's."

I stood up and started walking, expecting that the dog would follow. It had tracked me to my apartment, after all. It seemed to be attached. Yet when I reached the corridor between the two sides of the floor, I looked back and saw it still sitting there. I motioned for it to come to me.

"We'll take the elevator." I raised my free hand and slowly lowered it to demonstrate. "No steps. Just sit. Ding! Ground floor!"

Whatever it made of this performance, it stood up and limped down the walkway toward me. When it reached me, I instinctively reached down to pat its head. I just didn't think about it. The dog flinched, and I pulled back my hand.

"Sorry! I just wanted to touch you. I shouldn't have assumed that you'd be cool with that."

I held out my offending hand for the dog to sniff. It did so and then looked up at me. It glanced at my hand and then back at my face. I swore that it had just given me approval to pat its head.

"Yeah? Okay. Nice and easy."

I slowly moved my hand to the top of its head and gently rubbed. The fur was softer than I'd expected for a dog living on the streets. It felt like silk sheets, or at least like how I imagined that might feel. The dog groaned happily and leaned into my side.

The elevator in the hallway opened, and Maggie stepped out with a ladder. She nodded at me, and the dog tried to hide behind me as I stood up.

"It's okay, pup. Just Maggie, on her way to change a light-bulb or something. She's perfectly nice people."

"Damn, but that makes me sound lame."

"Sorry. Keeping it simple for the pup. You are, of course, a fucking delight."

She was, too. The complex was in need of major repairs, but the owners wouldn't pay for them. As the sole maintenance worker, Maggie was constantly running between emergencies. Despite the hectic schedule, she always took time to talk to me when we ran into each other. I figured she'd resolved to break me out of my shut-in lifestyle.

"Who's your new friend?" she asked, peering at the nervous dog behind me.

"No idea," I confessed. "Found it at Remembrance Park last night, gave it some ground beef, and this morning it was waiting outside my door."

Maggie laughed.

"Yeah, that'll do it. That's your dog, now."

I held a hand down for the dog to sniff or rub against, and it licked me instead. Kind of gross, but completely awesome.

"I won't say I haven't thought about paying the pet fee, but we're heading to a vet to check its back leg. Plus, if it's chipped they'll be able to find out where it belongs."

"Poor thing! It's so great you're taking it on yourself to get it cared for. You'd make a wonderful dog mom. Y'know, if there isn't a chip."

"I dunno. But I could be talked into trying it out."

Maggie readjusted the ladder. She was only half a head shorter than me, but she looked too small to be carrying that around so easily. She packed some impressive muscles under her sleeves. During the summer, her sleeveless garb revealed them. Now that it was cooling off, she wore three-quarter sleeve shirts under her overalls. Sometime next month, her flannel jacket would complete the ensemble.

She paused before moving along to her work.

"Blueberry Nipples is playing The Lez tomorrow night."

The Lez was a bar that was infamous in my college days. The boys all drooled over the thought of lesbians making out. From what I gathered, it was nowhere near that wild or fun, but I'd never gone there. I still worried that I wasn't enough of a woman to be welcome. There was no way I'd feel like risking it now, but Maggie had made me curious.

" 'Blueberry Nipples'?"

She laughed.

"Yeah, they're a side project for the bass and keyboard players from Strawberry Headache. More techno and less pop."

"I graduated a decade ago, and I'm already completely out of touch with the local scene. I've never heard of these bands."

"They're both great. Their albums are up on Broad Banned, if you want an idea. The Nipples always put on a great show."

This felt like a joke, but she acted like these were very normal things to say out loud. I smiled politely and promised I'd think about it.

"Cool. See ya there," she said, grinning and waving goodbye as she left.

The dog and I looked at each other.

"Let's go for a ride," I told it.

I swear the dog sighed.

CHAPTER TEN

Wolf

The door of the small elevator opened, and the woman urged her to enter it. She looked up at the human to try to uncover motive and saw only the same concern as before. She placed a paw inside to test the floor. It felt slightly unsteady. She glanced back, and the woman nodded encouragingly.

"That's it. Go in. It's okay."

She entered the cell and sat down, watching the woman follow in after her. The door closed, leaving them trapped in the tiny space, but before she could complain, the floor shook. Sounds of whining protest surrounded her as the cell continued to shake. She looked up to the human, adding her own whine to the chorus.

"It's okay," the human said. "It's just going down."

She remained deeply suspicious, but the woman's own calmness did help her weather the experience if not relax. Elevators were human contraptions, and she'd never been in one before. They felt too confined. When the cell stopped and the door opened, she raced outside to freedom.

The human followed her out, laughing.

"It's okay, pup. No more elevator. But you might not like the car."

The wolf hung her head in embarrassment. The woman looked at her strangely, as though noticing something about her, then reached down to pat her again. Then she smiled and knelt down, moving her hands to stroke the wolf's back and sides before encircling her in a hug. The animal groaned contentedly. It had been many lifetimes since a person had embraced her like this, and she'd missed the contact. She'd prefer a mate, but this was quite lovely.

"Do you want a name?"

The wolf had a name, or rather a feeling that she associated with herself. It combined her scent and her memories, and it varied slightly depending on mood. She looked at the human curiously. She knew that these ungainly creatures preferred to identify each other with purely verbal names, and she couldn't recall ever having one of those. There were words used to define her or to get her attention, but they were not personal identifiers.

She found her front lifted, and she complained as the woman craned to look underneath her.

"No block and tackle," was the pronouncement as she was lowered back to the ground.

She demanded more petting to atone for this unwelcome inspection. While the human made up for her transgression, she also mused aloud.

"When I was a kid, I got into constellations. I'd go outside at night and just stare up into the sky, tracing the figures in the stars. Reciting their stories. Cassiopeia was the most beautiful woman in the world. Her constellation is a W for some reason. I think she's meant to be sitting or something."

She put her hands on the sides of the wolf's face.

"How about it. Do you like 'Cassie'?"

She didn't care what the human decided to call her, but receiving a name was a rare honor. She might have found the one to help her host. She nuzzled the woman, who grinned broadly and rubbed her head some more

"Hi, Cassie. I'm Dale."

She licked Dale's face in greeting. The human's smile looked forced, but she didn't complain.

"Okay. That will take getting used to."

Dale stood up.

"Now, let's take you to the vet."

Cassie didn't know what that meant, but it didn't matter. Now that she and Dale were on good terms, she needed to get the woman to help. Cassie started trot-limping off away from the building. Dale called after her but eventually hurried to catch up.

Cassie led her human back to the small park where they'd met and continued from there, backtracking to where her host still slept. They traveled several more blocks and made a few turns before arriving at the stone building where her host lay hidden. Eager now, she ran ahead across the grass. Dale yelled for her to wait, but she didn't care. She ran to the hole her host slept in and released her from sleep.

CHAPTER ELEVEN

The Package

I woke up, confused by my bed of crunchy leaves and the smell of dirt. My dream of a friendly stranger in a purple shirt and hat bumped against my memory of how I'd gotten here. I'd never had so much happen in a single day before. A woman was shouting.

"Cassie! Where'd you go?"

The name seemed important. I thought about it and remembered the woman calling me that in my dream. It was a voice I wanted to trust. I was hungry and frightened, and cold from sleeping outside all night. My foot felt worse this morning. The tightness of the skin around my ankle made every heartbeat hurt. I crouched, balancing on my right foot, and lifted the grate. There was a gasp from above, and I felt like I was making a mistake by leaving my hole. But that sense of kindness and affection carried over so strongly from my sleep. I made enough room to get out and raised myself into the daylight, such as it was.

The woman of my dream stood on the grass nearby, staring at me with her mouth open.

"Dale!"

I'd never had a friend, and what the guards had said about them wasn't very useful for knowing what to do. The only reason I even thought of her as one was because of how she'd treated my dream self. I let those memories direct me.

She cried out as I crashed into her, hugging her tightly, rubbing my face against her, and licking. She smelled like I remembered, a mixture of spring flowers and something sweeter and fruity.

"Get off!" she cried.

She started to push against me. I was taller and stronger, but I let her shove me away. I'd never met a friend before. Maybe I hadn't done it right, but she'd teach me how to act. I smiled, thinking about her showing me how to get food and where to find beds.

"Who the fuck are you?"

I'd made a mistake. She'd met the wolf I was in sleep, not me as a person just like her. Maybe I smelled different to her.

"You called me Cassie this morning," I explained. "For the woman who sits in the stars. In front of where your cell is. After you hugged me."

Dale took a step backward, her face turning white. She began to smell sour, like fear. She still didn't know me.

"Where did you hear that? Did you follow me here?"

I wanted to walk toward her, but she was scared of me.

"You followed me here. I led you."

She stared at me, but now with some interest. The smell of fear was starting to fade a little as she examined me. It wasn't the way the doctors did, that made me feel somehow broken. Dale's gaze was open, looking at what I actually was. That's what I sensed, anyway. Her eyes stayed on my hurt foot, which I was mostly using to help with balance.

"That's the same leg that's hurt on Cassie," she said. "Looks like it hurts."

I nodded. It did.

"May I examine it?"

I didn't know why she'd want to look at it, but if it made her comfortable I didn't mind.

I sat down on the grass. She joined me, and I carefully put

my left foot in her lap. I hadn't looked at it yet, and I didn't know why my ankle was so big and red. It didn't look right at all. I'd only ever bumped into things before or had injections. This was new, and I hoped it would go away soon.

"Tell me if this hurts," Dale said.

She touched one of my toes. Her skin was lighter than mine, but she was allowed to leave her cell. That made no sense, unless she liked to stay in there. Some of the guards would go away for several days in the summer and return with darker skin, talking about having gotten out in the sun. Sometimes they were red for a while, but most of them were just tanned.

After wiggling a few of my toes, Dale had wrapped her hand around the front pad of my foot and squeezed it just a little. She looked up at me, and I remembered that the doctor would often do that when he wanted me to react. I shook my head, and she seemed to like that response.

Her arms had small dark hairs on them, darker than the long brown ones that stuck out under her hat. The hair on my legs was blonde and a little longer, and it covered my body. Her chin and neck stubble confused me, because I'd never met another woman who had as much hair there as I did. I wondered why she shaved it, but people did a lot of interesting things with the hair on their faces. Maybe she just liked it that way. After all, I kept my head shaved.

She'd worked her way up the foot, and although it started to become less comfortable for me, it didn't hurt. I just kept shaking my head whenever she looked at me. Then she reached my ankle. All she did was touch it, but that's all it took. I whimpered.

"I think we should get you to a hospital. It might not be broken, but it could be a sprain or maybe some kind of tear. I don't remember enough first aid, but even with treatment it might take weeks to heal."

She sat back a little, my foot still in her lap. I felt bad that I hadn't been able to wash off all the dirt from running. People didn't like dirt.

"Okay," I agreed.

I didn't know what that meant, but she was my friend. I trusted her. She frowned at me and pinched her lips together. Had I not been supposed to agree?

"Have you been to a hospital before?"

I shook my head.

"I don't think so. Is it a cell by a loud road?"

She opened her mouth and shut it without saying anything, then frowned deeper. It wasn't fear exactly, but something else that I'd never picked up before. Something similar to worry but a little different.

"Could you describe that cell to me?"

Dale's voice had become quiet and tense, and she smiled in a way that felt like a lie. I wanted her to be happy again and take me to the hospital to make my ankle better, but all I could think to do was to tell her what she'd asked about. I closed my eyes and thought about the moments before everything got scary. The cell really had been great. I smiled at her as I described it.

"It was really nice. It had a smaller attached cell for the toilet and shower. The floor was soft. It had a screen that showed *Major Indictments,* and a bed so wide that I could have rolled back and forth on it. I didn't though, because the guard had already yelled at me for playing with the pillows."

She held up her hands and waved them.

"Hold on. Guard? What guard?"

I'd thought she'd just assumed there'd been a guard watching me from outside. It had been weird to have one in the cell with me. Maybe that was confusing her.

"It was a fancy cell, with no bars and cloth over the windows. They had to put a guard inside with me."

"They—" Dale started. "Never mind. We can sort this out at the hospital. Right now, we have to get you to a doctor."

"No!" I yelled.

I nearly kicked her as I scooted backward. Doctors were worse than the guards. Sometimes they ignored me or yelled or threatened, but the guards knew I was there. Doctors just came in, pushed me around, poked me anywhere they wanted, and shoved things into me, like I wasn't even a person. I don't remember everything I said, but I kept yelling. Dale tried to come near but I waved her off. I hadn't had a reaction like this in a long time. I had to calm down before I drove her away.

I closed my eyes again and focused on my breathing. In, hold, out. Slower. Slower yet. A guard had taught that to me years ago. She hadn't stayed long. The other guards said she was weak. My anger shrank, and my heart slowed to normal. I took a few more breaths and opened my eyes. Dale was very close and watching me.

"Are you okay now?"

I nodded.

"I just. I don't like—"

"Got it," she said quickly. "Not... one of those."

She looked at my ankle, again.

"You shouldn't walk on that, though. I'll go fetch Queen Vic… uh, my car, and come pick you up. Just wait here."

"No," I said firmly. "I'm coming with you."

She frowned again.

"It could be easier with more legs," she said.

"I guess. But I only have two."

She pulled her lower lip into her mouth.

"You're Cassie, right? So turn into the dog again."

"I don't... That's not how... It's a wolf, and it only comes out when I sleep."

"And you're too wound up to sleep."

That wasn't the problem, but I felt strongly that I needed to leave. It was making me very nervous, staying in the open. I didn't want to lie to my friend, but I needed to leave.

Without agreeing to what she'd said, I stood up and started hobbling toward her cell. We had a long way to go.

"Hold on," she said.

She ran up next to me and put my left arm around her shoulders. I leaned against her on the way back.

CHAPTER TWELVE

Mike Lakeland

He'd been walking for hours and seen nothing. That was good, because he didn't want to see the girl killed. He hoped she'd been smart enough to go into hiding. Unfortunately, there was every chance one of his people would find her first. He couldn't risk telling his people not to follow through on the hit. If word got back to the boss that he'd changed the order on his own authority, that would be it for his generous salary. Admittedly, he'd rarely been asked to murder anyone to earn it before.

He had reached the edges of the campus when he heard yelling behind a two-story building with an awful stone facade. A sign in the yard identified it as the Banneker Mathematics Building of The Shale School of Engineering and Technology. It sat on the corner of the block, and apparently a narrow band of grass between the building and hedges wrapped all around the property. He crept carefully along the path, noting the window wells that the package could have slept in. He hoped he was wrong, but this wouldn't have been a terrible spot for her to have hidden.

He hadn't brought any of his scouting gear, so he risked a quick direct glance around the back corner. Two women were walking to the sidewalk on the other side. His target was one of them, still in her gray dress. She was limping, which might explain why she hadn't gotten further away in all the time he'd given her. The woman assisting her was shorter and fuller, clad in jeans, a purple tee, and a purple knit cap with some kind of white design on it.

Now he was screwed. Another party had involved herself, and his boss would likely want her killed too. He needed time to think. There might be some way to convince them to flee the city before the rest of his team found them. He waited for them to disappear, heading into the downtown area. Following at a distance, he called Markham.

"Yeah," she said.

"Anything yet?"

"Just sore feet. You?"

He paused to let the pair get a little more ahead of him.

"I have a hunch. Checking it out now. Have you tried the school yet? There are a lot of shrubs."

"How about I check this drug store and see if she's hiding in the pop cooler instead?"

He let her have a half of a chuckle for that. She could take all the breaks that she wanted.

"Heard from the cars?" he asked.

"Saw Tallman drive by an hour ago. Nothing since."

"Okay. I'll call them, too. Let me know if you see anything."

"That's the job," she replied.

He hung up and resumed tailing the women. He needed to come up with an excuse to tell the drivers to avoid this area of town. Hopefully they were as tired of the search as Markham was and wouldn't need much persuasion.

CHAPTER THIRTEEN

Elena Arana

Charli hung up the phone and sat back on her chair dramatically. She clearly wanted Elena to ask.

"So?" she asked.

"Well," Charli said. "They were supposed to be returning the trailer later tonight, so the original intent may have been to start driving back to Massachusetts yesterday or very early this morning. Assuming, of course, that they planned to take breaks."

She leaned forward, waving a finger for emphasis.

"But! Yesterday afternoon the rental company received a call asking to extend the rental for another day. Seems their plans changed once they arrived here."

Elena nodded, thinking.

"The timing seems to fit, so it's one possibility. Fastest nonstop route between here and the rental company is thirteen hours, nonstop. Maybe they were just exhausted and wanted to sleep before turning around."

Charli dismissed that explanation with a hand wave.

"The way they were armed, they planned out whatever they were doing. They'd have made reservations in advance instead of counting on getting adjoining rooms on demand.

No, something unexpected came up, forcing them to stay in town."

Elena shook her head.

"Maybe. We still don't know much, including what was in the trailer. The techs said the blankets looked matted down, but they haven't had time to process them for hair and fluids."

Charli snapped her fingers and clapped. Elena had come to recognize that as the sign of a newly half-formed thought, but this time it seemed to mean she'd remembered something. The Paris Code remained inscrutable.

"They get any hits on the fingerprints from inside the trailer?"

Elena had grown tired of Charli's impatience. All of these things took time. Crime rates in the city were reasonably low, but lab work still stacked up. They could leverage priority for a mass murder, but people still had to wrap up other things they were doing before they started processing new evidence.

"An assistant said that a lot of the prints were probably too layered or smudged to be useful and couldn't confirm how many people left them or how recently they did so. This is a rental. Who knows how often they scrub it out?"

Charli let out a big sigh and threw up her hands.

"Now what, Lena? We just wait for everyone to get on board?"

Elena took some satisfaction in knowing how much her partner would hate what she had in mind. She considered it payback for all the whining.

"Now you get histories on our victims, while I look through reports of the woman seen fleeing the area."

Paris sulked for a moment, then grinned broadly.

"Five bucks it was sex trafficking and she escaped in the confusion."

Elena refused to acknowledge that.

CHAPTER FOURTEEN

Dale Alexander

I dug through my pile of clean clothes, searching for something that might fit Cassie. The sounds coming from the bathroom implied that more splashing than washing was going on in the tub. She had leaned on me all the way home, never once complaining about the pain she felt. In the face of that stoicism, I really couldn't bring up the musky staleness that had surrounded her. Any amount of cleaning that was accidentally happening would be welcome.

She was taller than me, but more of her height was in her legs. Lean legs, full of tight muscles. I shook my head to dislodge the thought. I was trying to help her, not get her into bed. Besides, she clearly had issues. But godDAMN, she was built like an Olympic swimmer. One who would probably fit in any of my shirts, which I preferred on the large side. Her broad, muscled shoulders might make it look weird, though. My chest, belly, and upper arms all made themselves known under shirts, but she'd basically look like a boy, especially with her closely cropped hair. I didn't want to expose her to that kind of attention.

Come to think of it, I didn't know how she felt about her gender or much of anything, really. Doctors bad, me good, ankle sore... The splashing escalated briefly before settling down to a less worrying level. Bath fun. There'd be time to talk later, when she was comfortable and rested.

For now I just needed to find her something to wear. Near the bottom of the pile I found a dark red tank. It came from the fundraiser for a book that had sounded better than it turned out to be and featured a bright green image of a smirking mummy. I wore it once, inside the apartment, and had never put it on again. This would solve the sleeve issue, and drawing attention to her guns might distract from her slight chest.

Who was I kidding? She'd still look masc, just hotter than in a T-shirt. I felt bad about dressing her for my benefit, but she did need clothes, and I only had so much to choose from. Just tees, hoodies, sweatpants, and a few pairs of jeans. And this awful tank that she'd look great in.

None of my jeans would work. A belt would help with the waist, but I was wearing the only one I owned. Sweatpants would work. They'd be short on her, riding up on her shins. That could just be cute, though. I found an older pair, light gray, from when I first started hormones—before Liz left me, and I developed "an unhealthy relationship with food." They should look less ridiculously wide on my guest than my newer clothes would.

I took the outfit, such as it was, to the bathroom door and knocked.

"How are you doing in there?"

There were a few more splashes and a brief silence before she answered.

"I'm wet," she said. "And my foot still hurts."

I really didn't have an answer to that. She'd been used to showers but had never taken a bath, which I thought might be better for her injury. I'd had to run it for her and answer some questions about the soap (she'd never used a pump) and washcloth (a completely unheard-of implement). Given the novelty of the situation for her, I'd expected some kind of indication of whether she'd worked out how to handle everything. I guess as long she hadn't drowned it was okay.

"I've left some clean clothes for you outside the bathroom door for when you're done. There's no underwear, sorry. Mine would, ah, probably fall off you. I'll go order a pack for you, along with an ankle brace."

There wasn't any answer.

"Did you hear me, Cassie?"

"Yes," she said simply.

I had to remind myself that someone who called every room a "cell" might not have expertise in social etiquette. In my mind, I stood before a giant, sinister robot that had angry red eyes and carried a massive war hammer, with a head that crackled with dark energy.

"SHE IS TAKING ADVANTAGE OF YOU! SHE MOCKS YOUR AID! SHE WILL HURT YOU! ALLOW ME TO STRIKE FIRST!"

I squinted up at its head, some fifty feet above.

"Okay, pal. Thanks for looking out. I think there could be other explanations, but I'll keep your warning in mind."

It glared down at me in silence.

"We good?"

"YES! I JUST... WANTED TO HELP!"

I patted a hand gently on the front of one of its feet.

"I gotcha, big guy. Thanks for looking out."

"YOU'RE WELCOME! DON'T BE A STRANGER!"

That went well, and I got a little thrill thinking about telling Bastian tomorrow in therapy. I should probably talk to him about my sick craving for his approval.

Now, though, I had to take the opportunity to communicate my needs. Jesus, I was starting to think in therapy-speak.

"Cassie? Can I ask a favor?"

Silence.

"When I can't see you, I can't tell how you're reacting. It would help if you said something like you heard me or agree or whatever. Just a comment so I know you're not asleep or something. Do you understand?"

There was more silence, and I started to wonder if she had actually fallen asleep in there.

"I understand," she said at last. "I will obey."

"I... Just call for help if you need it. The clothes are by the door, and we'll do something about that ankle when you're dressed."

"I understand," she said quickly.

Someone or something had done a number on this girl, and I was the one left feeling guilty about it. I slunk back to the couch and picked up my laptop. It was time to take down that post about the dog. She was actually a wolf that was also a young woman that was currently in my bathtub. A woman with hints of a dramatically fucked-up past, who I should definitely ask about having been down in a window well at the good old Banneker building.

I logged into the Shale message board and my eye was drawn to the red notification circle over my message inbox. That was unusual enough that I had to see what it was about before doing anything else. I figured it was probably just an ad, but maybe someone knew about Cassie and didn't want to spill in the open channel.

The message turned out to be from a user with the handle Livinia. Unusual enough name, but she still must have been in the system fairly early to snag it without resorting to variant spelling, extra identifiers, or numbers. The goth scene struggled here, but it wasn't dead, and someone would have stumbled on the name within a few years. Livinia had no icon, but neither did I.

The message itself was brief, in meaning if not length.

"Dearest Child," it read. "Your charitable impulse to help this lost creature is worthy, and it speaks well of your character. In ordinary circumstances I might not have sought to contact you, although I certainly would still have appreciated your effort. However, in this instance I must impress upon you that this creature you have found is no animal suited to be a companionable house pet. I do not know how you captured it on film as well as you've managed, but I assure you that its transparency under the flash of a bulb is no trick or accident of the light but an innate quality of the beast. I implore you to remove your advertisement seeking the creature's owner and to put it from your mind.

"Yours, Livinia M."

What the actual fuck? Who was this freak? I clicked on the username, but Livinia M. had not filled in her profile. Undeterred, I searched for Livinias and Livs in Shale, filtering on the initial M. Nothing turned up in the local news sites or community pages. Telephone records turned up a Livinia Miller, but a cursory check revealed that she'd died almost thirty years ago. I broadened the search, looking for the name within ten words of another word starting with M. This got a shit ton of results, and I started refining the search to exclude words that weren't names.

This narrowed the results enough that there were only a few pages of them to examine in closer detail. There were Livinias with Marks, and Matthews, and Michaels, and one with a Maxwell. The only one that seemed to match what I was after was an Albert Monroe with his wife Livinia. I opened the reference to investigate further.

The article was from the society pages in the summer of 1921. Albert and Livinia Monroe were photographed attending a party in honor of a celebrated Canadian spiritualist, Maria Cullen. It seems Mr. Monroe was a wealthy local aficionado of occult matters and was even reputed to have conducted successful seances himself.

Assuming that they were freshly married and that Livinia had been about twenty at the time, she'd be over one hundred years old now. She could have very good genes or more probably was a younger relative. I keyed in new parameters to uncover more about the Monroes. Lots of articles from the early 1900s, petering out in the 1920s, and disappearing entirely until 1953, which was the final story in the list. Albert went missing in 1923. Livinia made fewer public appearances and eventually secluded herself in the mansion of her father, Colonel Aldous Jessup. Col. Jessup had disappeared at the same time as Mr. Monroe. The last mention of Livinia Monroe was that her estate had been placed in the hands of a private foundation. No descendants. No other family in the public record.

I'd stopped thinking that this lead might be going anywhere, but I'd become fascinated by this grand old family of Shale. I opened up more tabs as I pursued information about Col. Jessup; the spiritualist movement of the nineteenth century; a countermovement of skeptics investigating claims of the paranormal; an elusive organization called the Society for Preternatural Investigations—ominously abbreviated as SPI—that some labeled antagonistic skeptics and others claimed were waging war on immaterial forces; rumors of Jessup's and Monroe's attachments to SPI; and one conspiracy-minded blog that claimed Jessup, Monroe, and others were kidnapped by extra-dimensional beings that were still preparing for their assault on our planet. The language conflated galaxies with dimensions, and it was difficult to tell what the writer meant by either.

I was just starting to trace the language to old pulp fantasy stories when a voice broke my concentration. I looked up from the computer in confusion and struggled to understand why a young blonde woman was standing in my apartment with some of my clothing sticking damply to her.

Right! The wolf girl. Cassie. Context reestablished, I closed the laptop and stood up.

"Sorry, what did you say?"

CHAPTER FIFTEEN

Cassie (Human)

Dale led me to the couch and instructed me to lie down. After I obeyed, she put some pillows under my sore foot. This didn't seem to have a purpose, but I'd learned not to question guards. And Dale was my guard now. Much better than the others, who'd starved me and yelled and thrown things and kept me in much emptier cells. I was disappointed she was just another guard, because she'd been so much nicer than anyone I'd met, but this was still a big improvement.

I was hungry. And my foot still hurt. I wouldn't have bothered my former guards about those things, but Dale had instructed me to say what I thought. I did.

"My foot hurts, and I'm hungry."

Dale stopped whatever she was doing with the pillows and stared at the wall above the couch. There was nothing there that I could see, and when I looked back her eyes seemed unfocused.

"Okay," she said suddenly, coming alive again. "Foot first, then food, *then* order supplies. And take down the post. Fuck."

She walked across the floor and opened a small door near the top of a metal cabinet. A light came on inside it, and I realized that this was like the refrigerator in the guards' cell. More than twice the size, but very similar. The floor over there was different than where I was. Most of this cell had a giant rug, like the one where I'd gotten to watch the show yesterday. The floor where the bath and toilet were had been covered in hard small pieces. Along the wall where the refrigerator and other odd cabinets sat, the floor was bare but had a pattern drawn on it. I'd never seen anything like it.

Dale pulled a bag out of the refrigerator. Whatever was in it was in hard pieces that rattled as the bag settled in her hand. She opened a nearby drawer and got a small towel that she wrapped around the bag. Then she walked over and looked down at me. I figured she didn't want me on the couch after all and started to get up, but she only frowned.

"Hold still."

She was a lot nicer than any of my previous guards, but I needed to keep paying close attention to figure out her moods.

She put the wrapped bag under my sore ankle, and I flinched from how cold it felt. It was like the bars of my small window in midwinter. Dale placed her hand on my lower leg and smiled oddly at me.

"Yeah, it hurts at first. The cold should help with the swelling, though."

She headed off to the cupboards again.

"I think I still have some aspirin," she said.

I'd heard the word before. It was something guards used whenever they felt any pain, and I'd never expected to get any. I'd never really been hurt before, so I didn't know if they would have given me any of the medicine.

"You'll need something to drink. I've got diet pop, 2% milk, and a juice box. And tap water, I guess."

Guards drank pop. I drank water.

"I drink water," I told her.

She filled a large plastic cup at the sink and brought it over with a few pills.

"Take these," she instructed.

This I knew. I'd only been given pills by doctors, never a guard, but Dale was not a normal guard. I swallowed the pills, but I wasn't thirsty. I took a sip to show that I was grateful. She frowned, which meant that I had done something wrong again. I smiled. They liked me to smile, and I wanted her to like me. She seemed satisfied, and sat on the floor, leaning back against the couch.

"Let's get some orders in," she said, opening the gray case on her lap. "What do you like to eat?"

I'd never thought about food being something to like. It was necessary. I ate what I was given. One time a guard had given me something from his lunch. Said it was mealy. It was the sweetest thing I'd ever eaten, the only food I'd ever enjoyed. When I tried to eat the whole thing, he'd laughed and called me stupid. I'd kept eating anyway, despite having reached parts that weren't nice to eat, because I'd wanted to experience the whole thing. It had been my only chance to do that.

"I like apples," I told Dale.

She turned to me, with that strange look she'd used before. It wasn't quite a frown, and her eyebrows curved up at her nose. She didn't sound upset, though, and she smiled with one side of her face.

"I think you'll need a little more than just that," she said. "Do you have any dietary restrictions? Food allergies?"

I had no idea what she meant, but she hadn't said no to giving me an apple.

"Is pizza okay?" she asked.

The guards sometimes had pizza. It smelled really good. I couldn't believe my luck. She'd offered me guard drinks and now wanted me to eat pizza? I kept waiting to be punished.

"Yes," I said.

She tapped at the inside of the case, and I watched the image on its monitor change. I wondered if she watched *Major Indictments* on it.

"Meat Lover okay?"

I was determined to agree to whatever would get me food.

"Yes."

More tapping, another change of the screen, and she turned to me again.

"Okay, they usually get here in about twenty minutes. Don't worry, I added an apple and a bottled water for you."

"I understand."

Dale continued to type, and I decided to try to make sense of the cell. On the far end, with the cabinets, the counter, the sink, and the odd floor I thought I recognized a microwave. That's where guards warmed things like pizza and coffee, and sometimes they popped corn. The counter was full, mostly with dishes and tall, colorful boxes. There was also a coffee maker. The guards had been very excited about getting one like this, with no pot to keep clean.

In the main part of the room, there was only the couch and lamp. The large rug was almost completely covered. There were loose piles of books, which let me know she was very smart. One of the guards had spent a lot of time reading, and he told some of the others that made him smarter than they were. I'd guessed that was why he didn't stay long. There was also loose paper everywhere. Some of it was stacked, but mostly it was one or two sheets that had been folded in thirds. They were usually near or sticking out of paper wrappers. The rest seemed to be clothing. I'd never seen so much in one place. I'd only ever had one gown at a time, but the guards had worn different clothes every day, however similar they seemed. Most of Dale's were gray or black. Some blue or green. Guard colors. There were some that were other colors, like the shirt she was wearing now, but there weren't many. I did wonder what she kept in the cabinets. It seemed like a lot of them could go in there. Maybe she used those for more books.

My guard had stopped tapping and turned toward me again. I looked back at her. It felt weird to have her sitting below me. I wondered if the couch was where she slept. Sharing a bed with her didn't sound bad, but this was too small. I might be curling up on the clothes later tonight.

"I ordered an ankle brace and a pack of panties for you," Dale said.

She seemed pleased, so I smiled. I didn't know what that meant, but she'd said it was for me. There was only one appropriate response.

"Thank you."

Compared to previous cells, this was big and comfortable. It was dark, but not so much that I couldn't see. The toilet was separated from the bed. My foot had started to feel a lot better, and I had my new guard to thank for that. These clothes weren't as comfortable as my gown, and having my legs wrapped in fabric felt very strange. I was more aware of them than I'd ever been. Yesterday I could not have thought of a place this nice.

"I'm going to catch up on some work chat while we wait on the food," Dale told me. "Let me know if you need anything."

What I needed was food, but that was coming. I hoped that twenty minutes wasn't a long time.

"I understand," I said.

She sighed and returned to her monitor.

I looked at the light peeking around the cloth over the window, wondering if it would be okay to let it in.

CHAPTER SIXTEEN

Annette Kuiper

The boardroom was stuffy, but it always was. Father liked it that way. He claimed that people talked too much when they were comfortable, but after all these years under his thumb she saw through him. He treated his staff as he had his children: as occasionally useful servants that required constant instruction. It wasn't the talking that bothered him so much as the potential for dissent or worse, better ideas.

Annette Kuiper was the sole executive at Kuiper Innovations who was not a yes-man. This was not, as her father often joked, because she was the only female executive. Having reported to him for forty-eight years, from childhood and through her entire work history, she knew precisely when to object and how to phrase her objections for maximum effect on the old bastard.

There was a cost for this. As the Chief Human Resources Officer, she was a high-ranking executive, but her influence was extremely limited. That wasn't so bad, since no one but her father had any power, but he'd really screwed her over on this latest venture. This was a family meeting, and the topic was the escape of the wolf bitch.

Her younger brother David was talking. He was a CEO

himself, of the subsidiary company Kuiper Aeronautics, but of current import he led the effort to retrieve the girl.

"Our computer experts are identifying the individual who posted the image to the Shale community forum. Once we have that identity, our agents will detain and interrogate. Meanwhile, we have investigators searching the area for our property. Knocking on doors, asking questions."

Father nodded grumpily. This was how the old man showed approval.

"What are the Massachusetts branch doing? It's their goddamn mess."

David looked at his hands. Clearly, he did not have good news to share. Annette glanced at Tobias Jr., the eldest sibling, whose slight smile showed that he too smelled blood in the water.

"Well," David said. "They claimed that the attackers would not have been able to strike if we had been ready to receive the package as planned. They say it's our problem to resolve and that they expect us to do so promptly."

Silence fell as Tobias Kuiper Sr. glared at his second son. His lip curled in contempt.

"Nonsense!" he spat. "They look for external excuses for their own incompetence! Put them back on the search! Nathaniel's only fucking himself by refusing to complete the transfer!"

His mouth continued to work behind compressed lips. He glared at David as though expecting immediate action.

"Yes, sir. I'll tell them that."

"You'll do nothing of the sort! You'll make them locate, retrieve, and deliver it to us!"

David grimaced but immediately assented. Annette seized the small opportunity to ingratiate herself to their father before Tobias Jr. could do so himself.

"Perhaps," she said in the slow, soft tone she used to project reasonableness, "we should curtail our own efforts to find her. Since it's their responsibility."

Father squinted at her, which meant she'd given him something to think about. Tobias Jr. covered a snort with a few dry coughs.

"No. No, not just yet. It is their problem, but if we fix it before they do, that's egg on their face." He grinned his nasty mirthless smile before turning back to growl at David. "So get those smug assholes looking! It'll be more humiliating for them if they are trying when we pull their fat out of the fire!"

"Yes, sir. Of course."

David shot a resentful glance at her across the table. She looked back impassively. There was no need to gloat yet. She'd only added to his pain, not achieved her end goal.

"Get out," their father grumbled. "I don't want to see you until this is resolved. Toby!"

Tobias Jr. answered promptly.

"Sir!"

"Get that hatchet man of yours. Rosenberg."

The man's name was Robinson, but none of the siblings were unwise enough to correct their father. They knew who he meant.

"At once, sir."

"Have him ready. If anyone *has* taken our delivery, we'll need to be rid of them."

"Of course, sir."

Father waved his hands irritably.

"Get going, boys! No time to waste!"

Annette watched her brothers stand briskly and leave with purpose. She had not yet been excused, and the heat of the room had risen significantly. Being singled out could be very bad or very good. She doubted that this would be very good. No matter. She could handle a setback if the family at large continued to flounder.

"I might've respected your balls if you'd killed the little bitch."

She froze. How did he know so soon? Her men had been sure not to be identifiable.

"You didn't want your precious Kevin to fuck the dog, so you humiliated our branch and set the damned thing free!"

Her mind whirled through options for getting back on more solid footing.

"Sir, we can use in vitro fertilization. This isn't the seventeenth century. There's no need—"

He pounded a fist on the table. She couldn't avoid flinching, and she struggled to tamp down her panic. He was in a foul mood, and all of her patient scheming had amounted to nothing.

He stood up. A cheap dominance display to tower over her, but also a threat of the real violence that he could still unleash. She was a child again, crying beneath his broken grandfather clock, about to be thrashed and thrown into the cellar for a day. The blood drained from her face, and her world became his shouts and her own bile.

"It's fucking magic! He has to keep fucking her until she produces a little bastard cub! Then he can do whatever the fuck he wants! We can all do whatever the fuck we want!

"Do you understand that we need this?! Our branch of the family is on the brink of fucking collapse! The entire purpose of the exchange is to restore good fortune to us! And you! You decide your boy's too good to be a dog fucker, so you set it free!"

He stood, panting and red-faced, glaring at her.

She had no response. There was nothing left for her to say in the face of his rage, and she doubted he'd believe that she'd meant for the bitch to be killed.

He took a few deep breaths and straightened his clothes. He ran a hand through his hair to put it back in place. When he spoke again, it was in a normal conversational tone, his fury expressed through his precise control.

"I have not told your brothers of your obvious treachery. If they can't figure out something this simple, they're of no use to me at all. You." He shook a finger at her. "You've always been the smart one. The clever one. Full of schemes, ruthless, and patient. But you blew it this time. I chose your son because your line would continue to benefit from this wolf crap. This was a gift, and you threw it in my face!"

He sat down. Annette couldn't look at him. The immediate danger seemed to have passed, but she knew he wouldn't let her go unpunished.

"So. It's a three-way race. Make this right. Find the girl before the others, give her to Kevin, raise the whelp, and prosper as my heir."

It was a command, not an offer, and she knew it.

"Yes, sir," she said meekly.

"Now get the fuck out of my sight."

Annette left hurriedly, already pulling out her phone.

CHAPTER SEVENTEEN

David Kuiper

He in no way needed this shit. He had his own company to run, one whose profits kept the core family business afloat, and dear old dad had given him the shit end of the stick again. This whole wolf girl nonsense had nothing to do with him, but it was on him to fix it while his idiot brother and sister played with spreadsheets or whatever the hell they did instead of work.

He'd been very content to have this part of the family heritage go to sweet big sister Annette. His own children were in Boulder with their backstabbing mother, and they were both girls, incapable of breeding with the infernal creature. As for the supposed financial gains, he'd proven that he didn't need any luck there. With just some startup cash and the family name, his business acumen had propelled him to a position to rival Mr. Nathaniel Kuiper of the Massachusetts Kuipers, who'd screwed up a simple transfer of goods. And that was without keeping a wild girl in a cage.

Now he needed to call that prick, and he was tempted to just drop the whole affair right there. Unfortunately, he had to continue sucking up to dad until the old bastard died or agreed to let him split Kuiper Aeronautics off from its failing parent company. He told himself again that dad kept the others close because they couldn't be trusted, whereas he had proven himself time and again. There had to be a payoff.

Toby slithered up alongside him as he approached the elevator. His older brother was every bit as vile as their dad, but he fancied he was subtle about it. David didn't want his help and certainly didn't want his pet assassin. But dad would have his way.

"I'll let Mr. Robinson know that his services may be needed, little brother."

Always asserting dominance. Toby'd get his. David had proof that his brother had been embezzling funds from Kuiper Innovations, and once Tobias Sr. was in a receptive mood...

"Would you prefer that I remain your point of contact with him? He can set up a burner number just for you."

David pushed the elevator button and turned to face his brother. He reminded himself to be patient for a little while longer as the thought of Toby's pending downfall filled him with confidence. He patted his elder brother's shoulder with a beefy hand and shook his head slightly.

"He's your man. I'll let you do the honors."

The elevator opened, and he got in, punching the lobby button. He had a lot to do, and chatting with a hit man wasn't on the list.

"Let's just hope we won't need him," he added as the doors closed.

During the descent, David rehearsed what he'd tell Nathaniel Kuiper about the state of the search and his dad's ideas about how invested the Massachusetts branch should be in completing their delivery. He thought through whether Nathaniel would be more susceptible to reason (unlikely), bullying (absolutely not), or pleading (possibly) before settling on an approach of sharing frustration about Tobias's demands.

He left the building and was walking to his car when his phone dinged. It was a text from Toby. With no context or explanation it was simply the name Dale Alexander and an address at a cheap apartment building downtown.

He'd wound up owing that smug son of a bitch after all.

CHAPTER EIGHTEEN

Mike Lakeland

Nothing much had happened after his target and the other woman entered the apartment. Someone had come by and dropped off a plastic bag at the door. Residents trickled in and out of the parking lot, but it was mostly quiet. Which is why he was so curious about the woman in the black Saturn who'd pulled in twenty minutes ago and still sat in her car, watching the same building through some device.

His phone vibrated. It was his boss.

"Yes, ma'am," he answered.

"I don't suppose you managed to do your fucking job yet," she snarled.

"I—"

"Never mind. I'm withdrawing the order."

"Ma'am?"

He dared to hope that the entire matter would be dropped.

"Find it. Bring it to its cage. If David or the Massachusetts Kuipers find it first, we're all fucked."

"Yes, ma'am. I think we're getting close."

"Pray that you are, because that asshole Robinson is in it now."

She hung up, leaving Mike relieved that he didn't have to

kill the young women but worried about Robinson's involvement. Their paths had crossed before, and they'd gotten along well enough, but the man was a killer. If the order came down, they'd all be in trouble.

It was time to call his team to the Fuller Apartments.

CHAPTER NINETEEN

Dale Alexander

The shopping order had come first. The delivery service was expensive, but it was worth the cost to stay inside, safe from disease and judgmental eyes. I even tipped heavily, grateful for the people willing to shop for me. I hoped they at least believed in vaccination. None of them in the last few years had been wearing face masks.

Getting the ankle brace on Cassie had been easier than I'd expected. The swelling had gone down considerably, and the skin had turned a more subdued shade of angry. I'd gently touched her injury and had been amazed at her lack of response. She'd just kept watching me. When her expression had become more curious, I realized that I'd been unconsciously stroking her shin. I'd withdrawn my hand guiltily and put on the brace, shuffling off quickly to stick the bag of peas back in my freezer.

Getting underwear on her had been worse. Cassie hadn't understood the concept and then had tried putting the panties on over her sweatpants. I'd had to walk her through the process of removing the sweats, stepping through the right holes, and pulling them up, trying the whole time not to look at her. I'd been afraid of looking directly into the sun, but in a pervy sense that made me very uncomfortable. If that had all been a put-on, she'd really committed to the bit. I'd even had to remind her to put the sweats back on. After I'd gotten her stretched back out on the couch, she'd picked at her underwear and shifted uncomfortably until the arrival of our lunch had distracted her.

I got out two paper plates and put a few slices on each of them. The grease was already seeping through, so I gave up and put them on real plates. I normally ate right out of the box, so this felt really extravagant. After Cassie sat up, I handed her a plate. She smelled the pizza but didn't touch it. I sat down on the other side of the couch and watched her observe me.

"Have you ever had pizza before?"

She shook her head.

"I have not," she added.

I was starting to believe that she really had been extremely sheltered.

"Okay. I'll teach you how I do it. If that doesn't work, I can find you a fork."

She watched me.

"You have used a fork, right?"

She shook her head again.

"The guards use them, but they didn't want me to have one."

The poor girl. Where the hell had she been?

"Let's try to save that for a later lesson, then."

I set my plate on my lap and waited as she followed suit.

"Good. Now we're going to fold one slice over on top of the other, like this."

I demonstrated, trying to be slow enough so she could see how I did it. It's a simple move, but I wanted to make sure she could copy it. She did so easily, but the look of intense concentration on her face was so adorable that I had to suppress the urge to tease her. It helped that I barely knew her, so I couldn't be sure whether she'd be okay with that or take it as an aggressive act. For myself, Liz had ruined my affection for being teased with her vicious jokes about my lack of femininity. In about an hour Cassie had made me feel so comfortable that it had felt natural to be playful again. I needed to calm the fuck down and remember that this woman on my couch was someone that I didn't actually know who claimed to be a wolf. That demanded at least a small degree of reservation.

I shook my head, prompting her to examine our plates again. Apparently she thought I was unhappy with her pizza folding.

"Sorry," I said. "Just got a little distracted. It happens. The folding gives us a way to grip the slices on the top and the bottom and hold it like a sandwich, but the point of the bottom slice tends to sag and let the toppings slip out. If you don't care, that's fine, and you can pick them up off the plate later. Me, I have... I don't like getting my hands too messy, so I use my thumbs to hold it up."

That was a lot of lore, so I demonstrated picking up the slices a couple of times. It took her a few tries, but she was persistent and finally managed to get similar results in her own style, which abandoned the finesse of my approach in favor of just grabbing the pizza with one hand at the back and the other in front. Hey, whatever works. I admit that I felt a little bit of pride in that moment.

"Great work! Now, the cheese is really hot, so take small nibbles first. From the, ah, from the tip."

For once I actually did take a very small bite, avoiding the usual damage to the roof of my mouth from molten cheese. Maybe I should be this careful more often. Cassie took a small bite, but as luck would have it the cheese just kept stretching between her lips and the slices. She looked up at me in alarm, her eyes wide in response to this food that had somehow bested her.

"It's okay, Cassie. That happens. Do you want the thread of cheese cut?"

She nodded quickly, adding "Yeph, pweaph."

That nearly destroyed me, but she was so earnest that I had to just suppress my laughter and help. Setting down my slices, I reached over and grabbed the cheese about a half an inch away from her mouth. I pulled it away from her, breaking the string, and coiled the rest back on the top slice. She chewed her bite of pizza and beamed at me, while I licked my fingers and forgot completely about her being anything but completely adorable.

We managed to get through the rest of the first serving without more excitement. She seemed to enjoy it, making silly noises of satisfaction as she ate. I grabbed another pair of slices for myself as she finished licking her fingers.

"Ready for some more?"

She looked pained, furtively glancing at the apple that lay on the floor beside the pizza box. Well, on the pile of mail that covered the floor.

"Or did you want the apple now?"

Cassie's face lit up with pleading excitement. She might be a wolf, but she was a total puppy girl. I hoped absently that I wouldn't have to house-train her.

"Please?" she begged.

I felt ashamed of my sudden urge to make her keep pleading. This couldn't be a healthy dynamic. She needed to be removed for her own safety.

"Of course," I managed to squeak.

Swallowing hard, I reached down for the apple and handed it to her. She took a big bite, and her eyes got bigger than I'd ever seen them. As she kept chewing, she reversed course and closed them tight. Probably to focus on the flavor. It was by no means the best looking piece of fruit I'd seen, but she was enjoying the bejesus out of it.

With her injury and hunger addressed, it was time to start finding out what Cassie's deal actually was.

"What do you usually eat?" I asked by way of a sly opening.

She kept chewing as she thought.

"There's hand food," she said. "Mostly bread and cheese. Sometimes broth in a paper bowl."

She took another bite and chewed happily, like what she'd said was perfectly normal. I was beginning to think her thing about cells was both real and extremely dark. Munching on more pizza would fortify me.

"Nothing in the broth?" I tried to ask casually.

She shook her head.

"Nothing."

No wonder she loved apples so much. I wondered where she'd managed to get one before. For that matter, how was she so generally cheerful? If this was a facade, I didn't want to risk breaking it.

"If you can," I asked as gently as I could, "could you describe your cell to me? You totally don't need to! But if you're up to it, I'd like to understand."

She cocked her head and looked at me curiously for a moment. She really was a puppy girl. Then she enjoyed more of the apple while looking around my apartment.

"It was a lot smaller than this one. Maybe from the far wall to the door and over to that blue coat."

I figured she meant the sweatshirt on top of a pile of yuri manga that had once been stacked. That would make it about five feet by eight.

"It had a bed stuck to one of the short walls. A toilet and sink on the other. A window, much smaller than the ones I've seen since. I could see out of it if I jumped and grabbed the bars. Oh! And it was part of a larger cell that the guards came in and out of. There were bars between us."

She happily polished off her dessert, leaving me to struggle with the emotions boiling within me. Sadness, for how she'd been living; anger, toward the guards who'd kept her confined and for whoever was behind them; and incomprehension, of how anyone could do that to someone—I wanted to scream and cry and console her, but I let her apparent calm guide me.

Luckily, my busy brain had been worrying at a detail in her description. She was tall, maybe about six feet, and the bed was along a wall that was roughly five feet long.

"Weird question, but did you sleep with your feet through the bars?"

For the first time, discussion of her cell struck some kind of nerve. She nearly flinched, and all the joy in her body and expression fled. Shrinking into herself, keeping her gaze lowered, speaking quietly but clearly, she seemed to disappear as a person and become a prisoner.

"I obey the rules. I do not stick anything through the bars anymore."

I died a little inside, knowing I'd done this to her somehow.

"I'm so sorry, Cassie. I shouldn't have asked that. I shouldn't have asked anything. You're safe here."

She seemed confused, which was at least better than intimidated. I cracked open her bottled water and handed it to her, and her mood immediately shifted to wonder. She handled it carefully, staring through the clear plastic as she slowly turned the bottle. At last she sniffed at the open top and, apparently satisfied, attempted to drink it. Water poured down her face, and she glared in shock at the bottle's betrayal. I choked down another sympathetic laugh, knowing I'd had to learn all of this a long time ago and had probably looked just as ridiculous.

"Put your lips all around the top," I suggested.

Cassie had more luck this time, and she looked much happier for having successfully had a drink.

"I didn't mean to upset you. I just wanted to understand more so I could help. I'll stop."

She cocked her head again and frowned a little in concentration.

"What's up?" I asked her.

She hesitated but answered with another downward gaze.

"I've heard it before, but I don't understand the word 'help.' "

This girl was going to kill me. My heart ran into my bedroom and slammed the door to have a good cry, leaving the rest of me to deal with explaining human kindness to a person so abused she didn't know anything had been wrong.

"Well, help is when you do something for someone just because it needs doing, not because you were told to or expect something in return. Like when I got meat to give Cassie. Wolf Cassie, I mean. She'd looked so lost and alone that I wanted to help. So I bought the meat and went to give it to her. It wasn't everything she needed, but it was something she needed. That's helping."

She was still frowning in thought.

"Go ahead," I told her. "You don't need my permission to talk or ask questions."

She looked doubtful, but she took a deep breath and spoke.

"She wasn't hungry, Dale. Cassie, that Cassie, doesn't need food. She doesn't have a body."

Now I was lost. I felt my face go slack.

"But I hugged her this morning," I said quietly. "And she ate right in front of me."

"I don't know how it works," she said. "I only see her in dreams or get a sudden feeling about something that she wants me to know."

She stopped talking and seemed to be focused elsewhere. I got a third pair of slices and realized that there wasn't going to be enough left for dinner for both of us. Maybe I could introduce her to burgers and sweet potato fries. Cassie came back to herself as I started to eat.

"Cassie wanted to share some things with you. I'll try to explain. She can touch whenever she wants to, but only if she allows herself to be seen. It feels like there's something wrong, but I don't understand. She's always here, but she can't make herself seen when I'm awake. My hunger and pain affect her. She likes you because you saw her when she wasn't trying to be seen and were kind to her."

Having finished her list of thoughts to translate, she smiled at me.

"She thought you'd help me."

I could feel the tears welling in my eyes, and I took her hand as much for my comfort as for hers. She was startled but smiled more broadly.

"It's okay," she said. "You already helped by bringing me here. I thought you were a guard, at first, and those are most of the people I've met. A few doctors," she said through a shudder, "and once a keeper came in and spat at me. There were other people who came in to fix or clean, but they never spoke to me."

I squeezed her hand. She didn't seem to know what to do about that, but she let it pass.

"You aren't any of those, are you?" she asked.

I didn't know how to explain my job to someone who didn't even know about the internet.

"I'm just a woman who found a wolf and couldn't get her out of my mind."

I didn't deserve to live after throwing out a line like that. Luckily, she didn't understand how appalling and desperate that had sounded.

"Most people aren't guards. We're not much of anything, really. We live our lives, make ourselves as comfortable as we can, and ignore everyone around us. Even most guards probably don't care about much aside from themselves.

"There's a whole separate discussion about restorative justice and the ethics of prisons, but currently people are put into cells when they've gone through a system that supposedly determines whether they've been bad enough to deserve it. It's not a great system, and good people get put in prison, but it's what happens.

"What was done to you was completely outside of the

system, and it should never have been allowed. Everyone who put and kept you in that cell is awful. So I want to know whatever you can tell me about the assholes and how they treated you so I can help you. Whether that's to stay free of them, seek justice, or just learn to live as a free woman."

I'm not sure that she got all the implications of what I'd said. Her experience had been so limited that she couldn't know the range of possibilities before her. But she was overflowing with emotions. Her eyes threatened tears, and her eyebrows wrinkled in uncertainty, but her smile recast everything as hope.

She looked behind me and started to get up from the couch. I let her hand go as she made her way haltingly past me, but I tensed to be ready to help if she stumbled. My floor was a damned mess. That didn't usually bother me; just now I felt guilty in advance for any misstep it caused. It dawned on me that she was heading for the window. I stood up, but I didn't press her. There wasn't much distance between me and where she was going, and I didn't want to make her think I was planning to stop her.

When she reached the curtain, she looked back at me. Keeping them closed helped me feel safely isolated from reality, but if she wanted to let the world into my apartment, I wasn't going to say she couldn't. I nodded to her. She took one end of the curtain and held it aside. I knew that there wasn't much outside to see, but she stared through the window like a house cat looking for birds. Trying to avoid startling her, I approached and reached for the rod to the side of the curtain.

"Here, let me open it for you."

I drew the curtain fully open, and she pressed herself against the window. We stood there for a while, just watching nothing much happen. There weren't many people hanging around outside now that the weather had gotten chilly, although I saw a few just sitting in their cars. Cassie turned and smiled down at me, tears running quietly down her cheeks.

"I'm glad you're not a guard," she said. "I think I'd like your help."

Impulsively, I gave her a supportive hug. After a moment, she wrapped her arms around me and began to cry in earnest. I held her until she was ready to return to the couch.

CHAPTER TWENTY

Janice Altura

It folded the magnification glasses and put them into its work bag. One of many devices it'd had in its possession when its home dimension had disappeared, they were designed to look like mirrored aviator sunglasses—if shades had thick lenses that were cameras in front and screens behind, with a cord on one side sending images to a five-pound box to be processed and returned via a cord on the other side to present for viewing. Clunky, yes, but cutting edge for 1987 and still perfectly functional.

Janice had been about to approach to see if anyone was there when the curtain of the Alexander woman's apartment had opened. With proof someone was present, it'd taken the opportunity to spy, magnifying its view of the apartment until the window filled its vision.

What it'd seen had been not only Dale Alexander herself, uncharacteristically out of a hoodie, but also a taller young woman with a shaved head. It had wondered if she was the "bald girl" seen running from the Kersh Inn. That would be enough of a coincidence that Livinia would have to take notice. Whoever she was, she and Miss Alexander had hugged before withdrawing from the window. Janice didn't know what to make of that. It'd never quite understood human emotions.

With two people in the apartment, it'd have to abandon the thought of breaking in for a look around. It would have to use social engineering, which was not where it shone—unless the occasion called for a flat affect and the hundred years' worth of conflicting social rules rattling in its memory. A quick check in the rearview mirror assured it that its smile was nearly pleasant and its makeup would hold up. Deathly pallor was an improvement over its usual sickly yellow-tinged whiteness. Large sunglasses would conceal its eyes. Armored against scrutiny, it got out of its old black Ion and walked across the parking lot.

A young woman was walking in front of the apartment building. She seemed underdressed for a human; it would expect to see at least a light jacket over the tee and coveralls. Mixed with the toolbox, that was a good sign that the woman might know something about Miss Alexander and Her Amazing Fading Wolf. It veered to meet this woman, pulling out its phone along the way.

"Excuse me," it called out. "Perhaps you can assist."

Filtering its speech to avoid using outdated language was just one more thing it hated about this sort of playacting. It was much easier to sneak in, poke around, and slip away. Those were the jobs it preferred.

The young woman stopped and waited for it to catch up.

"Hi. I don't think I've seen you around before. New resident?"

"No, I'm just looking around."

Janice showed her the image of the wolf it'd downloaded from Miss Alexander's post.

"Have you seen this dog? I was told there'd been a sighting near here."

The woman peered at the image, frowning in concentration.

"Maybe," she said. She looked at Janice closely, and it

thought her genial disposition might have faltered. "Is it yours?"

"Yes," Janice lied. It thought that its eyebrows might have flattened, so it raised them a touch. "A Miss Dale Alexander saw her near here last night."

That put the woman at ease again. Janice wasn't going to question its luck.

"Yeah," she said. "Yeah! That's right. I saw her with your dog this morning. I think she was leaving, but I'd expect her to return soon if she hasn't already." She shook her head. "Sorry she won't be able to keep it. Between you and me, she needs to get out of that apartment more often, and a dog's perfect for that."

Janice put the phone back in its purse.

"I'm in the right place, then. Thank you..."

The woman shifted her toolbox and held out her hand.

"Maggie. Glad to help. It's what I'm here for."

"Janice. I appreciate it."

Janice felt that went well, and as it climbed the steps it hoped the rest of the excursion would go as smoothly. It had only wanted to find out whether Miss Alexander knew anything more about the "dog" she'd found and try to locate the beast. If it was in her apartment—well, that would be very convenient, even if it would make retrieval more complicated.

It reached the apartment and knocked. Sounds of a quick conversation came from inside, too muffled to make out anything but the tone, which it wasn't able to pin down. Panic? Confusion, maybe? There were a few footsteps, and Janice turned its smile to the peephole to reassure anyone looking out. It was just a friendly young brunette with an ashen complexion. Nothing to worry about.

A lock turned and the door opened a few inches. Miss Alexander peered through the crack, holding a hand over her lower face.

"Yeah?"

"Hi! I'm looking for my dog, and Maggie said she thought

she saw you with him earlier. Are you the one who posted the picture to the community page last night?"

Miss Alexander stared at it for a moment, then glanced back into her apartment. She turned her attention back to Janice, looking... skeptical? Hesitant?

"Yeah. That was my post. Sorry. The commenters were right. It was a stupid prank. I couldn't even get the superimposed image to work right. I hope you find your dog, though."

"Oh!" Janice said quickly. "But Maggie was so sure! Please!"

Miss Alexander's eyes darted frantically, seemingly past Janice.

"What does your dog look like?" she asked slowly.

"Mid-sized. Light yellow. Fully solid, ha ha."

"Name?"

"Janice."

They looked at each other for a moment, Janice trying to maintain its smile and Miss Alexander watching through narrowed eyes. Then she raised an eyebrow at her guest.

"Not that I'm judging, but your male dog is named Janice?"

"Oh! Ha ha. No, I thought you wanted my name. His is Rocky. I love ice cream, you see."

Miss Alexander glanced inside again.

"Well, I did find a dog up here this morning. Seemed friendly. We went down the elevator, and it ran off. No collar, though. Did Rocky have a collar?"

Janice nodded, still smiling.

"Have to hang the tags on something, am I right? He's gotten out of it before, though, the little scamp."

Miss Alexander straightened, and Janice guessed that the conversation was at an end.

"Well, I hope that helped. I gotta get back to work. Hope you find your pup."

"Thank you. At least I know I'm in the right area."

The door closed, and Janice finally dropped its smile. Its facial muscles hurt, and it wasn't altogether certain this had been worth the effort after all. Maggie, the woman with the toolbox, had given it more. It decided to keep watching the apartment while pondering its next move. Walking briskly back to its car, it dialed Livinia's number. The call went straight to voicemail, as usual.

"Checking in, boss. Miss Alexander claims the snap was just a giggle, but when I said someone peeped her with the woofer, she fessed up to being with one this morning."

It paused while getting into its car.

"Haven't clocked the beastie, myself, but dig this. I scoped another missy at her pad. Dunno if she's the chick who amscrayed from the hubbub at the Kersh Inn, but she's nearly a cue ball. I'll keep my lookers on them for a spell. Give me a jingle if you noodle something better."

It hung up and set its phone down, pausing as it switched back to the magnification glasses. There seemed to be more people sitting in parked cars than there had been earlier. It decided that this was more curious than concerning but made a mental note to keep a better eye on its surroundings. Glasses on, it settled back into watching the apartment.

CHAPTER TWENTY-ONE

Dale Alexander

I closed the apartment door and relocked it. The woman looking for her dog Rocky had been disturbing, and not just because she'd clearly been fishing for information on Cassie. Something about her had been uncanny valley. Her light grey eyes, not entirely blocked by her sunglasses, had been in stark contrast to her dark hair. Likewise, the sternness of her brow seemed at odds with her wide grin. I tried to not use ableist language, but the best description that I could think of for her was deranged. Her weird vibe aside, it was what she meant for Cassie that was my main concern. What I couldn't figure was just what she'd been after. Was it that she really did not know anything and was hoping to get me to talk; was she just trying to gauge how much I knew; or was she really just looking for her ice cream dog. She had mentioned talking to Maggie, so I could ask about that later. If I remembered.

The dog's name continued to bother me, like a fruit fly that thought my nose was a rotting morsel. If Rocky had been named for an ice cream, the only one that I knew of would be rocky road—a good name for an animal with a coat of dark brown mixed with white and maybe some orange or tan. A light yellow dog, as an ice cream, should be something along the lines of eggnog or honey. On the other hand, she hadn't made much sense to me in general.

With lunch over and Cassie back on the couch, it was time to drop in at work and see if I was needed for anything. That meant returning the apartment to my preferred working conditions, at least temporarily.

"Do you mind if I close the curtain? We can always open it again later, if you want."

"When I want," she corrected, stretching happily.

She was learning quickly. Thankfully, I'd clearly underestimated her.

There were a lot of cars in the parking lot for midday. Probably nothing, but it was the type of nothing that set off my anxieties. I hastily removed the outside world from view.

Cassie was dozing off again when I sat on the floor, my back resting on the couch. I opened the laptop and checked my work messages. There was nothing that needed my attention, so I looked for a small task to do. As my guest lost consciousness, her hand slid onto my shoulder. I'd forgotten how nice casual contact could be, and I let the joy of simply being next to another person again fill me with warmth.

But thinking of Cassie reminded me that I still hadn't taken down that post about her. Nice to know the meds weren't helping me stay on task. I logged into the community forum, and there it was—telling whoever she'd escaped from that I had seen her. I'd consider forgiving myself only if this didn't draw them to her. For all I knew, that woman with the creepy smile was one of them. There were new comments on the post, but I deleted it without looking at them.

I reread the message from Livinia M., and it was just as overwritten and condescending as I remembered. "Dearest Child" set my teeth on edge right at the start. I was thirty-one and a professional consultant. Companies trusted me to come in and get their system issues worked out. Tamping down my defensiveness, I reminded myself that Cassie needed help.

This pompous prophetess sounded like she knew what the fuck was going on. I started drafting a reply.

"Who the hell are you, lady? What do you know about this creature? Could you be more cryptic? Are you threatening me or genuinely concerned for my safety? What the fuck is going on?"

No, that wasn't good at all. Way too desperate and hostile.

"I tried to help the dog, and now scary people are coming to my apartment asking questions about it. Can you help?"

Better, but it could be more informative.

"Creeps are coming around to my place because of that picture. I deleted the post, but I'm afraid they'll keep coming. You seem to know something. Please tell me what's going on."

I read it over again, and it sounded direct but urgent. Satisfied, I hit send.

Now I could do some work to the sound of Cassie's gentle snores, interspersed with an occasional whine.

CHAPTER TWENTY-TWO

David Kuiper

His phone rang with the creepy tone reserved for his older brother. This mess with the wolf girl meant that he had to pick up, which rankled him even more. This business couldn't end fast enough.

"Toby," he said curtly on answering the phone.

"Little brother," came the patronizing reply.

David bristled, as always, but reminded himself that he owed the bastard for providing that address earlier. Forcing down his irritation, he assumed a more polite tone.

"To what do I owe the pleasure?"

There was a slight pause, and he hoped that Toby had choked on the word *pleasure*.

"Do you have it?"

He didn't need to ask what "it" referred to. There was only one topic on all of their minds today.

"When I do, you'll be the third or fourth to know. Thanks for the address, but I have people on this. If there's nothing else...?"

He wasn't exactly sure that they had done anything yet, or that they would be doing anything very quickly. His friend had given him the number of Wes Utley, a less than reputable cousin who was not above breaking laws for fun or profit. He'd also warned him that the man lacked any sense of urgency or subtlety but would eventually follow through. David had assumed that offering five thousand dollars would be motivating, but perhaps he should follow up.

"I see. Tell me, does one of them happen to be a dark-haired young woman who drives an old Saturn?"

He had no idea what Toby was talking about, but just knowing that he was leading to something made David's stomach churn.

"I don't care to know specifics. My man can use whoever he wants, but the price for services has already been set."

"I see," Toby said, and his tone conveyed his condolences. "Little sister was just telling me that her people—who are watching the apartment but have failed to act for some reason—saw such a person knock on the door, speak with someone inside, and return to her car to wait. I assured her that, as you are fully aware of the location, it's most likely that this woman is one of yours. I'd hate to think that you'd let some other party, even our dear sister, be the one to retrieve our asset."

If she wasn't one of Utley's people, and Annette had told their brother the truth, then she could be one of Nathaniel's. The bastard had sworn that it would take several days to mobilize a search from his end, if he even bothered, but who else could it be?

"Your concern is touching, but I'm sure everything is under control. Now, if you'll excuse me, I do have a business to run."

"Certainly, little brother. I apologize for taking you away from your important work. You know I worry about you and Annette, taking on so much responsibility."

Ah, the solicitous insinuation that the younger siblings weren't nearly as capable as Toby. A specialty of his back-handed approach to the family's dysfunction. David's own preference was curtness in the guise of efficiency.

"Yes. Well, thank you for thinking of me. Goodbye, Toby."

He hung up before he could hear whatever his brother said in reply and immediately called Utley. If that hadn't been one of the man's associates, then that meant two competitors were already on the scene.

CHAPTER TWENTY-THREE

Cassie (Wolf)

Her host had fallen asleep, and she could be present again. She walked behind the couch before doing so. Other creatures seemed alarmed when she simply appeared among them, so she'd long ago built the habit of revealing herself by emerging from concealed places.

She padded out from hiding, her paws treading softly on the carpet. Her gaze shifted between her host, asleep on the couch, and Dale, the woman who could see her. Watching them bond so quickly was encouraging. After being attached to so many hosts in captivity, here at last was a chance to experience a life of relative freedom.

It was too bad that the agent of their rescue wasn't male. The woman would have made a good mate for her host, but unless there was a pup to move on to, it would be back to the family that kept her hosts locked away. Still, her current host would be able to find her own mate, and that was a pleasant thought. There'd be plenty of time for preparing a new vessel, so why not allow this one to enjoy her life while she could?

Feeling optimistic about the future for the first time since her binding long ago, she approached Dale. The woman sat on the carpet, back to the couch, frowning at her laptop and occasionally typing. The wolf spirit stood beside her, peering at the screen. She'd learned to read English several hosts ago, but this looked like some form of structured poem mixed with math.

"Gimme a sec," the woman said.

She turned back to the human, leaning in to sniff. Finally noticing her, Dale turned, startled, and received licks of greeting. Once again, the woman refused to open her mouth for grooming. The wolf spirit was disappointed, but she sensed that this human didn't trust easily. She understood that. Most of the species were largely untrustworthy, which was why this one was so special.

Dale scratched her behind the ears, and she crawled into the woman's lap to accept more. At least they'd come this far. There was time to bring her more fully into the pack.

First Interlude: Livinia Monroe

Livinia had gone back to the beginning in order to experience the life she'd lived after casting the spell. In the immediate aftermath, things had gone on much as before. She'd spent her days in isolation within her mansion walls. Long a hermit in practice, the sudden inability to leave the house had made no difference in her behavior. What it had altered was her perspective. The loss of her family and inner circle and the collapse of the Society for Preternatural Investigations had prompted her to withdraw to the solitary comfort of her library. What the spell had accomplished was to create a new being out of her old, brooding self and the very house within which she'd hidden. Though her consciousness resided within a body not altogether different from her human form, her senses had grown to encompass the house. Her spatial awareness had expanded to include complex new layers that determined the position of her bipedal form within her larger body. She could feel where objects lay within her and monitor the approach of humans and animals.

The footprint of her home, her body, had not changed, but her beloved library had enlarged to contain every word ever written. There were sections for every topic, from botany to the writings of Millicent Webster, a seaman's wife in eighteenth-century Falmouth who composed beautiful sonnets in the margins of her papers, all of which were lost in a dreadful storm. It contained every Sumerian tablet and every message of beads. If it was written, it was in her small library. She just had to locate it.

There was no formal guide for navigating this archive. The room remained as it always had, with a desk and lamp along the wall to the left of the door. Shelves covered the other three walls—one of which had held windows long ago—and two sets of floor-to-ceiling shelves stood between them, bearing books on either side. There were a few small display cases to hold artifacts that couldn't fit comfortably on a shelf. Typically these bore cuneiform tablets or oversized tomes, but she had discovered small stelae and folded quilts there in her wanderings.

That was the trick of it. As she walked though the shelves and thought about what she was after, the library's contents shifted toward her goal. Although she could feel every plate, every candle within her walls, the library stacks lay beyond her sense of self. She suspected that their contents were so vast that she would be unable to spread her awareness over them all. The stacks changed every time she turned a corner, never while she watched. After some practice, she learned to focus her searches with some precision. The greatest difficulty lay in knowing what she sought. Greater specificity yielded the best results. The more that she knew about the work's author and origins, the easier it became to track it down. To find the first written communication, she would have to know when it was written, where, and by whom. In other words, she had to do exhaustive research in order to find the information required to locate anything. Given that data, she could simply enter the library and reach for it.

She had amused herself for months by starting with a particular English translation of Plato's series of dialogs about the trial and death of Socrates and followed its citations backward in time until finally losing the trail in Byzantine texts of the eighth century. It was during this exercise that Livinia established a procedure of taking extensive notes about where sources were found. These then appeared in the library, creating an easy-to-locate personal index for the materials she'd already found.

Access to the entire history of human writing had been her goal, and having time to dig into it had been a key motivation for casting the spell. In her time as the research librarian for her father's House of the SPI, she'd examined and translated dozens of occult tomes. Magic became more unreliable the further it got from its primary sources, and most of those were no longer extant. Copies and translations always introduced variance even with the best of intentions, and the versions generally available to modern practitioners were dangerous to attempt. It was only after she'd lost everything that she had felt any temptation to try one herself. She'd had nothing more to lose. Only her books and research remained to her, and the potential for expanding her collection of knowledge had been incalculable.

The biggest drawback had been discovering just how exhaustive her library had become. In addition to all of the manuscripts she could ever want, she had every note, every edit, every childish scribble in a margin. Graffiti, bills of sale, initials etched in trees—if it was written, it was here, somewhere. Her store of all human wisdom drowned in the trivialities of mundane lives. In the quiet of the mansion, she could hear the constant shifting of the library as it collated the daily written output of a few billion people. It had been maddening.

She'd needed a focus, a way to approach the massive influx of information, and she'd begun to read the local papers. Having spent her life in esoteric circles, the matters of the public record were mysterious to her. Arguments over proposed ordinances. Notifications of store openings. High school sports scores. Crime reports.

The SPI had sought to protect the world from dangers

outside the normal experience—creatures from other worlds and dimensions, things that crept in the shadows and crawled underground. Perhaps she could bend her talents toward the more prosaic hazards of ordinary experience.

Livinia followed the crime sheets until she read about an arrest for a robbery. She shifted her consciousness to the day of the theft and sent word to the manager of her foundation. When he arrived, she entrusted him with a note to hand the police. It contained the name of the perpetrator, the time and location of the robbery, and the few pieces of evidence mentioned in the article. She recalled having experienced a memory from a later point in her life that she should not attempt to use future knowledge, but it had seemed simple enough to accomplish.

She returned to the day of the original arrest and hastened to the library to see what had changed. Nothing. All was as it had been. The crime had still occurred, and it had taken the same amount of time to discover and capture the criminal. Perhaps the police had not read her note.

She went back to the papers. Weeks later, she read a report of a fatal traffic accident. This time she sent notes to the police and the two drivers. Again, there was no change. She began to form and reject theories. These were only memories; she could not do anything that she had not already done. (Nonsense. She had not sent out the four notices until she replayed those moments.) Her actions might differ, but fates could not change. (It was inconceivable to hold that one person had free will in a world governed by destiny.) She existed outside of the flow of time, so any change she made was rapidly erased.

That last thought was interesting. Her agent had confirmed on both occasions that he'd delivered the notes, and he remembered having done so when questioned later. It was true, however, that she existed apart from time. What if she couldn't change events because she'd already changed them? Then she had lived twice through those periods of time, but the future she'd tried to prevent had happened precisely because of that intervention. She wasn't sure of the physics; that had been Rudyard's area of expertise, and he had been lost with the rest of her SPI House. Her specialty had been research and legends, and she'd found many references to prophecies that came true despite or because of attempts to circumvent them. Foreknowledge caused the actions that brought about that fate. Of course, another interpretation was that any action at all would lead to the same outcome, but that implied only some events were large enough to be predetermined and the details between them were mutable. In that event, it was peculiar that she had found two such unchangeable moments in quick succession.

She needed to learn more.

Some days later she found another opportunity: a blaze that had hospitalized a responding firefighter. As she read about the incident, she thought about how to stop the fire from starting or at least keep the responder safe. A simple notification wouldn't be enough. She'd need to know the cause and find a way to convince someone to ensure it didn't happen. As she thought about the alternatives, she felt the now-familiar tug in her mind that indicated a related memory. Though she tried to experience her memories in linear order, she had made exceptions. Intrigued by this feeling of a connected event, she decided to explore it.

This other recollection took place in her library, where she read the same paper, but details of the fire were different. No one had been injured, but an additional three homes had burned. Not an ideal outcome, but one that spared physical injury. What had happened differently? Livinia recalled that in the first version the hurt firefighter had been hailed for leading a desperate, risky final push into the home. Now, there was criticism of the response, as the unit had used a more cautious approach. They'd allowed the fire to burn and focused on minimizing its ability to spread. They considered the loss of four houses a victory under the circumstances. It seemed that the outcome of the incident hinged on the choice of one person.

She wasn't comfortable choosing between the versions, but here was an event that could help her to understand her relation to fate. Since the injury had occurred in the first iteration, she would select the second to be real. But how would she bring it about? Assuming that her prior notes had reached their intended readers, the warnings had not been read. She might suggest that the firefighter be cautious, but that's exactly what she'd have done having never seen the account where he'd come out of the incident unscathed.

It occurred to her that on the previous occasions she'd written the warnings from the perspective of future knowledge. Telling him to be cautious would reinforce the injury narrative. She'd have to write from the knowledge of the future in which he was not in danger. She could hear Rudyard grousing about his beloved Scientific Method, and the Colonel lecturing her about controls and hypotheses. She could do that. But this was about magic, a subject notoriously immune to scientific analysis.

Livinia went back to the day of the fire and wrote a brief note to the firefighter. All it contained was the short sentence "You'll be fine." She summoned her man to deliver it. As soon as he left, she went forward to read how it all turned out. Four houses lost, no injuries.

Speak the future you want to see.

Part Two

THE CURIOUS MANSION

CHAPTER TWENTY-FOUR

Mike Lakeland

Miss Kuiper had demanded that he move in now before that woman who'd knocked on the apartment door came back. He'd ignored her, partly because their target would be difficult for such a small person to control but mostly because he'd rather not work for her anymore. It wasn't easy to think of what other jobs he could perform that would pay so well, but he'd socked enough away that he could afford a lower salary. The tricky part would be extricating himself from this mess. The greater Kuiper family had a long reach, but he had to hope that his direct employer lacked the influence to wield it. For now, he was content to continue watching. The target or the apartment's owner would leave at some point, and they would have an opportunity to act.

A white Chevy Colorado pulled into the lot and parked right in front of the building. Two men in hunting camo and brown jackets got out, and he watched as they went up the steps. They looked at the door numbers as they passed and stopped directly outside the apartment under observation.

"Fuck," Lakeland said.

Behind the wheel, Fielding simply shook his head.

"What now?" Markham groaned from the back seat, where she'd been napping.

"More company," Fielding summarized. "And they look like assholes."

Markham sat up to look and watched with them as the men broke through the apartment door.

"Huh," she said. "Couldn't we have done that an hour ago?"

"Sure, if we wanted to be noticed," Lakeland answered testily. "But what do they plan on doing once they grab her, toss her in the bed?"

He pointed at the truck, and she laughed when she saw it.

"Try driving with six feet of angry woman sitting bitch," Fielding said.

Markham laughed again.

"You're gonna have five and a half feet of angry bitch behind you if you keep that shit up, Paul."

They fell silent as the woman from the Ion hastened past them on the way to the apartment.

"Mike?" Fielding asked.

"Let them fight it out," Lakeland said. "We'll follow whoever manages to come out with our target."

He called Tallman in the other car to relay the instructions. Maybe real estate wouldn't be a bad gig. He had a cousin who could give him pointers.

CHAPTER TWENTY-FIVE

Dale Alexander

It was the wolf's reaction to the knocking that pulled me out of the package release notes I'd been digging through. We'd settled on an arrangement where she rested her head on my left thigh while I balanced my laptop on the right one. Since I was mainly reading, it had been working well. Then she jerked her head up and growled.

I patted her on the head and closed my laptop.

"I'll be right back," I told her.

I got up and looked out the peephole. There were two large men outside, wearing dark knit caps and light brown jackets. They had that two-day stubble look that I never understood. Of course, I had my own feelings about facial hair.

"Who are you?" I asked through the door.

"We're here for the dog."

That answered my next question without addressing the first, but it seemed that taking down the post hadn't been enough. I imagined that Cassie's pursuers would arrive soon, if they hadn't already. Would we have to leave my apartment? This was the only place where I felt safe to be who I am, whatever that was exactly. I had to make them go away.

"There wasn't any dog. It was just a stupid joke. I'm really sorry you thought it was your pet."

I glanced back at the couch, taking in the wolf's alert stance.

"She's not a pet, ma'am. Escaped lab animal. Very dangerous. Need to retrieve her before anyone gets hurt."

I backed away from the door, and I started to feel faint. Their story was nonsense, but they were closer than the last visitor in some alarming ways. The growling behind me had grown hotter.

"Haven't seen it!" I yelled, panicking. "Go away!"

The wolf came over to my side, fur bristling, her growl deep and threatening. I could hear them talking outside but couldn't make anything out. They fell quiet, and I dared to hope that they'd decided to leave. There's a reason I don't make bets.

The door shuddered as they slammed into it, and my knees gave out. Cassie's wolf moved slowly and deliberately in front of me, hackles raised, lips curled. She'd gone silent. The door shook again, and this time I could hear splintering wood. I couldn't think of anything useful to do but call the police, but they'd want to take Cassie away. If they discovered what she was... And so I watched as the little chain that held the door ripped away and the men came inside.

Cassie puffed a few times and ran for the bedroom. The sense of abandonment hurt more than the realization that a moist warmth had spread down my inner thighs. The men pushed past me and headed for the couch. I buried my face in my hands and hoped the end would be quick. My mental robot protector was nowhere to be found.

CHAPTER TWENTY-SIX

Janice Altura

It crouched in the doorway and fired two quick rounds from its somnumatic pistol. They hit the man grabbing the sleeping woman's shoulders, and he fumbled for his gun. His friend, with his back to the door, moved quickly. This one spun and drew his pistol fluidly, firing before he could see his target. It wasn't afraid of being hit, but regrowing skin was itchy and slow. Staying low, it rolled into the room and fired a shot at the second man.

The first one had gotten his pistol out, but he was already unsteady from the doses of somnusol. He fired wildly as he veered to face Janice. The resident, Dale Alexander, crouched sobbing on the ground in the midst of what had become an active fire zone. It felt bad about that, but when the men had broken in, it had felt the time for observation had passed. It grabbed the woman and pulled at her.

"Get out of here! Now!"

Dale was unresponsive, and Janice decided it needed to move the lines of fire away from her. A bullet tore into its upper arm as it loaded three more bullets, and it lost some control of the limb. Dangit. It crab walked toward the first intruder, firing a few shots at the second. Only one hit, and it cursed its many years spent in semiretirement. At least his return shot missed again. The first one, meanwhile, lost his balance while turning and fell onto the couch. Janice took cover where he'd been standing and paused to see how the other would react. With two doses in him he should be pretty wobbly soon.

"We just want the girl," the second said from his end of the couch.

It glanced between the two young women and figured he meant the one on the couch. Were these guys involved in the shooting at the Kersh Inn?

"Well," it said. "You need some new kicks, pal. How about coins? I held onto a few steelies, myself."

He fell silent, and it wondered if he'd passed out as it seemed his friend had. Then she saw the tip of his gun stick out from behind the couch, pointed toward the center of the room, where Dale was trembling.

"Throw out your gun, or I shoot her," the man demanded.

It heard soft footsteps approaching from behind. Not knowing there was anyone else in the apartment, it turned to see who was there. Pale blue eyes, under a furrowed brow, stared at it over a blonde muzzle. The wolf had been here after all. Hooray. The creature was nearly fully visible in the gloom of the apartment, and it would prefer to not test the solidity of those teeth. Feeling the hot breath of the wolf, Janice thought the odds against the gunman were a lot steeper.

"One sec," she called over the couch. It lowered its eyes, vaguely recalling that canids saw eye contact as a challenge. "I'm in a tight spot."

He laughed.

"She has until I count three."

Still looking down, it tilted its head back and to the side, exposing its throat. The wolf sniffed and gently placed its jaws over the drab gray flesh.

"One!"

The wolf withdrew, seeming uneasy but no longer interested, and stalked around to the front of the couch.

"Two!"

Janice refocused on the situation. The wolf had moved on but there was little time left in which to act.

"Thr—"

"Okay!" she called out. "I'm out of the corner now! Thank you!"

"You're—? Throw the gun!" he barked. "Now!"

"Here it comes!"

It powered down the somnumatic and threw the pistol high over the couch, angling it to give him time to see and focus on it. Hopefully that would allow enough time for Janice to move.

It darted from behind the couch, but the fight was already all but over. The back end of the wolf moved behind the other edge of the couch, while the screams of the man dwindled into gurgles underneath its weight. Figuring that the creature had him under control, it hurried over to Dale.

"You're in the clear. It's all gravy now." There was shouting outside as panicked residents tried to figure out what was happening. "More like drippings. We need to skedaddle."

It looked over to the corner of the couch but only saw the mangled gunman. The wolf had disappeared. Livinia would blow a gasket. The girl on the couch groaned and pushed at the man who'd fallen on her. Janice helped Dale stand up and patted her back in an attempt to encourage her.

"Good girl. Pack your bindle. Phone, wallet, birth control, whatever. We need to jet."

It left Dale to go to the couch and help remove the unconscious gunman. Freed of his mass, the girl immediately rushed to Dale and held her, glaring back at it with familiar pale blue eyes. Janice swore that a small growl came from her snarling mouth. The pieces didn't all fit, but it could see the shape of the puzzle.

"Oh," it said. It had never encountered anything like this

wolf girl, but it had seen far stranger things over the last century and change. Janice looked down again and spoke quietly, making itself use much more direct language than it preferred.

"I'm not here to hurt you. Either of you. I was investigating the phantom wolf sightings, but that's all. When these mooks... when these men broke through your door, I thought you could use a hand. If you want me to leave now, I will. I'll just go, no questions asked."

It paused. The wolf girl had stopped snarling but continued to radiate hostility. Livinia would be upset if it returned empty-handed, but Janice felt that returning with both hands and its face would be nice.

"But I hope you come with me. Not because my employer is curious about you, but because you need someplace to hide. Whoever sent these two isn't going to give up, and right now a whole lot of scared people are calling the cops. This apartment is about to be crawling with officers who won't ask questions until after throwing you into a cell."

The wolf girl had been starting to calm, right until that moment. Janice didn't know what had changed, but there wasn't time to reflect. The girl started thrashing erratically and screaming. Much of it was incoherent, but a few words stood out.

"No! No cell! No guards!"

While Janice tried to figure out how to regain control, Dale came out of her daze, hugging the girl and murmuring reassurances.

"No guards, Cassie. No cells. No doctors. Just us."

Janice noted the name while retrieving her somnumatic.

"Dale," it called out. "Time to move. If you want to protect Cassie, we have to get her to safety."

Dale nodded distractedly.

"Okay. Okay. Cassie, she's right."

"Not right," Cassie said, muffled by Dale's shoulder. "She's not right."

Janice glanced at the pair. The clever woofer had clocked her. It found a bag and stuffed in some clothes that seemed relatively clean.

"'It/its', and I'm no normal deb, true, but I'm the street peddler selling the swell idea to book it before you're pinched."

Dale frowned, but she continued to reassure Cassie.

"Anything else you absolutely need?" Janice asked.

"Laptop," Dale answered. "I'll get my med kit. You okay, Cassie?"

Dale disappeared into the back of the apartment while Janice crouched over the unconscious man.

"Do you know who sent them?" it asked Cassie.

"No," she said flatly.

The man's pockets were nearly empty. No wallet. No keys. But it did find a picture of a young woman with a shaved head, wearing a drab simple dress. Cassie. It took the photo. Livinia might be able to do something with it.

"Cassie, could you help me lug this dope? I'd like to crack his nut."

Cassie approached uncertainly, but she did help lift the man. By the time they had him upright, Dale had come back, sporting a dry pair of gray sweatpants, pink Vans, and a black backpack. She put on her knit cap and a dark blue hoodie, glanced at the others, who were still propping up one of the intruders, and picked up the bag Janice had packed. They left wordlessly, no one bothering to shut the door. As they walked to Janice's car, the sound of sirens grew closer.

CHAPTER TWENTY-SEVEN

Annette Kuiper

"Do you want the good news first, or the bad?" Lakeland asked.

Annette gripped her phone harder.

"Don't waste my fucking time," she answered. Her voice was quiet. She'd long since learned that yelling at work would be used against her, and she refused to raise her voice enough for it to escape her private office. But her displeasure made itself felt in razor-sharp enunciation.

"Right, okay. The tl;dr is that the agent who approached earlier took the package. We have two cars following them."

Annette smiled despite herself. She'd hoped all along that the woman had been working for Toby. It had simply been too soon for Nathaniel's people to arrive. There'd be a price, but at least her dear older brother would be willing to part with the creature. Of course, this did not counteract her displeasure with Lakeland's performance. As soon as this affair was over, she planned to cut him loose.

"Send around a description of the new agent. Let's get identification and known associates for her."

"Right away," Lakeland promised. "We have clear shots of her and her car from when she approached the apartment earlier."

Lakeland paused, and Annette once again had to push aside a flash of anger. He always had one more bit of information but wouldn't just say it.

"Good work. Let me know what you find. Was there anything else?"

"She didn't take only the package. She has the woman who found it and one of the idiots that broke in."

"Who?!"

"Sorry, ma'am. We were preparing for our own grab when these two guys drove up in a pickup and charged into the apartment. That's when the woman entered and, well, it looks like she won."

David had always held himself separate from the rest of the family, so it made sense he'd send amateurs. That much made sense, but if the woman was working for Toby she wouldn't need anyone but the target. She was the only leverage necessary to squeeze either her or David.

"Was she holding a gun on them?"

"No, ma'am. She had some kind of pistol when she entered the apartment, and there were shots fired inside. Cops are crawling all over the place now."

"Lakeland," she growled.

"Yeah, sorry. She came out carrying the guy with, ah, the package's help. The resident followed along with a couple of bags. Everyone conscious seemed to be together willingly."

A DM from Kevin popped up on her monitor.

Hey mom

"Hold on," she told Lakeland.

She typed a quick response to her son, letting him know she was wrapping up a call.

"Okay. Thanks, Lakeland. Call me when you have anything on this mystery woman or where she's taking the package."

"Will do, boss."

She hung up and took a deep breath. This had already gotten messier than she'd wanted, and she'd have to sort it out before she lost the prize. But her son came first. This whole business was for him.

Annette told her phone to call Kevin.

"Mom, I texted 'cause I can't really talk."

The noise of a van load of high school golfers verified his claim. A chorus of loud, exaggerated greetings emerged from the general commotion. "Hi, mom!" they yelled. Annette smiled, imagining her son blushing at the attention.

"I just wanted to hear your voice," she told him.

Kevin's teammates laughed as he shushed them.

"Bad day?" he asked her, his voice quiet but closer. She realized he'd pressed the phone to his face.

"I've had better," she admitted. "But it's under control. Don't worry about me. Keep your mind on your swing."

He groaned dramatically.

"I know. Between you and Coach, how can I forget?"

"Right. You're so abused," she remarked, and if there was a touch of acid in her voice it was surely a release for her stress over the wolf affair.

"Anyway, I just wanted to let you know we're on our way to the course."

"Thanks for checking in. I'll be there shortly to applaud wildly to the extent it's allowed. I just need to wrap up a few outstanding items."

"Okay. See you there."

"I love you, Kevin."

She knew she'd put him in an uncomfortable position by saying that. Would he respond in kind and risk the ridicule of his friends, or would he finally break her heart and deny their close bond?

"I love you, too," he said, as quietly as possible. His teammates heard it, though, and the background erupted with sarcastic endearments.

Satisfied, she let him go. She had more calls to make.

CHAPTER TWENTY-EIGHT

Cassie (Human)

The creepy woman's car was small and I never wanted to be in one again. At least she'd let me sit where I could see outside, but I could barely see anything before it was gone. The bench was comfortable, but I was pressed in between the bench ahead of me and the guard sleeping next to me. Dale had strapped herself in front of me. I reached out and tapped her right shoulder. She turned, but only a little, so I leaned toward her.

"I don't like her," I whispered. "She's not right."

"It," Dale said. "Not 'she' or 'her.' "

I sat back, frustrated and a little hurt.

"I don't understand," I said. "You say you want to help me, and I should say what I think, but when I tell you I'm worried you ignore me and just say 'it.' "

"Cassie, I—" Dale started.

I could see her look at our driver with concern, but the woman didn't seem to notice.

"You probably didn't hear much about pronouns in the... where you were. They're the general words you use in place of names of people and things."

I didn't see what this had to do with anything, but I

trusted her and hoped that she'd come back to what I'd said about the thing sitting next to her.

"I understand," I said, lying just a little.

"Okay, so until very recently you'd use the pronouns 'she' and 'her' for anyone you thought was a woman. 'She called,' 'I talked to her'—that sort of thing."

I did understand that, but I hadn't known the word. There was a guard who'd complained about pronouns, I remembered, but he hadn't said anything about what they were. I still didn't know why we were talking about this. To the best of my knowledge I'd been speaking correctly.

"Yes," I said. "She upsets me."

"It," they both said.

"What the prof here is trying to break down for you is that even though your peepers see a woman, you should use 'it' and 'its' pronouns for me. 'It upsets me' and 'I'm in its back seat' and 'I should thank it for saving me.' "

I thought about that. It didn't make any sense to me, but that was okay. A lot of things didn't. If she... if it wanted me to use those words for... it, I could learn to do that. But now I didn't know what that meant.

"Okay, so is it a man or a woman?"

"Neither," it said. "I'm nonbinary."

"That's an umbrella term," Dale said. "There are a lot of identities under it, but in general enbies don't follow the strict gender roles of their culture."

I was more confused than before, so I said back what I'd understood.

"Nonbinary people aren't men or women, and I should call them it."

The driver made a barking sound that could have been a laugh. We still needed to talk about how much I didn't like it.

"There are a lot of different pronouns," Dale said. "And also you can still be a man or woman. There's a lot of nuance, but it comes down to personal preference."

I wanted to ask more questions, but she seemed to have

gone blank again. After a moment, she came back and glanced around the car.

"Since you're genderqueer too..." she said, looking at it before turning back toward me. "I'm trans nonbinary, but I use feminine pronouns. So you'd use 'she/her' for me, even though I don't call myself a woman. Most of us won't get offended if you accidentally use the wrong one—like, obviously not out of malice—but we'll let you know what to use. Everything was so fucked up that I didn't stop to think you wouldn't understand our corrections. Sorry about that."

Somehow this whole thing about pronouns had become an apology. Dale was incredible. I could feel the happiness flow up from my chest into my face.

"Anyway," she added. "You were saying something?"

I couldn't remember what I'd wanted to talk about. There was only this warm feeling that made my eyes water.

"No, go on," I told her. "I'd like to know more."

CHAPTER TWENTY-NINE

David Kuiper

It was Toby's ringtone again. Given everything, he answered anyway.

"Yes, Toby," he said.

"Little brother, things have gotten busy at that address I gave you. Have you heard from your man who was handling this for you?"

David took a deep breath.

"No, but I'm certain I'll hear from him once he's done the job."

"Oh! I hope for your sake he's not the one who died."

David felt the blood drain from his head. His stomach immediately twisted.

"Dead?" he choked.

"But if he is alive, he was taken by the dark-haired woman. I suppose that would be good, if she were working for you, especially since she took your package."

The phone slipped, and he had to grab it with the other hand.

"I see," he said. "Well, I'll look forward to hearing from Mr. Utley."

"In that case, little brother, it's time for me to send in Robinson on your behalf. Our sister's operatives are currently in pursuit of your prize, and I want him to take charge. For you, of course."

David couldn't control his anger anymore. He supposed that made him more like their father than the others were. They prided themselves in hiding their rage and contempt, even though they fooled nobody. At least he was honest about his feelings.

"Fuck you, Toby! I don't need your goddamn help! Keep that Robinson fuck out of it!"

"Well, if that's the way you feel, little bro—"

He hung up.

This needed to stop. Not just the wolf business; it was well past time to be rid of his brother. He'd need to deal with both quickly, and it seemed that the people he'd hired weren't going to be useful.

He called Nathaniel again.

CHAPTER THIRTY

Dale Alexander

We pulled into a small driveway nearly hidden between the parking lots of the emergency vet clinic and the small strip mall, which only had a tanning salon still open. It led back behind the two buildings to a circular drive around a fountain, which appeared to be well-maintained despite having no water pumping through it. Given the late October chill, I figured it had been turned off for the winter. Beyond this feature stood an imposing structure—a mansion in the Victorian style, two stories at least (I couldn't tell if it was topped by a diminished third floor or an attic), with a wraparound porch and a tower on the right side. It was a pinkish purple with lavender trim, and I recognized it from my browsing this morning.

"Here?" I asked. "Jessup's mansion, Aletheia?"

The car pulled in on the curve in front of the walk.

"Bingo bango," our driver said.

We got out of the sedan and opened the rear doors. I pushed down my seat so Cassie could climb out. This car might work for clowns, but it was ridiculous for the rest of us. Cassie helped Janice haul Sleeping Beauty out of the car, and I followed them toward the porch steps with my bags.

"Do you work for Livinia Monroe?"

It glanced back at me as it and Cassie hauled the guy up to the porch.

"I'm just a friend doing a favor."

"Whose friend?"

The door to the mansion opened. I craned to look inside, but there didn't seem to be anyone in the doorway. Maybe there was still a butler here, or whoever's job it was to greet people. I wondered just how well-funded the Jessup Foundation was. At least this validated the research I'd done on the family this morning. Whatever "Livinia M." had tried to warn me about, I was in it now.

We went inside, passing through a dark entryway. It was like going through an airlock before entering the actual house. The next door, also opened to us, led to a large room with a grand staircase and openings to other areas. I grew up and lived in apartments, so I'm not really sure about fancy room names. There were some ornate chairs and a small table by the staircase, so I thought it could be a waiting room of some kind. Here, the heavily clouded sun came through the windows and brightened the gloom somewhat. I doubted that even the chandelier (currently unlit) could do much to counter the heaviness of the ornate wallpaper and busy decor. My apartment resembled a gloomy trash heap, and the only difference here was that all the clutter was neatly displayed on the walls and tables. Even the ceiling was decorated with what looked like stamped tin squares.

Whatever this room was, it was roughly the size of the public space in my apartment. The hall—was it a great hall?—had nobody but us in it, and I could see a sort of living room through a large opening in the wall to our right. The wall was very thick, housing a wooden door that presumably slid out. The other room looked smaller, but that might be just that it was crowded with chairs and couches. It was also much brighter. The dim outside light had plenty of windows to seep in through, particularly from the tower. My bags were becoming unbearable to hold, and I was sure the others would have liked to set down our captive. Before I could move toward the living room, the doors behind us swung closed. As Cassie and I recovered from the surprise, a woman came down the stairs with all the grace and poise of Hollywood's Golden Age. We watched in silent awe as she approached.

She was small, somewhere between me and our diminutive driver in height. Her outfit was an older style—a matching pink jacket and long skirt, with a white shirt and narrow red tie. My mom loved Katherine Hepburn, and the woman before us reminded me of her presence. Refined and elegant, this was no well-bred actress; she was a socialite, even after all these long years. This was Livinia Monroe, more than twice as old as in the picture I'd seen, but far younger than she had any reason to be.

She looked us over, her eyes absently wandering to the side of us, before she focused her polite smile on her helpful friend.

"Perhaps, Miss Altura, you'd care to explain."

CHAPTER THIRTY-ONE

Janice Altura

Janice adjusted the weight of its captive. Its wounded arm had improved but wasn't back to full functionality yet.

"Got anywhere to stick this lug?"

Livinia looked him over indifferently.

"There is some rope in the pantry. You may leave him in the kitchen for now. He'll be moved downstairs shortly."

It looked past the unconscious man at the wolf girl.

"Let's make tracks, Cassie. Two more rooms."

They carried their burden into the dining room and maneuvered around the table. It was a large room, but between the massive table, the elaborately carved chairs with arms too large to slide under the table, and the sturdy side cabinets, there wasn't enough room for three people to pass easily. They shuffled along sideways, rounded the corner, passed the entrance to the sitting room, and left through the tiny back hall. Barely the size of the entranceway, this was a glorified connector between the dining room, the back stairs, and the kitchen. Once in the kitchen, Janice guided them to the small table in the corner and pulled out a chair with its foot.

"Here."

They lowered the man into the chair, and Janice retrieved the rope from the pantry.

"What's that for?" Cassie asked.

It finished tying the captive's arms behind him and started working on his legs.

"Just making sure our guest sticks around," it said.

"Why?"

Janice had never had children. That likely wouldn't even be possible, and it had certainly never felt the desire to try. All of its coworkers who were parents talked about the "why" phase, when their offspring were either challenging authority or really struggling with understanding the world. Janice stared into Cassie's eyes, wondering for the first time just what was going on in their shaved head.

"Here's the dope. When a goon throws slugs at you, and you want the skinny, you make sure he can't skedaddle."

They looked skeptical.

"But his gun is gone. You could just put him in a cell."

A human might laugh at that, and Janice had never fully understood why. Some people seemed to need that to release tension or frustration. Or express a sense of irony. Ted had always laughed, and that might have been its favorite thing about him, back in the day. But it didn't laugh. It could grin well enough, when feeling honest joy or happiness, but it had never worked out a proper laugh.

"Yeah, okay. Got a cell in your pants?"

Cassie frowned.

"Just my legs. And the panties Dale gave me."

That wasn't enough to make Janice grin, but it did decide that the wolf girl was fun.

"Rope will have to do, then," it declared. "Let's scoot. The others are probably stuck scoping each other."

CHAPTER THIRTY-TWO

Livinia Monroe

Livinia led the young woman into the parlor while the others carried the criminal off to the kitchen. It was an overcast day, so she chose the curved bench in the arc of the tower. The three windows let in what little light there was to be had, and she suspected that her visitors would feel more comfortable on the sturdy wood than perched on ornate chairs. She seated herself at one end, and her guest immediately took the opposite position, gazing intently at the late-blooming flowers outside. This gave Livinia an opportunity to appraise her.

She thought that the young woman was unhappy—not just with the present situation, but in her life. She'd made herself as small as possible on the bench, and her stare was wild-eyed rather than curious. She looked trapped, and her disheveled clothing made her seem feral. Livinia wanted to tell her that she'd be okay, but that was only one possible future. She needed to work out how best to ensure it. There would be a trade. There was always a trade.

The other returned with Miss Altura, and the extra presence still accompanied them. No one had mentioned it, and it seemed likely they didn't know about it. She herself could barely discern that *something* was there, but it remained impervious to her scrutiny. Not that she had no suspicions of its nature. There was a high probability that this was a spirit that had attached itself to the girl with the shaved head. Livinia would confirm that shortly enough.

Livinia motioned the visible entities to sit on the bench. The wolfling approached her friend cautiously, but getting no reaction she settled for sitting a small distance away and pulling her limbs in close. Miss Altura, more aware of social cues than it would ever admit, sat directly between the two women and threw its arms around their shoulders, sticking its legs out in a relaxed pose. It glanced at each of its new companions before addressing Livinia.

"I can explain."

Livinia smiled very slightly but with genuine affection. She raised her hand to her friend, palm up, offering the floor.

"By all means," she said. "I'm eager to hear this." This was true whenever Miss Altura spoke. Its speech frequently revealed an inner mirth that contradicted its flat affect. These were the moments in which it fully engaged in life, and they would be among Livinia's fondest memories.

"Firstly, did you play the message I left?"

"I did," she said, but her memories clashed on this point. She knew she'd listened to it, but when she tried to revisit that memory, it wasn't there. She was on a different timeline now. What had she changed? What had been the price? She'd find out, but she needed to pay attention to this moment. She hadn't heard the message anymore, so she would need the information anew to stick in her memory long-term. "Perhaps you should remind me of the pertinent facts."

Miss Altura gave her a quizzical look, only identifiable from long acquaintance, but it did as asked.

"I bombed out trying to get in the pad, but Miss Alexander and I had a face-to-face." It nodded toward Dale, who had turned her empty stare from the garden to the floor. "She claimed the snap was bogus but fessed up to being with a buff woofer earlier this morning. I could tell she had a gal-pal in her digs, but I didn't eyeball them until later. Their name's Cassie, and they just decided in the horseless to try on nonbinary for fit." It squeezed Cassie's shoulder lightly. Cassie flinched and snapped their head to gape at it. "I rang to tell you that, minus the deets about Cassie, and to give you the scoop I was keeping my spyholes on the nest."

"Eminently reasonable, Miss Altura. I presume something transpired under your watchful eye."

It nodded.

"That heavy in your kitchen broke into the joint with a friend. I had to dive in." It raised its hands behind the other women in a small shrug.

"I see. And what of your prisoner's friend? Did he 'leg it,' as you might say?"

It glanced at the people under its arms.

"Long story. Wolf ate him."

Livinia looked at her visitors, still sitting quietly and uncomfortably.

"The phantom wolf?" she asked.

"Its chompers were solid enough."

Livinia looked Cassie over, paying close attention to their build and body language. While Dale tried to shrink into herself, her companion's tightness was ready to explode into motion. Their head was lowered, but their eyes continued to flick up in developing challenge.

"Where are my manners? Ladies, my name is Livinia Monroe, and this is my home. Welcome."

Dale finally looked at her but remained silent. Cassie continued to surreptitiously scan the room.

"Did you pause to introduce yourself before whisking them away?" Livinia prompted.

Miss Altura closed her eyes for a few seconds, her small gesture of annoyance.

"Hiya, pals. I'm the groovy gal that pulled your keisters out of the kindling."

Livinia continued to watch it sternly. It closed its eyes for slightly longer.

"Janice Altura," it said grudgingly. "Apologies for the circumstances of our meeting. Charmed, I'm sure."

Livinia nodded approvingly and turned her gaze on Dale, who quickly looked away.

"You already know me," she mumbled.

"Please. I'm afraid that I insist."

"Dale." Her whisper was nearly inaudible.

"Look at me, Dale." She did so, very slowly. "Head up. Do I frighten you?"

Dale stared, swallowed and stiffly shook her head.

"You're safe here. Please speak clearly and try again."

"I'm Dale. Dale Alexander. Are you really Livinia Monroe? Daughter of Colonel Jessup?"

Dale trembled, but her determination was impressive. As was her information. Livinia smiled warmly.

"I am. My husband, wherever he may still exist, is Albert Monroe. We, along with several acquaintances, investigated reports of preternatural incidents. The picture of your friend attracted my attention. Before we speak of that, I believe that we have one introduction yet to make."

Everyone turned to Cassie, who continued to act trapped.

"It's okay," Dale told them. "Just say your name, and we can maybe start getting some answers."

Cassie raised her head defiantly and announced herself.

"I am Cassie Kuiper."

CHAPTER THIRTY-THREE

Cassie (Human)

It surprised me that the others didn't react to my name. I'd always thought the Kuiper family was important and powerful. The guards talked about how they were afraid to make them mad and what could earn their favor. The rest of the family, not me. As long as I was in my cell and unhurt, no one cared about me. They hadn't even given me a name. I was just "the beast," "the bitch," or, to one guard, "the cub." Until the night my father's wife came to my cell, I hadn't even known I was a part of the family.

She'd come in, unsteady on her feet—because of the small sticks under her shoes, I thought. It was the first time I'd seen anyone else in a shirt like mine, but it was much more than that. It was green and shiny, sticking to her body instead of just hanging like mine. Her hair was like nothing I'd seen before. Long and brown, it covered her shoulders and much of her back. She was beautiful. When she'd entered, the guard had stood up.

"Mrs. Kuiper!" he'd said. "What can I do for you?"

She'd ignored him and stumbled over to the bars. I'd come forward to meet her and waited for her to speak. At first she'd only stood, watching me angrily. With the height from her shoes, we were nearly eye-to-eye.

"It's your birthday," she said at last. "Did you even know that? You're old enough to be fucked now, so we should be able to get rid of you. Guess what, honey? We're stuck with each other for another nine or ten years! Your chosen mate has to ripen more, and your new keeper hasn't made your boudoir yet. So here we are."

She spat on me.

"Little bitch! Do you know how much this is worrying Nate? He had to fuck a dog-woman for his family, and he did what he had to! Your worthless life was supposed to bring us fortune, but you're a curse! We only found more misery because of you!"

I stood still, letting the spit run down my cheek, trying not to react in any way. The guards had made it clear that this was the safest way through angry moments. Wait for the yelling to end, and accept whatever was said or done.

"Money? Our net worth has fallen by twelve percent over the last eighteen years. The companies aren't struggling, but they've stagnated, and investors don't like that at all. Not! One! Bit! And children!"

Tears ran down the dark streaks under her eyes, and I realized that she'd been crying for a while.

"You're it! You're his only child. We tried everything, but he's shooting blanks. There's nothing to work with. You shouldn't even exist! You can't! There's no way you're his! Even if you are, you're less Kuiper than I am. You're a womb with skinny legs, a possession to ensure the unbroken family legacy of bestiality! Other people could use sperm donors. Not us! Can't raise a kid without wolf blood in its veins."

She glared at me, wobbling.

"Happy birthday, you piece of shit. You don't have that many left."

She cried again, or maybe laughed.

"Fuck you," she said, then turned and left.

CHAPTER THIRTY-FOUR

Elena Arana

By the time Detective Arana arrived at the Fuller Apartments, the unidentified victim had been taken away. This was Detective Horst's case, and she was only here to see if it was related to yesterday's shooting at the Kersh Inn. There would be no reason to suspect that the incidents were connected, except that she'd heard a description of the persons of interest, and one of them had stood out. Sightings of the bald girl in a gray dress had been leading her to this part of town, and it felt too coincidental that a similar person had been sighted in connection with another shooting death so nearby.

"Why the fuck are you here, Elena?"

Detective Horst was examining the refrigerator and closed it as she approached him.

"Frank," she said. "I heard you're looking for a young bald woman."

"Who isn't?"

He crossed his arms and leaned back against the counter.

"What's your interest in her, anyway?" he asked.

Elena glanced around the apartment, where a tech was shifting through piles of clothing and pizza boxes for anything useful.

"Jesus, Frank. Don't you listen to the morning updates? A bald girl in a gray tee dress was seen fleeing my crime scene yesterday at the time of the shooting. We don't have leads on the paramilitary assholes yet, but we've had interviews with witnesses that saw her coming this way just this morning. So, how about it?"

He shook his head.

"I passed the info along, because it's easier than explaining why I didn't later. It sounded like complete bullshit to me. The only one who claimed to see anything was the dyke who does maintenance here. She said that the guy who lives here left carrying bags, along with two females carrying a dead or unconscious male. One, the driver, looked like a cartoon beatnik. The other was some bald jock. They all squeezed into a black Saturn and drove off together, happy as sardines."

He sighed theatrically.

"Some people just have to feel important. I took down her story and what little she saw of the license plate and reported it in. Probably it's all crap, but if we're lucky the car was real. Though I doubt it had leopard print above the doors."

Elena rubbed the back of her neck.

"That sounds weak all right," she admitted. "Don't suppose anyone saw play soldiers here?"

He laughed.

"Yeah, I think I saw one under a pizza box." He waited for her to laugh, and she smiled slightly so he'd move on. "Anyway, our dead fella was wearing hunting camo. Dunno if that's what you mean. Whatever he was after tore him apart."

That got her interest.

"I thought this was a shooting."

"That was the report. Multiple people heard shots. There are a few bullet holes in the walls, and we're searching the trash for more. No blood anywhere but the corner. Looks like a pack of dogs tried to eat him."

"Dogs? When did dogs get involved?"

He sighed again.

"That same maintenance worker said she saw the resident with a large dog earlier this morning."

"Shit. I'll stick with straightforward militia-on-militia violence."

"Detective Horst," the tech called.

She was crouched over a book, her digital camera still pointed at it. Frank picked his way through the trash to bend over and take a look.

"It looks like blood spatter, Detective."

"It looks like ranch dressing," he scoffed.

Elena came over and crouched down to see. Frank had a point. Whatever had landed on the book was white. But it was a lot more watery than a creamy salad dressing, and it did resemble blood spatter. She stood up and patted Frank on the shoulder.

"Good luck with whatever the fuck this is," she told him.

He looked sourly at the messy floor.

"Fuck you, Elena."

CHAPTER THIRTY-FIVE

Cassie (Wolf)

Her host followed the others into another room, and she joined in order to continue to observe these new creatures. They weren't human, although one looked less convincing than the other. Janice, the one who'd assisted against the intruders, smelled more like damp soil than any living creature she'd encountered. Its flesh had no melanin at all under the makeup, its paleness that of a fat spider. The strongest odor came from the wound on its arm, which had briefly bled a white liquid before closing. The thing was a poor mimic of humanity, but so far it had proven useful. Perhaps it could be made into another ally.

The other, the one they'd met here, she found more unsettling. The woman looked perfectly human, but she blended into the background of the house as though she wasn't there at all. At first, the wolf thought this meant Livinia wasn't alive, that the woman was a puppet of some kind. Yet the entire building felt oppressive and watchful, and it became apparent that the very house and the majority of its contents were one living entity. They were all inside of this creature, and it knew that she was here. So far there hadn't been any evidence that they were in danger here, but she felt uncomfortably as though they had walked inside of a giant maw. The question was whether they'd be swallowed.

After everyone had said their names, Livinia had asked them to follow her to the sitting room. The wolf had decided to accompany them in order to gather more information. The new chamber was much as the other but with less natural light. There was also a larger fireplace, centered on the wall rather than tucked into a corner. All of the furniture here was oriented around this fixture. As she entered this new area, the wolf saw that a chair now stood before the hearth. No one else appeared to notice that it hadn't been there a moment earlier.

She watched Livinia guide Cassie to the chair. The wolf remembered being given that name, but it now belonged to her host. That was fine. She knew who she was. She knew less about what she was, but she'd managed to survive for hundreds of years without that information. She only cared that they remained free of the Kuiper family.

Dale and the Janice creature sat on the couch facing Cassie, while the object called Livinia collected items from a nearby cabinet. The wolf watched closely as she gathered a boxy camera, a magnifying glass, a pair of scissors, a bit of yarn, a box of matches, and an ashtray.

"How's your foot, Cassie?" Dale asked. "Do you need a footrest?"

"I don't think it's sleepy, but it's fine. It stopped hurting before I woke up."

"It was so swollen!"

"I understand," Cassie said.

The wolf's hosts had always healed quickly, which she appreciated. They were her anchor to the physical realm, and she felt their injuries.

Livinia set the items she'd assembled on an end table that hadn't been next to Cassie's chair. The wolf had not detected the furniture moving or appearing, and her unease intensified.

"I need to assess your nature," the woman told Cassie. "When Miss Alexander posted your photo, I warned her to be cautious." The wolf noticed that she glanced to Janice for confirmation before continuing. "Unexamined apparitions, such as a phantasmal wolf, can be dangerous. Hence, an examination."

The wolf felt her host's discomfort and alarm, but before she could think of how to help, the creature next to Dale spoke.

"Liv just wants to be hip to whether you'll off us. It's no sweat; she gave me the once-over ages ago. Just waved doodads over me."

"Doodad?" Cassie asked.

"Any one of a number of arcane devices, the use of which Miss Altura has never attempted to learn," Livinia replied, picking up the camera.

She opened it, and the wolf recognized that it was one of those that printed a photo immediately.

"Close your eyes, Cassie. Think about your wolf, how it feels when she's free. I'm going to photograph your thoughts. You'll feel the camera against your forehead, and when I say 'now' you'll hear a noise. May I proceed?"

The wolf felt Cassie's hesitancy as they studied the camera, but in the end the attitude of acquiescence learned in captivity made their decision.

"Yes," they said.

Livinia pressed the camera against their temple and gave them time to gather their thoughts.

"Now," she said.

The camera cracked sharply, causing Cassie to flinch. When the photo finally emerged, Livinia shook it vigorously.

"Not to second-guess you, Mrs. Monroe," Dale said, "but if you need a Polaroid for this, the newer models are a lot better."

Livinia gave her a thin-lipped smile.

"Better for some uses, I'm sure, but less effective for others.

Changes to the autofocus in the 1970s destroyed its ability to pick up on psychic auras."

The camera was another piece of the house, the wolf saw. She knew little of magic but wondered if it actually mattered what form the instrument took.

"The lab coats back at Madru Harbor Security could whip up a gizmo for this that anyone could use."

Livinia stopped shaking the picture and looked at Janice sadly.

"Perhaps they could. I'm sorry we can't ask them."

A pall spread over the room, and no one said a word. Dale and Cassie glanced uncomfortably between the others. The wolf shared in their confusion. Finally Livinia examined the developed picture in her hand.

"The image suggests that your companion spirit is agreeable by nature, albeit capable of intense aggression. I'm not amenable to sheltering a creature of unrestrained violence, so this is somewhat in your favor. The spirit is also prone to deep loyalty. It's possible that she's influenced by your feelings and desires."

The wolf felt that was overstating it, although she tended to identify with Cassie more than she had most of her hosts.

Janice turned its head and looked Dale up and down.

"Someone just became a key player. They're in mad puppy love."

Dale shrank into the couch as much as the thin cushions and hard wood allowed. Livinia exchanged the camera for the scissors.

"I need a small quantity of hair for the next test," she said, looking unhappily at Cassie's bare head. "The scalp is the preferred source, but that's not an option. Is there anywhere that you grow longer hair?"

Cassie nodded. They reached for their sweatpants.

"I need to stand."

CHAPTER THIRTY-SIX

Cassie Kuiper

I didn't mind being naked in itself. I'd always worn the clothes given to me because it had been expected, not because I'd felt any need to cover myself. What bothered me was being inspected. The normal guards, for all their distance and authority, hadn't cared much about me. The guards had their limits, but I'd learned to pay attention and could sing or talk or dance for a long time before they got agitated.

Medical exams had been different. Doctors had demanded silence and stillness. They'd treated me as a thing that needed to be controlled. Livinia was very nice about it, but I still felt that fear. I had to behave or there'd be punishment. I closed my eyes while she selected the hair to cut and just breathed.

There was a small tug and a sharp noise, and then I heard her shift to stand up.

"Thank you, Cassie. I appreciate your willingness to endure that."

I pulled my clothes back up and sat down, still feeling uncomfortable. Livinia acted like I hadn't had to obey. Like I was a person rather than an unruly animal. Had I actually had a choice?

Livinia placed the hair in the small dish and opened the cardboard box. She pulled a red-tipped stick out of it and scraped it along a band on the side of the box. After a few tries there was a crackle, and there was a tiny flame on the red end of the stick. I watched it burn. I'd seen similar fire when a guard would light her cigarette, but that had come from a small plastic container. There could have been a red-tipped stick inside of it, I guessed. This smelled different—sharper and less sweet—so maybe not.

My eyes followed the fire as she put it into the dish. Smoke rose, and it smelled awful. Livinia blew out the stick. She picked up the glass circle with the handle and watched the smoke through it.

"The bond is weak. Your spirits are aligned, but they are not as one. You influence each other, even share memories, which assists in creating unity of purpose, but like all alliances it may fracture if stressed."

"Is that bad?" Dale asked.

"It's a matter of perspective. You're familiar with the expression about whether the glass is half empty or half full?"

Dale nodded. I didn't know what she was talking about, but I kept quiet. Livinia felt similar to a doctor or a keeper to me, and I wasn't sure how she'd react to my questions. Something was odd about her smell, too, but I couldn't figure out what.

"The phrase is merely an illustration of the difference between pessimistic and optimistic thinking," she said, "but there are interesting questions underlying the scenario. To wit, which state is desired? Was the glass being filled? Was it being emptied? How had the state been changed over time? Without that context, we cannot accurately comment on the current state of the liquid in the glass."

"So you're saying that without more context you can't say if it's good or bad that their connection is weak?" Dale asked.

Livinia nodded slightly.

"Essentially, yes. Is it strengthening, weakening, or stable? What was the intent? Combined spirits can happen naturally or be brought together through ritual. It can be hereditary. All we can confirm at this stage is that the connection is weak, but the spirits are extraordinarily compatible. As Cassie's nature prefers calm, I believe that we have the time to uncover the history we would need to properly evaluate their bond before deciding what can be done about it."

"Do about what?" I asked.

It was uncomfortable asking Livinia to explain, but I just couldn't stand being talked around anymore. That was too much like where I came from. She didn't look angry, though. That was nice.

"It's up to you, of course," she told me. "Once I fully understand how you're linked to the wolf spirit, I can do research. Given the weak link, I may be able to find a way to sever the connection. It's also possible that I could alter it to allow a stronger bond. It's too early to know what the options will be, and it would be your decision whether to pursue any of them."

That was a lot, but I got the general idea. She didn't know anything, but if she ever did, she'd tell me.

"There's one more test," she said. "Open your mouth, please."

I did as asked before I could think about it. She popped something onto my tongue that felt fuzzy, and I reached to pull it out. She blocked my hand.

"It's a bit of yarn, Cassie. I need it to be saturated with your saliva. Please."

"She wants you to slobber on it," Janice said.

I glared at it, and it looked at me with its creepy blank face while I worked up some spit. Livinia held out a small plate.

"When you're done, please."

It was weird how much better a "please" made all of this. I felt more comfortable here, even being examined, than I ever had in my cell. At first I'd thought it was the newness or the larger space, and that did help. But what I realized, pulling the wet string from my mouth, was that nobody here was afraid of me. There were a lot of scents I didn't recognize, but the smell of fear was almost missing. There was some on Dale, but that was left over from the attack and not about me.

"I'm afraid I need some of your blood for this. Would you rather poke your own finger or have one of us do it?"

I didn't like either option. So far the worst had been cutting some hair, which was far better than I was used to. Active poking was too much like what the doctors did to me. I tried to say no without making her mad.

"Why?" I asked.

Janice barked.

"Good for you, sister."

"I'm trying to discern whether your connection is good or bad, to put it simply. The ritual is simple, but it requires the blood and saliva of the spirit host."

I thought about it. The wolf had never been a bother, other than how my family treated me for having it.

"They said the wolves brought fortune to the family. That's good, right?"

Livinia didn't answer that. I frowned.

"Mrs. Kuiper said it wasn't working, though. So maybe it's good but broken."

She continued to watch my face, not saying anything.

"She also said I was going to die soon, but that was many years ago."

Everyone stared at me. They didn't say anything, but they didn't have to. I held up my weak hand and looked at Dale for support.

"Go ahead," I told Livinia.

Dale smiled at me, and I held still as I felt a pinch on my fingertip. We kept looking at each other and grinning. I think I could learn to be happy anywhere if she was there with me.

Livinia mumbled some words I didn't know, and Dale broke eye contact with me to watch her. I looked too.

"Spill," Janice said.

Livinia set down the plate and glanced at the others before focusing on me.

"It's a bane," she said. "Whoever placed it on your family may have intended it as a boon, but the actual effect is harmful. Maybe not to the family, but to you and any others who bear it."

"I think there's just me," I told her. "But other than being kept in the cell I haven't had anything bad happen."

"Those guys broke into my apartment to get you," Dale said quietly.

"One of your relatives claimed you were going to die soon," Livinia added.

"Baned," Janice agreed.

"The active threat appears to be whoever sent those men to capture you, which has a high likelihood of being your family. We can return to studying the bane later. Janice and I will question our guest in the kitchen, but my house is largely open to the two of you. The only places off limits are locked. You may use the tower bedroom on the second story. You'll find a lavatory down the hall."

"Are we free to go, if we want?" Dale asked.

Livinia looked at her curiously.

"To where, exactly?"

Dale didn't answer.

CHAPTER THIRTY-SEVEN

Annette Kuiper

Kevin was at the second hole when Annette's phone vibrated. Seeing it was Lakeland, she walked away from the small crowd to answer it.

"Report," she said, firmly but quietly.

"Do you want to know where they went first or who took them?"

"Thrill me, Lakeland. Just fucking talk," she said.

"Sorry. So, they went to a Victorian mansion up in the Cobbleton district. Turns out to belong to a foundation now, but it used to be the local base for a global organization called the Society for Preternatural Investigations."

That was interesting. Annette walked further away from the golf spectators.

"This society, does it still operate?"

"Not officially, no. Apparently it all went to shit during World War II. The daughter of the last local leader created the foundation, but she disappeared around the same time. No way she's still alive; she was born in the 1890s."

"And the foundation?"

"It doesn't seem to do much more than preserve and maintain the grounds. Still digging into who runs it now. Maybe the finances will tell us more."

Their mysterious competitor took her prizes to a place that used to look into things like wolf-bitches. She wondered if Toby had anything on that house. She wondered again if the woman worked for him.

"Who else is in the house?"

"We've only seen one other person. Middle-aged woman, dressed like something out of an old movie."

A woman? Still, she could be reporting to Toby.

"Identity?"

"Still working on it."

His tone suggested there was more. She sighed in frustration.

"Spill," she commanded.

"We think she might be a granddaughter of the last known owner."

She'd reached the tall fence at the edge of the course and stood looking out at the grand old houses. Her quarry and the people who took her were nearby, perhaps only a few streets away.

"Continue."

"The likeness is remarkable, only there's no record of any more descendants. It's weird."

"One might say 'preternatural.' "

"What?"

"You said you had something on the woman who took the package."

There was a brief pause. She could almost hear the gears shifting in Lakeland's head.

"Sort of."

"Lakeland!" she snapped. "What do you have?"

"We're still looking, but so far all we have indicates that she's a local rumor."

"Explain."

"There are stories of a woman who appeared on the goth scene in the 1980s. Those who met her reported that she was attractive but somehow unnatural and didn't show any emotion. They started to call her a vampire. Thing is, the scene changed, years passed, and she's still around. Wears different clothes, but still the same disturbing presence. And she hasn't aged a day in forty years."

There it was. The start of another stress headache.

"A vampire. A fucking vampire stole the package."

"Rumored vampire," Lakeland amended. "Maybe. No one knows who this woman is, but they call her Janus. She's our best guess at the moment."

"Did she cart them off in a goddamn horse and carriage?"

"Old Saturn Ion. Black coupe with rear access doors and leopard-print trim."

Annette decided that once she was on the other side of this nonsense she'd have to replace him.

"Whose fucking car is it?"

Lakeland hesitated.

"It belongs to the foundation."

"Of course. Keep watching for now. Do not engage until we know who we're dealing with."

"Gotcha."

She hung up and walked back. Her son had moved on to the third hole, and the walk would cool her off.

CHAPTER THIRTY-EIGHT

Derek Robinson

Derek's business phone rang, so he muted the TV and picked it up. The caller used the burner given to Tobias Kuiper Jr. He'd hinted that something big was in the works. Definitely one to answer.

"Yeah," he said, watching his character get torn apart by ghouls.

"Aletheia, old mansion. Extraction only. Co-ordinate with Lakeland. You're in charge."

"On it."

Derek hung up. His vault dweller was dead, and he'd have to start over. He had an ethic: one character, one death. It kept him smart and careful. Too much so to rely solely on Mike Lakeland and his gang of amateurs. He'd want at least one capable operative to manage a strike inside a house. Someone with cool nerves and no compunctions, who he could trust to make use of a few weekend warriors.

He texted Brianna Katt, the best private security contractor he'd ever worked with.

U up?

Less than ten minutes later, he got the response.

No plan. U?

House hunting

Call me

CHAPTER THIRTY-NINE

Dale Alexander

I'd settled onto the four-poster bed with my laptop. The mattress was a double, which was pretty small but felt enormous after sleeping on a single for the last four years. The thick, elaborate cover and canopy made the bed seem luxurious. The room itself was large and had the same tower extension as the first place we'd sat. There was a fireplace in the same corner, which made me wonder how exactly that worked out, architecturally. Did they share a chimney?

Cassie ran all over the second floor, shouting in wonder at everything they found. Their enthusiasm was adorable, and honestly I was amazed at how positive their attitude was to a completely unfamiliar environment. If I was on the run, I'd be freaked out and afraid of everything.

Of course, I was on the run now, right alongside them. I didn't regret helping them at all; it had been the right thing to do, and I liked to think I'd have been brave enough to do it knowing where it would lead. My temporary inconvenience wasn't anywhere near as awful as what they'd been through, and I assumed that I could crawl back into my dark hole at some point. Cassie would have to find an entirely new home, if their family would even allow such a thing.

I knew all of this consciously, and yet my overwhelming

feeling at the moment was frustration. Despite the businesses nearby, there was only one Wi-Fi network visible, and it was locked down too tightly for me to mess with. I had some tricks, but they mostly relied on terrible security. My phone couldn't get a single bar either, so there was no hope of using it as a hotspot. This house was in a complete dead zone.

Carrying my laptop into the hall, I saw Cassie trying to open a door at the top of the grand staircase.

"Is that one locked?"

They turned to face me, pouting a little.

"It won't open."

I put a hand on their shoulder, then felt self-conscious about touching them and pulled away.

"Mrs. Monroe is being incredibly generous, letting us take shelter here. I don't think we should complain about a single door being locked."

Cassie thought about that and nodded somberly.

"Okay. I understand."

Then their eyes glinted as they grinned slyly.

"What if there's a second door I can't open?"

I smothered a laugh.

"Come talk to me about it when you have a final count."

They nodded seriously.

"I found a way upstairs. I'll check there."

"You do that. I need to talk to Janice for a sec. See you in a bit."

As Cassie ran off down the hall, I went down the winding stairs. Janice and Livinia had headed to the back of the house when we split up, so that's the direction I went. The dining room off the main hall was where they'd gone on leaving the living room or whatever the hell it was called. There were two doors from there, and I heard the loudest noises from the one closest to me. I stepped through that into a back hallway behind the living room. There were stairs leading up, and I wondered if they were the same ones that Cassie had found to get up to the third floor. There was also a door that opened on a large kitchen. At least it was larger than any I'd been in before.

The noises were louder here, the loudest sounding like a clap of some kind. The room was empty, and although there were an alcove and a few closets, I didn't think anyone was there. After a brief walk around to look over the stove, sink, and what turned out to be separate pantries—one leading back to the dining room—I decided to check the alcove. That turned out to be some kind of mudroom, with a door leading outside. I was sure they hadn't left the house, so I added that exit to my mental map along with the one I'd spotted behind the big staircase in the front hall.

The sound was almost behind me, so I walked along the outside wall back toward the hall with the staircase. There were doors on that side of the kitchen, and I chose the one closer to the windows. Behind that was a passage to another set of stairs below the ones in the hallway. Now I could hear voices, some low and insistent and one that was loud and anguished, and I could make out that the noise I'd been following was most likely a whip.

I hesitated, but I really needed internet access. There wasn't anything too urgent that I needed to take care of at work, but I couldn't just disappear entirely. I went down the steps. They were what I called monster stairs, those bare wooden slats that you just knew the monster or killer would reach through and grab someone's ankle. They led down to a small cellar with a packed dirt floor and stone walls. One long wall was made of concrete blocks, and it had a metal door built into it. There was an old wooden door along the opposite wall, but the noises were definitely coming from behind the first one.

Janice slipped out from behind the door before I could knock.

"Everything copacetic?" it asked tersely.

The hanging bulb down here was off, and the darkness turned Janice's unsettling appearance into a threatening presence—even if she was half my size. It was too late to mutter an apology and go back upstairs, so I handled my discomfort the way I always did—with deflection.

"Did you hear me coming?" I asked.

It didn't move.

"You're in Liv's house," it said.

That explained nothing, but I wasn't up to asking further than that. I just needed to be out of this creepy cellar with a person who suddenly struck me as potentially dangerous.

"So, ah, I need internet access."

I heard a slap from behind the door and Livinia commanding someone to stay awake. What the fuck were they doing to that guy? He'd attacked us, so it's not as though I was worried for him, but what sort of people had we taken refuge with?

"For work," I added. "Or I can just tell them tomorrow that my power went out."

Janice moved toward me, and I fell back to the staircase. It kept advancing, and I held up my laptop as a shield. I trembled as Janice passed me and headed up the stairs. Surprised, and more than a little embarrassed, I followed it.

It led me up the back stairs to the second floor, and I confirmed that they led to the third as well. Out in the narrow passage, I could see the front main second floor hall to our left. We went right and immediately turned into a room with computers and a sewing machine. A dressmaker's dummy stood in one corner, garbed in an open leopard-print vest, short neon pink scarf, and cat-ear headphones. Computer peripherals and bundled cords were stacked alongside bins of fabric.

Janice sat down in front of a keyboard and monitor, reached under the table, and turned on a custom tower filled with purple lights. It logged in and pulled up a network account management dashboard that I didn't recognize.

"Is your laptop work or personal?"

Janice remained focused on the screen, which was comforting. We were just two professionals setting up access.

"A bit of both," I admitted. "It's managed by my client, but they don't seem to care about security."

Janice created a new account and set up permissions.

"MAC address?"

"Hold on."

I set the machine on a stack of bins, opened it, and brought up the information. Janice typed it in as I read it out loud then read it back for confirmation.

"Okay. You should be set. Try joining Charon's Boat."

I side-eyed Janice, who had now turned to watch me. As ever, its face was a mask. Maybe a death mask. Compared to the eeriness of its friendly smile, this was something of an improvement. I found the network and joined it. After a few moments the Wi-Fi indicated it was connected. I brought up my browser and clicked the bookmark for itch.io. The page loaded quickly. Leery of instant success, I scrolled down and selected a game at random. The game's page loaded just as rapidly as the home page had. Excellent download speed. I wondered what the upload was like.

"It works. Thanks, Janice!"

Janice shut down its computer.

"Of course. We'll get a personal account set up later for your phone. Do you have a tablet? Other devices?"

"An e-reader."

I hadn't used it in some time, but I was sure it was still in my backpack.

"We'll make it a password account then. Do you need anything else right now?"

"I'm good. I know you're busy."

I saw what might be blood on Janice's shirt, and I didn't want to know any more about it. I already felt conflicted. Turning a blind eye to the torture in the basement was horrible. At the same time, that motherfucker had broken into my home to kill or kidnap Cassie. I'd felt so damn helpless during the assault, and now I was too scared to even voice my objections to what these strange people were doing. I always had been a coward.

Footsteps thundered down the stairs, and Cassie poked their head into the room, grinning broadly.

"You should see all the stuff up there!" They told me excitedly. "Dunno what any of it is, but it's great!"

Cassie noticed Janice sitting by the computer desk, and their mood faltered. They left quickly and ran downstairs.

"They've got pep," Janice observed.

I nodded and excused myself. Work awaited. There'd be time to think about what I'd gotten myself into later.

CHAPTER FORTY

Janice Altura

Janice returned to the basement, where its prisoner slept on a cot, and leaned back against the door. Livinia sat primly beside the cot, resting a hand on the man's forehead.

"What snake-oil were you selling Dale? She acted like I was gonna croak her."

"She needed to start acknowledging the danger she's in. Sheltering Cassie has involved her in affairs beyond her understanding with unknown but aggressive adversaries. Dale's response to her situation has so far been one of placid acceptance. She may need to be a participant before this resolves, and I want her to begin thinking about what that might require."

Janice continued to stare at her. Livinia relented.

"She thinks we were lashing him."

Janice shook its head.

"Never. He'd pass out too much."

It approached the cot and looked down at the man.

"He sing yet?"

Livinia shrugged.

"I believe I have everything he knows, but that's a disappointingly small amount. They were specifically sent to retrieve Cassie. He did not know she hosted an animal spirit. Nor did he know for certain where they were to deliver her. His associate, whom the spirit slew, had that information. He did know that they were acting on orders from a man named Kuiper, which is the surname that Cassie used. It would seem that her family is indeed looking for her."

"All that from just a little light petting."

Livinia smiled indulgently.

"Dream infiltration is a smidge more involved than that, but yes."

She frowned and looked at the sleeping man.

"The question now is how to dispose of him."

"The Passage," Janice suggested.

Livinia gazed at it critically.

"You thought my mere suggestion of torture cruel."

Janice shrugged.

"Easy peasy, boss. Door's right across the hall. We won't even hear him cash in his chips."

"After all these decades I still can't be completely certain that you're joking."

"I'm a gosh-darned stumper."

Livinia stood and walked to the exit.

"There are two options I'm considering at the moment. The first is that we keep him here, unconscious, until this Kuiper issue is resolved. We can't estimate at this point how long that could take. The other is to push him outside and let the people watching the house take care of him."

She opened the door and began climbing the stairs. Janice followed, closing the door behind it. This was unnecessary—the door would shut and even lock if Livinia wished—but it wanted to feel the problem firmly secured behind it.

"They found us already?" it asked.

"A car followed you from the apartment. The three people in it have been watching us ever since. Another three arrived shortly afterward, conferred with the first group, and took up a position on the other side."

They reached the first floor and continued upward.

"A six-pack. Gee, we're the cat's whiskers all of a sudden."

"We don't know if they work for the Kuipers, but if we put our captive outside this evening we may be able to find out."

"You mean if I do that."

Livinia took the second-floor passage into the hallway, approaching the library door at the top of the main stairs.

"I knew I could count on you. Make certain that our guests eat. I'll be conducting research."

With that, she disappeared into the heart of the house. Janice stood in the hallway, considering its options.

CHAPTER FORTY-ONE

Dale Alexander

Cassie had fallen asleep on the bed next to me as I worked, and their wolf had jumped up to join us for a nap as well. It was weird seeing them asleep together. Mrs. Monroe had explained that they were individuals that had been linked, but to me they'd felt more like two forms of the same, well, person. With them settled in, I'd fallen down a research rabbit hole looking for a way around a browser rendering error. It was only the movement of the wolf standing up beside me that made me notice that Janice was glowering at us from the doorway.

I guessed that was what it was doing, but its expression was as flat as ever. A person who'd help torture someone wasn't getting my assumption of positive intent. Plus its arms were crossed, and without sunglasses on I could see how light its eyes were. Its face almost completely vanished against the darkness of its hair and lipstick.

"There's our furry phantom. She really thinks I'm phony, doesn't she."

That sounded like an observation, not a question. I placed a hand on the wolf's back and felt her tension.

"To be honest, you're a little sketch. I mean, thanks for the rescue, and I appreciate the hospitality, but if I had anywhere else to go I wouldn't stick around the Jessup house of torture."

My heart pounded, and a wave of nausea prepared to sweep through my body. Janice watched me silently for an uncomfortable amount of time before responding. I regretted having spoken up, certain that I was about to be sent to the cellar.

"You don't need to be a nervous Nellie over us," Janice said at last. "Livinia put on a fright show because she wants you to dig the danger you're in, but she doesn't have a handle on people anymore. She's a little odd after seventy years cooped up in here with only me to stand in for humanity."

It came into the room and sat on an elegant chair by the tower windows. The wolf lay back down but remained alert and watchful.

"I'll give you the lede. Those bruisers who came for your blonde biter there were sent by a fella named Kuiper. We don't have the inside scoop on the family, or whether someone actually wanted her to flee the scene, but I'm assuming those gorillas were planning to throw her back in the cooler. Liv's hitting the books to ferret out the dirt on the Kuipers and suss out how to get them off of your backs, but I'd lay down money she's also snooping for the lowdown on that bane."

It gazed out a window, lifting a lacy curtain.

"We've got the Brady Bunch out there, hemming us in."

It leaned forward, resting its elbows on its knees.

"I knew I was poking a hornet's nest when I ran into your pad, and I knew dragging you here would set them on Liv. Sure, maybe I didn't think they'd be so zippy, but I knew we could take their stings."

It gestured at my guard wolf.

"You found a cute phantom floof and thought she made a pretty pooch. Quick as a flash you're in a killer chapter play. You've got the jitters, and you think maybe if you do a runner you'll get to split the scene, but the only way to get written out is a ride in the meat wagon. You gotta play a role to reach the curtain drop."

I stared at it in amazement. Sure, it had just told me that this whole situation was probably worse than I'd thought, and curling up into a self-wetting ball had probably been an appropriate response to the violent break-in. Yet my mind latched on to *how* it had said this. I'd grown up watching my parents' tapes of old serials with characters like Flash Gordon and Captain Marvel. They were goofy, and sometimes pretty cringe, but I still loved them. Just a lot of running back and forth, posturing, and the occasional trash-can robot.

"There weren't a lot of deaths in the serials I've seen," I told it. "I take your point and all, but there's usually a lot of knock-out gas and escapes from death traps."

"Some filled more coffins than others. I caught a bunch recycled on the idiot box, but Ted used to give me the skinny on new chapters as they rolled out."

I petted the wolf, who had decided that Janice didn't need all of her attention after all.

"Janice?" I asked carefully. "Not to be rude, but the serials I was thinking of were from the thirties and forties."

It nodded.

"Those were aces. There were silent stories, too, y'know. Lots of kooky crimes and mysteries. Death traps and secret passages. Also torch job dicks. Melodrama by the boatload."

"And this friend of yours," I said. "He told you about them. As they came out."

It stopped and stared at me. The wolf noticed I'd stopped petting her and licked me for attention. I scratched under her chin.

"Dale, look at me."

I turned back toward Janice, but I was afraid to meet its gaze. Things usually didn't go well when I expressed uncertainty about what people were saying.

"How old do you think I am?"

I swallowed. This felt like a trap. No one asked that out of curiosity. It had some point to make, and I probably wouldn't like it. Something about it was extremely off, and not because its brain was wired oddly. Janice just felt wrong somehow, as though it shouldn't exist.

"You look younger than I do," I said eventually. "If I had to guess, I'd say early twenties."

It nodded.

"Swell facade held together by a little spackle and a bear claw now and then. I've been a hot dish since 1896. My pal Ted was the dick behind *Ted Mars, Science Detective*."

" 'Police detective of the far-off twenty-first century'?"

"1920s Madru Harbor, anyway."

"I've only seen a few chapters, but they were un-fucking-hinged!"

"They stayed tops back home. Local hero and all. Plus, they're a goof. I've got the tapes, if you'd ever like to check them out."

Maybe my stay at Aletheia wouldn't be so bad after all.

CHAPTER FORTY-TWO

Annette Kuiper

Kevin rode back with his teammates. He'd played well but not spectacularly; it was enough to help his school eke out a win. He enjoyed golfing with his friends, so Annette reminded herself that he didn't need to excel at it. She was glad he'd had fun, but she also resented taking time off work to go support him when he wasn't taking it seriously. On some level she understood that it was selfish to think this way, but she couldn't help how she felt. At least she'd have time to put it aside before she saw him again later.

Now she could get back to work on securing his future. Lakeland had called again with even worse news. Now fucking Robinson had been brought in with orders to take over the operation and deliver the wolf-touched to David tonight. There was no way to keep the dreadful creature away from her son now without angering the family. So be it. She wasn't going to throw her son to that creature.

She sat in her car and called Derek Robinson on her emergency phone. He had a stronger working relationship with Toby, but she liked the odds of turning him against David. Her younger brother had never inspired loyalty in anyone of significance. It took several rings for Robinson to answer.

"Yes, ma'am. How can I assist you this evening."

"I have some trash that needs to be removed."

"How many bins do you need?"

"Just one, but you may have to take care of some to get to it. Up to four total. I'll pay for five regardless."

"I appreciate the generous payment, but I would prefer not to clean more than needed. How do I identify the trash you're interested in?"

"You should have been contacted about it earlier today."

Robinson fell silent. Annette almost worried that she'd overestimated his willingness to betray David, but he hadn't refused her outright.

"Ma'am," he said at last. "I'm picking that trash up tonight for another client."

Of course they'd ordered it for tonight. They couldn't wait to see their nephew thrown at the wolf.

"I don't want the trash delivered. I want it to be incinerated."

"I'd like to help you, but I've already received the intel on where it is and made arrangements for the help needed for the pickup. I can give you a discount on your next problem for the inconvenience."

"Payment for ten bins. Tell your other client that one of your workers screwed up."

Another pause. This time, she didn't even consider possible failure.

"I don't want to burn my relationship with my primary contact on this account. Get him on board, and I'll accept your terms. I'll need his verbal confirmation by eleven p.m."

"Thank you. I appreciate your services."

"Always a pleasure, ma'am."

She pulled into the Kuiper Innovations headquarters lot and found her older brother at his suite on the top floor. Having ruthlessly managed the company's finances to the enrichment of the stock holders—the majority owners being Tobias Sr. and his three children—Toby had used the leverage to turn half of the top floor into his personal quarters. He had, of course, provided a series of graphs detailing how this would benefit the company, but none of that had mattered so much as Tobias Kuiper's view that his namesake son had earned it. Coincidentally, it had made Toby even more dependent on staying in his father's good graces. Annette had always wondered why he'd want to place himself in that position.

It was an elegant apartment suite; he'd spent quite a lot of company funds renovating it. It had all been written off somehow with his balance sheets and his nested accounts. Annette would not have been surprised if Kuiper Innovations had ultimately made money from the expenditure. The space was ostentatious in a more sterile way than their father indulged in. Where Tobias preferred shiny gold and cluttered opulence, Toby favored an austere minimalism. It was a showroom more than a living space, and she always suspected that her rare visits to her brother's inner lair necessitated days of cleaning. The thought made her smile.

She walked into his office, signaling that this was not a social call. Not that Annette had ever made a social visit to these quarters. The siblings had never been close, united mainly in their contempt for their father and the extended family. For each other they felt a wary respect, an acknowledgment of capability and cunning. Within that framework, all visits were professional. Besides, she found stark minimalism to be incompatible with life.

Toby entered the room wearing a black kimono because he was that type of asshole. He sat behind the desk in a chair she hoped was at least as uncomfortable as hers, and his hands rested stiffly on the black lacquered desktop.

"Annette. A pleasure, as always."

"Older brother," she responded. It was a ridiculous affectation, but catering to his fixation wouldn't hurt her case. And she really needed him to back up her play.

"How can I help my little sister?"

She ignored the patronizing phrasing. Eyes on the end

zone. Straight to the point was her best play. If he was willing at all he'd keep talking.

"Robinson has agreed to destroy the package. He'll find a subordinate to blame for the unfortunate mishandling."

"I see," Toby said flatly. He steepled his hands before his mouth, because of course he did. She was certain that very soon he'd install small lights to reflect off his glasses just so. "I hope that he has other business lined up to replace ours. I'll honor the expenditure from your discretionary funds, but we cannot afford to do business with an unreliable contractor."

Annette smiled thinly.

"Oh, he's very reliable. His acceptance of my counteroffer is entirely contingent on the approval of his official contact, you."

"That does color the situation differently," he granted. "Perhaps we'll retain his services after all." He dramatically threw himself back in his chair, slumping because he thought it made him look dangerous. "But I haven't heard why I should authorize your offer."

She slid a thumb drive across his desk.

"That contains my findings about the efficacy of our family's breeding program. As each branch's lineage renews its connection, there is no pattern of significant gains to fortune. Contrary to the story that's been handed down, there is no correlation between branch renewal and branch wealth or overall stability.

"Simply put, there is no need to continue wasting resources on a failed experiment."

She knew Toby responded to numbers more than any other argument. He pretended to be unemotional, but data allowed him to express his feelings as irrefutable facts. Still, he didn't so much as glance at the drive.

"My own research supports your findings," he allowed generously. "However, I don't necessarily agree with your conclusion. Terminating the project without the approval of the other branches would at the very least jeopardize our mutual interests. While the main blowback would fall on our little brother, father would be the one doing damage control. He's many things, but he is not stupid. He'll know it was your doing because you have the most at stake, and he'll know that I assisted because Robinson works for me. To say that his reaction would be unpleasant is an understatement. It would be far less risky to simply refuse the package, and even that could isolate us from the greater family. So why in the world would I approve your bargain?"

He had delineated his concerns but hadn't rejected the idea outright. She had saved the bait for this moment. He'd done his initial analysis of the situation and found it lacking but worth discussing. She needed to change the equation.

"I'm offering to split David's and Father's shares. The two of us combined would control Kuiper Innovations."

He pushed his glasses up. They hadn't slid, but the gesture meant that his mind was engaged.

"That's an interesting thought. How do you propose stripping away their stock?"

She held up her left hand to start ticking off points.

"First, we don't attempt to suppress the fact of the termination. Instead, we pay Robinson to point to David. This establishes the second step, eliminating David on Father's authority. Third, we use the leverage to force Father to divest."

He shook his head.

"Never work. He's too stubborn. Even if he agreed he'd find a way to get even."

"Possibly," she agreed.

His eyes moved rapidly, unfocused, flitting as he thought. After several minutes he sat up and looked at her again.

"Yes to David. Let his death be his contribution to the family. But instead of confronting Father, we approach the branches with the evidence of his involvement. He's not well-liked among the family leaders, and I have some small influence. We should be able to use them to apply the pressure for us. He fears the real power they wield."

He looked at her pointedly over his glasses.

"As should you, little sister."

She considered his amendment. Pitting the council of elders against their father did leave them insulated from the fallout. Getting their hands on his shares would be more difficult, however. She saw no guarantee of gaining the control they desired.

"But will they kill him?"

He smiled, pleased with the future he foresaw.

"They'll do worse than that. It may take a month or so, but he will transfer his shares in order to retain some portion of his wealth, and of course his life. You may even become the head of the branch, which I would advise you to take."

"Do we have an agreement?"

He leaned forward and set his forearms on his desk.

"I want you to move up to CEO. IT will be moved under my control. I will also accept the remainder of this floor. We divide our shares equally, as you said."

She rose and gave him the silly deep bow he seemed to love.

CHAPTER FORTY-THREE

Cassie Kuiper

Eating at a table was strange. I'd always just sat on the floor with my tray. Pizza on the couch was odd, but I'd liked sitting next to Dale. These chairs were awful, and she was on the other side of the table from me. I picked up the plate and held it against my chest as I ate. No one said anything, but Dale kept hers on the table. Janice didn't eat, but it sat with us to talk. I wasn't happy about that, but it had given us food.

We were eating something it had called burgers, which were tasty. They'd come with fries and chocolate malts, which were also good. Janice had claimed one fry from each of us as "tax" for having ordered the food. So far it hadn't eaten either one.

"So what do we do about the people watching the house?" Dale asked.

"Zip, for now," it said. "You claimed sanctuary, so you're safe and sound. Liv may find a way to call off the riot."

"Do you believe that?"

"The eight ball says 'cannot predict now.' "

Dale sipped at her malt.

"I can't imagine them letting Cassie go. Or, well, the other Cassie."

When she said our names together, I realized that it was a little confusing. What if someone called for Cassie's attention and I thought they meant me? It wouldn't be terrible, but it was kind of my fault. Cassie was the wolf's name. I'd just taken it as well because I'd never had one.

"It's a tall order," Janice said. "Liv's a whiz, though. If there's a path to take the Cassies through the woods, she'll root it out."

I dropped my plate back on the table. It was louder than I'd expected, and the others stared at me. No one yelled. They were just watching me. Waiting.

"I need a name," I told them.

Dale had asked me to say what I was thinking.

"You said you're Cassie Kuiper," Janice said.

I shook my head.

"No. I did, but I was wrong. I'm part of the Kuiper family, but I'm not Cassie. Dale gave that to the wolf. I shouldn't take it."

Dale set down her malt.

"I get it. I went through a lot of names before choosing mine. It's important."

Janice shrugged.

"I picked mine in half a jiffy, but I didn't think it was a big whoop."

"When was that?" Dale asked.

"1896," it replied. "Dr. Madru was a stickler for red tape."

"I want you to name me," I told Dale.

She opened her mouth and tried to close it a few times.

"Me? Cassie, that's... sorry. I'm flattered, but a name is so personal. It should mean something special to you. I'd be happy to help you brainstorm, but I couldn't possibly tell you who you are."

I had gotten her chased out of her own cell. Maybe she had decided that she didn't want to be around me anymore. I'd understand, but it hurt.

"You named Cassie," I said.

"Oh, sweetie. I thought she was just a pup."

"One as solid as a dream," Janice said.

"I don't understand what happened with the picture I took of her. She always looks and feels solid to me."

"No fooling? She fell on that mook like a fuzzy fog."

"You were wearing sunglasses!"

Janice picked up one of its fries and started to eat it slowly.

"I liked the story you had about the stars."

Dale smiled and looked down at her burger.

"What story?" Janice asked.

"Just that I used to look at the stars a lot. I named Cassie for my favorite constellation."

"Cassiopeia," Janice said.

"Yeah."

"It's pretty," I said.

They both nodded.

"Weird thought," Janice said.

It picked up its remaining fry.

"Cassiopeia," it said.

It broke the fry in half and held one piece out.

"Cassie."

Now the other came forward.

"Pia"

It moved them together.

"Cassie and Pia. Make Cassiopeia."

"What? No, they make Cassiepia, which isn't anything," Dale said.

"Pia," I said, just to try it.

"That isn't even a name."

"Ever see *Voyage of the Rock Aliens*? Classic '80s goof, starring Pia Zadora. She's a triple threat: acting, singing, and dancing."

"That's what you have? Pia Zadora. The girl in green paint from *Santa Claus Conquers the Martians*."

"Another boffo flick."

"I like it," I said. "I'm Pia, part of Cassiopeia."

Janice popped the pieces of the fry in its mouth. Dale looked between us a few times and then smiled at me.

"Pia it is. This is why I didn't think I could give you a name. You're the best judge of what's right for you."

I grinned and picked up a few leftover fries. On a sudden urge, I dipped them in my malt before eating them. It was interesting enough that I reached out to try again.

"Is that right for you, too?" Janice asked.

I shrugged.

"Not wrong."

It made that barking laugh again, and I decided that was right for it.

CHAPTER FORTY-FOUR

Mike Lakeland

This was a shit show. Robinson had strolled in with his best ghoul Brianna Katt and started barking orders, acting like they were on a damn strike force. They were planning the extraction like a critical military operation, complete with contingency plans and lots of special signals. Mrs. Kuiper hadn't been pleased when he had updated her, but she'd told him to play along while she talked to her brothers about it. That had been hours ago. Now the late evening sun had nearly given up the struggle, and the "troops" were getting antsy.

Lakeland was on surveillance when the front door opened. He watched as the package and the woman called Janus brought a man outside. They dragged him down the steps and left him on the front walk. Janus looked out at the line of trees beside the yard and waved. He was certain she couldn't see him, but he wasn't happy she knew someone was probably watching from here.

He'd have to report this to Robinson. Once he saw them go back inside, he touched the call button on his headset.

"Lakeland," he said. "Need a substitute. Something happened at the front."

"Roger that," Markham said. "I'll let His Highness know."

"Careful. He'll have you court-martialed."

"Thank fuck."

Fielding arrived presently to relieve him, and Lakeland made his way back to the staff parking of the strip mall. Katt intercepted him before he could approach Robinson, who was busy glowering at map printouts.

"What happened?" she asked brusquely.

"The package and Janus pulled a man out of the house and left him. Looked like the guy they took from the apartment."

"That's all?"

He barely tolerated that tone from Mrs. Kuiper, and that was because she paid him generously. Rankled, he decided not to mention Janus's cheery wave.

"Not sure if he's dead or just unconscious," he said.

"Jesus, Lakeland. You're such a waste."

"So, you're just going to leave him there?"

She sneered at him.

"You want us to let them know we're out here? For that loser?"

He clenched his jaw to avoid inflaming the scene even more. Instead he shrugged stiffly.

"Not my call."

"Damn right, it's not."

Lakeland walked over to the back of the building and sat down. He powered up his phone and checked for messages. Still nothing. He leaned his head against the cool bricks and tried to catch a nap.

CHAPTER FORTY-FIVE

Derek Robinson

He didn't like how this job was going. Lakeland's crew were rank amateurs, but he'd need at least six people to sweep the house and three to guard the exits. He'd prefer more or better to hold the perimeter, but that just underscored the importance of the work inside. To boost the strike team, he'd brought in Henderson and Gordon. That tipped the balance in favor of experience while leaving three of Lakeland's fools to take the fall.

Kuiper had confirmed the kill order, which Robinson didn't entirely mind. The extra money made up for hiring three subcontractors, and they wouldn't have to try not to hurt anyone. There was considerable added risk, though. Not physically, that was the same no matter what. The aftermath was what bothered him. They'd have to kill at least one of the idiots they were borrowing. More if there were loyalties. They'd have to remove the bodies and torch the house, all of which traded off one trail of evidence for another. Then there was Lakeland. He wasn't afraid of the man at all, but he wanted him to stay in play. It helped to have weak competition. Hopefully the Kuipers would convince him to keep his stupid mouth shut.

They waited in the rain, watching the house until only a

few lights peeked through heavily-curtained windows. It was time to move. The air was heavy with ozone, and Robinson dared to hope that thunder would help cover the shooting.

"Lakeland. You, Markham, and Tallman cover the doors. No one should get by us, but we need you to stop anyone if they manage. Chalmers and Henderson, you take the downstairs. There's still a light in that front room, so be alert. The rest go upstairs in two teams. Fielding with me. Campbell and Gordon with Katt. We'll clear the second floor and go up from there. That's either a third floor or an attic space, and they could try to hide there. We need to eliminate all four that were spotted before we leave. Anyone else we find, we eliminate as well, but those four are the objective.

"Any questions?"

There were none, but he caught Markham and Lakeland sharing a glance.

"Lakeland, you're coming to the back door with us."

They walked low and quickly through the trees and across the lawn. Markham and Tallman peeled off to go to the doors at the front and the left of the mansion. Lakeland accompanied the rest to the back.

"This is where they're most likely to attempt to sneak out," Derek said.

He didn't believe it would come to that, but he thought a little implied flattery now would help control Lakeland later. Henderson broke the lock, and they went in.

CHAPTER FORTY-SIX

Paul Fielding

Robinson was an asshole, but he had way more pull than Lakeland would ever manage. Paul hoped that if he performed well while under direct supervision tonight he could move to the big leagues. He followed Henderson inside, watching him for notes about how to act.

They passed through a small mudroom into a kitchen, where he stuck close to Robinson. The two of them watched the hallway while others poked around the various other doors in the room. Of them all, only Chalmers had turned up anything interesting. He gestured that the door opposite the entrance led to a basement. From the consternation on Robinson's face, Paul doubted he'd known about that. Might not have been in the building plans. After confirming that Chalmers hadn't heard anything down there, Robinson led them into the small hallway.

This housed the back stairwell and served mainly as a junction between the kitchen, the dining room, and the upstairs. Katt, Campbell, and Gordon took positions guarding the three paths as the rest filtered into the dining room. From there, one door led to a darkened room—the sitting room, according to the house plans—and another to the front hall. Both revealed a light shining in what had to be the parlor.

Chalmers and Henderson split off to take the front hall, and Paul followed Robinson into the sitting room.

The two groups met in the parlor. No one was in there. The entire ground floor was empty, and one lamp in this room was the only light still on down here. Robinson sent Chalmers to relieve the three guarding the back. It was time to go upstairs. Henderson took a position in the front hall, and Robinson led the way carefully up the fancy staircase. Paul followed, imitating the low crouch.

They paused near the top and peered through the second floor railing at the main hallway, well-lit by a chandelier. The doors they could see were closed, but light bled through from under the one immediately to the left on the landing. Robinson carefully tried the knob, but it was locked. They peeked around the corner. Down the corridor there was a dim light. Robinson motioned for Paul to stay put and began to creep down the darker corridor. He froze when Janus emerged from the back room. After a few steps, Janus stopped and looked down at him.

"This is your lucky chance to rabbit," she said.

A pistol cracked from the top of the back stairs and the opposite side of Janus' head opened up. Small clumps of white matter in creamy pale liquid hit the wall. Watching from the landing, Paul thought wildly that her head was filled with cauliflower soup. Impossibly, the woman turned toward the back stairs, her ruined temple oozing lumpy white cream over a shredded ear. She raised a finger and pointed directly to Katt, who'd made the shot. Her lips opened in a horrific smile.

Janus lunged at Katt, who switched to aiming at her chest. Robinson tracked with his pistol but didn't fire. All the shots left Paul deafened, and he couldn't make out what Robinson was shouting. He couldn't see what was going on either, but he clearly remembered the woman calmly turning with a hole torn through the right side of her face. The allure of trading up to Robinson's team wasn't enough to make him move in closer.

Bullets struck Robinson, and he returned fire. Paul heard someone yell, possibly Katt. He retreated to the stairs and started to back down them as the shooting and yelling increased. Halfway down, he turned and ran. Chalmers stopped him at the bottom.

"What the fuck's going on up there?"

Paul shook his head. He had seen more than he could bear but couldn't articulate it.

"Cauliflower," was all he managed.

CHAPTER FORTY-SEVEN

Jason Henderson

The firing stopped suddenly, and in the quiet they could hear someone running toward the stairs. There was a cry of fear and surprise, followed by more running in the opposite direction, and then something landed to the side of Lakeland's clowns. It wore black clothing and looked similar to a small person, less one arm and most of a head. Above its neck there remained only an untethered jaw and a shallow bowl that held bone-white clumps of some unsavory substance. From several points on its body, most especially its torso, a thick white liquid oozed through tears in its garb. In its remaining hand, it held Katt's pistol, silencer painted with smiley faces in rainbow colors—one for every kill. It shouldn't be on its feet, and it shouldn't be aiming directly at Fielding.

In that moment of disorientation, the creature fired. Fielding dropped, his face torn. The tableau broke. Chalmers backed away, emptying his pistol into its chest to no effect. Henderson took a moment to assess before shooting. It had already taken an incredible amount of damage in the heart and lungs—if it had those—and didn't seem to have felt it. Robinson had shouted instructions upstairs that had been obscured by all the gunplay. What had he realized? The biggest effect on it so far had been the removal of an arm. Shoot to incapacitate, not to kill.

"Target the joints," he yelled.

Chalmers hurriedly changed magazines while Henderson took aim at its arm. He moved to the side to shift the line of fire away from Chalmers and let go a tight grouping of shots at its upper arm. Perhaps less effective than further down, but also easier to hit. Most of the shots hit, and its own uncanny aim faltered. Its next shot struck Chalmers in the upper chest rather than his head. He stumbled but managed to pump several more rounds into it, taking off its hand in a lucky shot. For his reward, the thing delivered a spinning kick to his head. His neck snapped with a sharp crunch, and he crumpled to the ground.

Henderson aimed for its feet, hoping to disable it before it could reach him. He got two rounds into its right foot before it turned toward him and charged. He backed away steadily, continuing to shoot when that foot was forward. Gun empty again, he turned to dodge around a corner, hoping it would race past and give him an opening to run. He'd only had the spare magazine out of habit. With seven guns for four targets there shouldn't have been a need to reload at all.

Its foot broke off when it next struck the floor, and the creature lost its balance. Momentum pitched it forward, and it landed on the floor beside him in the dining room. Henderson tried to duck into the sitting room, but it spun on the ground and hooked his legs. With a twist, it brought him down. He kicked at it and felt relief when it seemed to pull one leg away, but it was just maneuvering. It shifted the leg under his and brought the other one down hard, breaking his shin.

He screamed and grabbed the doorway for leverage to pull himself away. It was relentless, though, already positioning to break his other leg. He fought back waves of nausea but kept his focus on what it was doing. When it raised a leg to strike again, he moved his good leg out of the way and yanked on the doorjamb. Momentarily ahead of the creature, he tried to crawl toward the front door. The effort made his pain pulse. The nausea came in waves, rising higher each time, threatening to drag him under.

Henderson made it to the parlor before uneven footsteps came rushing from behind him. *Thump, squelch thump, squelch thump.* There was a louder thump and then a short pause. Before he had time to wonder what was happening, it landed roughly on his upper back, cracking his spine and pushing the air out of his lungs. He was in shock when it landed beside him and couldn't appreciate that it no longer moved.

CHAPTER FORTY-EIGHT

Christopher Gordon

He held back on the mid-floor landing as Katt and Campbell proceeded the rest of the way up. His job would be to guard the stairwell against escapees. The others would remain in the second floor doorway until they saw Robinson. Then they'd join the sweep, and he'd move up. Gordon didn't expect to be needed, which was fine by him. It was good pay for just standing around, and he couldn't get his adrenaline up to slaughter unarmed combatants. They had supposedly had a wolf with them elsewhere, but wolves were just dogs, and dogs weren't a problem if you kept your cool.

He heard the first shot from above and figured that Katt had already lowered the target count to three. This would all be over quickly. Then he heard several more shots in quick succession, which was all wrong for the situation. Maybe that amateur Campbell had panicked. The sound of impact from just inside the doorway above changed his mind.

Multiple shots came now from the stairwell and from the corridor, the echoes deafening him. He distantly heard someone shouting and bodies slamming, but he couldn't tell what was happening up there. A few last shots ended the burst of fighting, and the upstairs fell briefly silent.

He thought he heard movement, but he couldn't quite make it out. Then a noise like a stifled scream, and something landed heavily. He wasn't sure where. As he considered whether to advance, another suppressed vocalization came from the doorway. Quick footsteps followed, heading up to the third floor.

This was what he was here for. He'd move to cover the second-floor entrance to the stairway and make sure whoever was upstairs stayed there. This was supposed to be the only way to access the top level, so they'd just trapped themselves. Another spurt of gunshots came from elsewhere in the house.

He quickly advanced to the next landing and held fast, taking in the carnage. Two bodies lay there. Katt's neck had been twisted, and her head had landed at an impossible angle to her shoulders. Campbell had perished more cleanly, with a single bullet to the head. What the hell had happened?

Gordon checked their weapons and ammo, his heart racing. He was all in now and wasn't going to go down easily. There were two spare magazines on Katt, but her pistol was missing—possibly taken by whatever had done this to them. Campbell's gun was empty, and he had no spare ammo. A peek into the hallway revealed that Robinson was also down. There also seemed to be parts of an extra head out there.

The gunfire had subsided again. With the plan in shambles, he could just leave. He didn't even know who their employer was or how to get the money now that Robinson was dead. But this dull assignment had just piqued his interest. This was no defenseless prey they'd been after. Finishing a job that the top two contractors in the region had failed at would secure his reputation. He headed upstairs.

There was less room on the third floor. The footprint was the same, but multiple gables cut into the usable space. There was a large central area, with its own peaked roof above the others. Smaller, triangle-cut rooms circled it, except for the full curve of the tower's top. In the daytime, the windows would admit sufficient light to see almost everything up here.

Now, the storm clouds blocked even the moonlight. The rain slammed into the tiles above, masking any sound that might have otherwise made it through his temporary deafness. It would also cover a lot of the noise he'd be making.

He crouched and began to creep clockwise around the edges of the room. If he'd chosen the wrong direction they'd be able to slip out, but sometimes you had to just make a choice and go with it. He moved slowly and carefully, letting his eyes adjust to the darkness as much as they would and watching closely. The pace was excruciating, but he was confident that it would pay off.

The space was used for storage, but there wasn't a lot in it. Everything was pushed to the walls, leaving the bulk of the room open. Gordon passed an old chalkboard on wheels, a lectern, several wooden chairs, a few trunks, a wardrobe, small tables—nowhere did he see the targets, even inside the larger containers.

The room lit up for a second, and he analyzed the afterimage for signs of less angular shapes. There seemed to be some draping several feet away, and he trained his gun in that direction. Thunder rattled the window panes as he approached. The lightning had wrecked what night vision he had, so he relied on touch to investigate the form he'd seen.

Starting at the floor—wooden, in need of a polish—he explored until his fingers reached the fabric. It was heavy, like a curtain or a blanket. He slipped his hand beneath it and quickly found something wooden. Thinking it to be more furniture, he brushed over it to determine its type. The material quickly changed to a stiff, heavily-coated fabric. He reached to the side and found more wood, maybe two inches wide. A painting, probably several, protected under a dustcover.

He started moving again. Another flash of lightning illuminated the attic, and he thought there might have been someone peeking out from the tower. That wasn't far away, perhaps eight feet, and he considered his next action. How many of them had come up here? Gordon thought there were at least two. Had they stuck together? Impossible to guess. As soon as he fired a shot, he'd reveal his position—if they didn't know already. The thunder made his heart lurch. He had to decide.

If they'd come up here to mount some kind of offensive strategy, they'd have acted by now. Whatever had torn through the others was separate. These were likely to be simple victims, hiding in the dark. That meant he was wasting his time. The real challenge was downstairs, and he'd need to wrap this up to go confront it before Henderson got all the glory.

He broke a glow stick and tossed it into the tower. A red glow revealed two figures crouched there, one of which immediately ran toward him. He knelt, aimed carefully, and stopped her with two shots to the chest. She fell next to him, and he swiftly pulled out his knife and buried it in her. The other woman screamed, and he raised the pistol, aimed again, and fired.

That was his intent, and he got as far as aiming with no difficulty. Before he could pull the trigger, though, his pistol had vanished. The room filled with light again for an instant, and when it faded once more to the weaker red glow, there was a figure standing before him. He saw the outline of a small woman, primly holding his gun with just one finger and her thumb. She flung it away, and he heard it clatter on the floor. He started to feel lightheaded.

"I regret that my inattention allowed you and your comrades to enter my house and bring harm to my guests. All that you have done shall be undone, but I wish you to feel my displeasure before I set things right."

He was absolutely dizzy now, and he fell over onto his side. She continued to look down at him and express her anger.

"I control everything within this house. I am this house. I

can move through time within its walls. I can create anything I need, and I can remove anything I don't."

If he could only catch his breath, he could think straight. His gun had been taken away, but he had something else. What was it? A knife? No, it was in the girl he'd shot.

"At the moment, what I don't need is oxygen in the air around your face. You can gasp all you want, but it's useless. You are suffocating and will shortly die."

He weakly reached up to the indignant woman, but his body shook from convulsions. His heart sped up dramatically as pain exploded throughout his chest. He struggled to breathe, to stay conscious. Blotches with vague edges clouded his vision. His hand fell.

"I'll rewind this evening so this doesn't happen. I could simply choose not to let anyone pass through the doors, but unfortunately for you I'm angry. Your disappearances will serve as a cautionary tale."

She walked away, toward the red light.

"Hush now, Dale. I know it's been awful, and I'm so sorry I didn't stop it, but I will now. I'll make it all better, more like the way it was supposed to be."

More was said, but it slid off of him as he lost consciousness.

Second Interlude: Dale Alexander

It seemed like I'd just fallen asleep. I'd lain in bed, all too conscious of Pia sleeping next to me. By the time I thought that turning away from them would help, Cassie had already draped herself across my legs. It had only been one day, one very long and bizarre day. I'd been chased out of my home and taken in by unnerving strangers. Helping this incredible fugitive had robbed me of the security I gained from a stable routine and virtual isolation. I was completely out of sorts and agitated. My therapist would have to do some heavy patch work in the morning. My brain had finally quieted enough to sleep while I played through our probable conversation about the day's events. On balance I'd imagined he'd be pleased that I'd left my apartment.

My awakening was rough, and I struggled against it briefly. I found myself looking up at an older woman who was presumably the one shaking my shoulder.

"Dale, we must hasten."

She seemed familiar, but I couldn't place her. My eyes slid closed again.

"Dale!"

She pinched my cheek, and I swatted at her hand.

"What?" I asked, drawing out the vowel sulkily.

"We don't have time, dear. You and Cassie need to follow me. Immediately."

I sat up a little, since she was clearly not going to leave me alone. A large dog lay on my legs, watching us. The bed was wider than mine and had a canopy. Most curiously, a woman snored quietly next to me. My mind caught up and filled me in on what was going on, but I was still kind of out of it.

"You mean Pia? Cassie's already awake."

Livinia smiled tightly.

"Pia, then. I believe Cassie should be able to do as she wishes, but we need to get the two of you to safety."

The tension in her voice was convincing, although I still wanted her to explain the urgency. I rubbed the bristly hair on the top of Pia's head, petting them. They groaned and rolled over, cracking open one sleepy eye. The wolf disappeared instantly, her weight vanishing from the bed. They smiled up at me.

"Hi," they said.

I rested my hand on their cheek and stroked gently with my thumb.

"Mrs. Monroe wants us to get up."

"Mmm... what for?"

"Pia, please. I promise that I will explain this to all of you tomorrow, but I cannot do so now."

They peered at her closely, then grudgingly got out of bed. I climbed out myself and thought about throwing on more clothes. My pajamas, such as they were, were shorts and a tee, and while I'd rather wear more in company this was probably okay for a late-night emergency. Pia would need more than an inside-out pair of panties, though. I threw them my hoodie, and they sniffed it like a happy weirdo before putting it on.

We trudged after Livinia as she swiftly led us to the door at the top of the main stairway. Janice, who'd been leaning against it, slid off to the side. Its silence felt ominous. Our hostess stopped and addressed us.

"For your safety, I shall place you temporarily in my

library. It is a liminal space that I can navigate due my affinity for it, but others will quickly lose their way. That will protect you from the assailants who—"

"Wait, what?" I asked.

"People are breaking into my home to kill you. I shall attend to their incursion, but I need you to do exactly what I say."

I opened my mouth again, and Janice stopped me.

"Hold your horses, Dale."

"I need you to follow my instructions," Livinia continued.

She moved between Janice and the door.

"Miss Altura, your hand, please. Hold your other one behind you. Miss Alexander, you're next. Take its hand please. Thank you. Mx. Kuiper... excellent. Keep a firm grip on each other and follow along. If you get separated, it may take some time to locate you."

The door swung open for her, and she led us into her library. It was shorter than the dining room below it, likely because of the corridor leading back to Janice's combination sewing and computer room. A desk sat against one wall, an old lantern perched on it. There was a door opposite the entrance that probably led to a closet. The only thing that way was the sole bathroom in the house, and the only door to that was down the corridor. The remaining wall surface was covered in bookshelves. Three floor-to-ceiling bookcases divided the center of the room.

"Eyes on the floor," Livinia said.

I obeyed, and I hoped that Pia did as well. Whether Cassie did or not is anyone's guess, but since she was a spirit that hopefully didn't matter. We walked to the desk, and although I heard no match struck, new light shone in the room. I smelled burning kerosene.

"Now we can enter the stacks. You may feel some dizziness or nausea. If you do, try closing your eyes. It's important that only my mind directs our path, so please try to clear your minds, and don't talk while we're moving."

I thought about emptying my mind, but it's fucking cluttered in there. Bastian always asks me to picture my mind, and to me it's Willy Wonka's lab—from the ancient Gene Wilder flick, of course—only instead of orange muses singing judgmental ditties they're zombies occupied with dumb shit I've mostly lost track of. This one's been singing "Ob-La-Di, Ob-La-Da" since the eighth grade, no matter how often I try to put it down. Over there is one that's just thinking about the soft hair over Pia's muscles. It's drooling a bit. By the door is one that's got a reminder of therapy with Bastian tomorrow, and another keeps pushing it outside as part of emptying my mind.

As this visualization grew more complex, filling up with colorful zombies carrying out increasingly pointless missions, I realized that we'd already started walking. I dutifully watched the floor's wooden slats as we wound through the shelves. The direction of these structures was parallel to the planks, which I found very satisfying. We turned several times, more than seemed reasonable for three rows between bookcases. Was she just leading us in circles?

I looked up, just a little, scanning the bottom shelves to my left. From what I could glimpse, the books were about aquatic life: sharks, cephalopods, whales. Someone had a definite oceanic fixation. Not that I was less obsessive in my reading. A healthy percentage of the books scattered throughout my apartment were gender-swap manga. The thought of Livinia desperately wishing to live underwater actually humanized her. She could be masking regrets, grief, dreams, or anything behind that facade of bland decorum. After all, how could someone capable of photographing spirits not be harboring a deep secret?

"Whoever's thinking of mermaids, please stop. You're interfering with my search."

Guiltily, I snapped my eyes back to the floor. The grain of the wood created patterns I could follow, which helped to keep my mind busy. Every time I found my thoughts or eyes wandering, I returned to the swoops and lines. It was oddly peaceful. We continued without further incidents, and after a few more turns she brought us to a stop.

"We're here, ladies. You may open your eyes now."

Janice and I let go of each other. I tried to take my hand back from Pia, but they held on. When I turned, they were grinning at me. I had to let them win; they were too happy. It would probably be good to talk to them soon about setting healthy boundaries.

"I'll leave the lantern here for you. Please don't wander from this aisle. This shouldn't take long, and I'll come back for you when it's over."

She handed the light to Janice.

"One other thing: if you would like to join me, Cassie, I'd be delighted to have your assistance."

With that, she walked into the darkness, the sound of her steps fading quickly.

"What the fuck?" I asked Janice.

It placed the lantern on the floor between the bookcases and sat with its legs drawn up, back against the shelves.

"Plant it. For the pooch to help the boss, your pal's gonna need to nod off."

I sat cross-legged against the opposite stack. Pia looked between us and must have decided that it was correct. They curled up next to me and rested their head on my thigh. We so needed to discuss boundaries.

"I repeat. What the actual fuck?"

"Sure. I'll spill. What's bugging you? The library? Liv sticking us in here for timeout? Your baby doll's bane?"

Now that she mentioned it, yes. Pretty much everything. How was Livinia Monroe still alive? How could Janice itself be a hundred and twenty-something years old? Why did everyone say Cassie was see-through? There was so much weirdness all around me that I felt overwhelmed. Just pick one thing and start there.

"Okay. Yeah. Why did we have to stare at the ground while we circled the same three rows widdershins or whatever?"

Janice looked at me for a while, and I thought that it was going to renege. It glanced around the area lit by our small lantern and turned back to me.

"I'll give it to you as straight as I can. I don't think you'll like any of this, but if we're in here things are worse than we thought. She called this a 'liminal space.' You get what that means?"

I nodded. "Transitory, or something like that, right? It's used a lot to describe pocket dimensions and other overlapping spaces in fiction."

"The boss would go into lecture mode over that, but sure. Close enough. This whole house is magical, but the library is its center. This room holds everything that has ever been written by humans, and it's still growing. There's so much in it that there aren't actual sections. Think of the shelves as a web portal. Every time you look at a new one, you see a new search display. Liv's never adapted to computers, so she turns corners to filter her search. It can take a while, but she gets there. If we wanted something, we could think of a more complicated query and only have to check a few shelves, but of course we can't."

"Why the hell not?"

"We're not Livinia. We might get away with it briefly, especially if we don't make any turns, but it's easy to get lost in here. If you picked up that lantern and walked to the open end of this row, you wouldn't see the door anymore. It's only in the initial state of the room. You can't leave the library until all search terms are cleared, and that's an admin function."

"And she's the only admin," I said.

It nodded.

"Her house. Her library. She knows where she put us, and anyone coming in after us would get totally lost. The odds of them finding us before she returns are extremely low. Even if someone happened across us, I'd probably be able to take them."

"Then why are you in here with us? Couldn't she use your help?"

Janice hugged its knees.

"That's what worries me. I know her pretty well. Either she's actually worried that someone might find you after all or... things went very wrong and she's rewound to try again."

I felt a number of expressions vying for control of my face. This was getting weirder every time Janice opened its mouth, and the implications of what it had just said were unsettling. It was right; I didn't like this.

"Fuck the what, now?"

"The boss *is* the house. She controls everything in here, including time. There's a way that things are supposed to fall out. From hints, I think she's reliving memories. So when something goes wrong, she goes back and tries to fix it. It's risky, though. Her interference can throw things further off. I've been staying here for forty years, and if she's done a rewind to change anything in that time I don't know about it."

"So why do you think that's what's happening now? How would you even know?"

"She's agitated," it said simply.

If it had been living with Mrs. Monroe for that long, I had to take its word for her mental state.

"Okay, but we've seen you in action, Janice. You kick serious ass. Why wouldn't she want your help?"

"Ha! Those palookas were a cinch, but thanks. I'm tougher than I look, but I can be benched. My guess is that's what happened, at least in part. I got in the way or was too wounded to help. She wouldn't do a rewind for just that, no matter how I've grown on her. I'd get better sooner or later. But if either of you were taken out of the picture, she might care enough."

I frowned.

"Why us?"

"Memories are all she has. When I brought you in, I saw the look in her eyes. She knows you two, and she likes you. If anything took you away, all the memories of her time in the future with you would fade, and she won't allow that."

It glanced along the row again, and I swore it was nervous.

"She's lost too many people. It happens. We're pretty much both the same age, and I hate watching friends die. Hers, though, they vanished. All together, on a mission through the... never mind where. Point is, she talks about maybe finding them one day. But her eyes are dead. She knows that she won't. Loss like that—with no hope—it makes you cling to what you can."

I didn't know how to accept that. Someone valued us—*me*—enough to *turn back time*? In my experience, when people got to know me they pulled away. They didn't make memories they'd want to revisit. Yet more to discuss with Bastian in the morning.

"Cassie, on the other hand," it continued. "About the only thing that could happen to her is to be sent back wherever she came from. There may be some way to protect against her or keep her out of somewhere, but she's loads less vulnerable than I am."

I guess that made sense, given everything else, but one thing still stood out against the background of weirdness.

"If Livinia controls everything inside, uh, herself? Then why does she need to lock us away to handle them? Couldn't she just keep them from coming in?"

Janice just looked at me, an inscrutable mask of a face atop its more emotive body. Its hands had balled up with tension, and its arms pressed its legs together tightly. It was worried.

"She wants to," I said, trying the idea out.

It rested its head on its knees and gazed at the floor.

"Holy shit, she wants them to suffer."

I said that quietly, in disbelief that someone that seemingly calm and bemused could be overcome by vengeful wrath. What kind of horrors was she about to inflict on account of us?

Although, apparently they killed us first?

My therapy session couldn't come soon enough.

Part Three

THE PROBLEMATIC ACCORD

CHAPTER FORTY-NINE

Rick Chalmers

There was someone in the cellar, he was sure of it. He approached Robinson, who stood at one of the exits from the kitchen into the main house. Most of the team was clustered around him already, except for Henderson, still guarding the back door. Following the orders to stay silent as long as possible, Rick tried to get across that he'd heard something. Point down, cup ear, waggle hand like a sock puppet talking. Robinson glared at him and made angry gestures. Rick shook his head, not understanding the signals.

Henderson grabbed him by the arm and pulled him toward the cellar door. Rick followed, hoping he'd been wrong. Most of his work for Lakeland had been surveillance or guarding. The turn of this assignment to murder had not been expected or welcome. Technically, he hadn't broken any laws for work before—not serious ones, anyway. Wasn't everyone involved in a crime that led to death held responsible? At any rate, he'd rather not use his pistol tonight.

From the doorway, there were only a few steps to a small landing. Then a right-hand turn led to steep wooden planks down into the darkness. They both turned on their flashlights. Henderson held his up, like a cop, which heightened Rick's sense that Robinson's crew were pretentious idiots. Seriously, since when did hired muscle train to be movie space marines?

Before they reached the bottom, Rick could see light coming from under a door. He passed his flashlight over the area, revealing a metal door set into a cinderblock wall. Henderson passed in front of the beam, heading off to explore the room. On reaching the dirt floor, Rick went straight to the door and pressed his ear to it. A small noise filtered through: unidentifiable scuffling. Then the distinct, although muffled, sound of a door closing. He waited but heard nothing more. Thinking it was safe to proceed, he turned to wave Henderson forward.

The other beam of light had vanished. Rick scanned the room; dusty old shelves, the sagging remnant of a crate, a mousetrap with a piece of cheese that looked petrified—there was nothing here except for an open wooden door tucked just behind the steps. So much for teamwork. It seemed they were splitting up.

He tried the handle, and it moved smoothly. The door opened with little noise, and the room beyond was lit by a bare bulb hanging from the ceiling. Rick turned off his flashlight and entered. There was a cot in the back corner and a plain wooden chair next to it. A bucket completed the furnishings. The other door was unpainted wood, set into a plasterboard wall. The haphazard division of the basement didn't fit the fussy elegance of the upstairs, but he guessed it was because the owners never came down here. The kitchen and everything below it was simply for the people who kept the place running.

He listened at the wooden door. Nothing. The door behind him slammed shut, and he nearly dropped his gun whirling to see who was there. He remained alone. It must have swung shut on its own. Forcefully. Rick performed breathing exercises to bring his heart rate back down. Once his pulse dropped enough to hear over, he listened again. Still nothing.

It was possible there was another way out of the basement toward the front of the house. He readied his gun anyway.

This door opened on a small, finished room. The walls were drywall, painted gray. The concrete floor had been sealed. Tin tiles covered the rafters and pipes above. A set of fluorescent tubes hung from them, but they were turned off. The only light was what straggled in from the bulb behind him.

He turned on his flashlight again and played it over the walls. Yet another door. Lockers behind cages. No one in here. He took a deep breath. It was nice not having to kill anyone, but this was getting frustrating. Rick lowered his gun and entered the room. Halfway across, the bulb in the outer room burst. It was unnerving, but less so than the door shutting violently had been. He just needed to get back upstairs where everything was orderly and clean.

A clacking sound, like fingernails on a desk. Or claws on concrete. He whirled, his light falling on a large yellow dog—falling through it to form only a vague silhouette on the floor behind it. It snarled at him, silently but with clear anger, and advanced slowly. *Clack, clack, clack.*

Rick shot at it, missing wildly, the bullet chipping the painted cement next to the creature. It didn't react at all. He aimed more carefully, and this time he swore that he saw the shot pass through its shoulder into the chest. Another chip out of the floor. *Clack, clack,* it came implacably.

Rick fired twice more before it leapt at him.

CHAPTER FIFTY

Derek Robinson

Katt appeared at the corridor entrance to the back staircase, and they split to cover the floor. While she went to the back, Derek turned the glass doorknob of the room at the top of the main stairs. He carefully pushed the door open, revealing a library with a desk and multiple shelves of books covering the walls and floor. Light came from a lantern someone had left on the desk. The way it flickered meant it was oil. Someone was likely still in here.

He crouched down and entered the room, pushing the door gently shut behind him to slow anyone attempting to flee. Scanning for any movement behind the rows of shelves he saw nothing, but he heard soft voices beyond the first floor-to-ceiling shelving unit. He smiled. At least two of the targets were close at hand. He slid along the wall, using the books to hide his approach.

Derek waited at the corner, but the voices had stopped. They must have heard the door. It had hardly made a sound, but if they'd already been keyed up and hiding it wouldn't have been hard to notice. No matter. They were trapped. He pivoted around the corner, aiming along the new wall.

Nothing.

He moved forward, turning with his gun to look down the

new row. Just a lot of books and the gap before the far wall. Derek frowned and moved to the next row. Again, there was no one there. He could see the desk now in the space between this aisle and the far wall. Only one more row to check. Making sure of his grip on the pistol, he slid into the last row, against the outside wall. There was nobody there. Perplexed, Derek stood and walked toward the desk. At the end of the shelves, he peered toward the door.

There were shelves along the entire wall. Two turns following the walls should have left him opposite where he'd come in. The desk had been visible from the entrance, but somehow the reverse wasn't true.

Using the desk as his focal point, he walked across the room until it was how he'd first seen it on entering the room. There was no door. He looked along the whole wall. Solid shelves. Okay. First wall. He walked briskly along the shelves until he reached a corner. Second. This wall, too, was completely covered in shelves of books. Another corner reached. Third. He could already see the unbroken book-shelves. Derek half-ran to the last corner.

Books. Books. Books!

He whirled frantically, scanning the room for any sign of an exit. Everywhere he looked there were only books. The walls were all lined with books. There were six stacks of shelves on the floor, opposing each other in groups of three across a center divide.

Derek stopped. He recounted the stacks. Six of them. When he'd come in there'd been only three. Three stacks, and a desk. Undeniably, the room had changed. He let his gun fall to his side. There was nothing to shoot.

"Fielding!" he called out. "I'm in a trap of some kind! Open the door!"

Derek had killed for the Kuipers before. He'd destroyed evidence, blackmailed, threatened, robbed, burned, and done whatever else Tobias Jr. had paid him to do. None of it had bothered him. It was a lot of money for very little effort, and he enjoyed a lot of free time to practice and work out. This was the first time he'd ever felt, deep in his gut, that he was out of his depth. He needed to focus.

He went to the nearest stack and inspected it. Firmly attached to the floor. No mechanism for sliding or rotating. He hadn't really expected any, since he'd have heard it move. Nonetheless he methodically went over the other five to assure himself that they were completely stationary. That accomplished, he stood thinking for a while.

None of this made sense. Either the room had changed around him, or he'd moved into a different room. Neither seemed likely, but he couldn't consider options that meant his perceptions had been compromised. It was possible that something airborne had gotten into his system, but if he was hallucinating he had no way to recover. He'd be at the mercy of the people he'd come to kill. It was better for now to act as though this was real.

The walls. If he'd entered a different room it was through a wall. Maybe an optical illusion had fooled him. Derek went to the closest wall and began knocking books to the floor. If he clung to the walls, he'd know soon enough whether there was any architectural trickery going on.

Turn after turn, wall after wall, he circled the room, leaving tossed books in his wake, never finding books on the floor in front of him. After the fourth circuit he stopped. From what he'd seen, the library should be at most one fifth of the usable space of this story, somewhere between 150 and 200 square feet. There was barely space for a second copy of the room, and four was out of the question.

He was seeing things.

His frustration turned to fear. For the first time, he thought he might never escape. He unscrewed the silencer and put it in his pocket. The holster for his pistol was back in the van as he hadn't expected to need it, so the gun went into the back of his pants. It wasn't going to do him any good now. He was in a trap, and he doubted his captors would come for him while he could still fight.

He wandered the library for days, giving up on finding a way out. He'd lost complete track of time, but he knew a lot had passed because he could barely walk anymore. His throat rasped as he tried to breathe, and his eyes stuck to their lids when he blinked.

Over time, the bound books had given way to provide space for the curious and wonderful objects that he stumbled across: cuneiform tablets, elaborately drawn maps, engraved bones. As his thoughts turned to death he found a headstone.

It was a large piece of polished pink granite, engraved with a name he didn't recognize and dates that measured a lifetime of only a few decades. He stared at it, trying to extract some secret meaning. None of it meant anything to him apart from the gloomy symbolism. He laughed roughly, more of a shallow wheeze, thinking that his next discovery would be an open grave marked by his own headstone.

He didn't get much further before he needed to rest again. He could feel his strength waning from both hunger and growing despair. A nap would certainly help. Conserve energy while his body ate away at his muscles. He thought grimly that his starvation was less of an issue than his dehydration.

In his dreams, he continued pacing the narrow aisles of the library. He smelled food and heard water, but he found nothing. The shelves, laden with bones stored by type, became darker, mustier. Even in slumber his exhaustion couldn't be ignored. When he came upon an empty shelf, he crawled into the space. It felt good to stop and lay his head down.

Derek Robinson never woke up, in his dream or any other place.

CHAPTER FIFTY-ONE

Jason Henderson

Jason led the descent under the house, with Chalmers dragging his ass behind. Their flashlights revealed an old, dusty cellar with stone walls and a hard-packed dirt floor. He didn't notice anything remarkable right away. Moving into the room, he saw a door behind the open steps. It was old, cracked wood set into the stones. He lined up the first floor in his mind and figured that it was under the kitchen, leading outside the footprint of the house.

There might have once been a passage to an outbuilding—an escape tunnel perhaps, or possibly another set of stairs leading to another level not in the plans. More likely, it could lead to those slanted exterior doors he sometimes saw in movies. Jason tried to remember if he'd seen any as they'd come around the side of the house. He didn't think he had, and surely Robinson would have made someone guard that if there'd been one. Wherever it led, the noise Chalmers had heard could have come from it.

He looked to see what his partner was doing, but the man was gone. Jason had hauled him to the door and seen his light coming from behind him on the stairs. Had he turned around and gone upstairs? This was why working with new people sucked; you never knew when they'd flake.

He walked over to the wooden door. It had once been fancy. Hard wood, decorated with bevels and carvings. Lacquer crumbling over paint, with hints of a very old stain peeking through at the edges. Years in the cellar had not been kind, and it was now cracked and faded, covered in dust. It had an old brass knob set into a large, ornate plate—one with a large keyhole in it.

He reached out and tried to open it, but the door wouldn't budge. A quick search of the immediate area revealed several nails in between the stones to the right of the door. Most were empty, but an old brass key hung from one. It was ornate, with a handle design that resembled some kind of splayed bird. He held his flashlight in his armpit while he tried the key in the lock. It took a little fiddling, but he soon had the door open.

Complete darkness lay beyond it. He retrieved his flashlight and shined it into the space behind the door, but it never reflected off of anything. He pointed it at the ground, just past the threshold. Again, the light vanished. Crouching, he set the flashlight down and tried to touch the ground on the other side of the door. He felt wet earth, but he couldn't see his hand anymore. When he jerked it back, it seemed unharmed. Just an unexplained visual effect of some kind. Unpleasant but likely harmless. He walked in.

On the other side, the darkness was absolute. The weight of it surrounded him, pressing his clothes to his body, touching his skin with sharp fingers. Jason stowed the flashlight—it was useless here—and shoved his hand in a pocket. The ground was uneven and grew spongy after his first few steps. There was no humidity, though. The temperature was unremarkable, neither notably warm or cool. No air movement or odors. If it weren't for the soft ground and his own breathing, it would be a sensory dead zone. He reached out to either side but couldn't find a wall. Where exactly was he?

Patches of color seeped out of the void, pooling into abstract shapes around him. The darkness had been bad, but it hadn't hampered his sense of balance. These images floated everywhere, moving separately in all directions as he passed through them, diving below his feet and playing havoc with his spatial awareness. He stumbled a few times before learning to trust his feet more than his sight.

The odors crept in while Jason adjusted to the lights. Earthy at first, a mild hint of damp soil and mildew. Another step brought a sharp whiff of copper that made him flinch. Like the colors, the scents shifted constantly, as though they existed only in small pockets. One replaced another as he walked through the tunnel—methane, cotton candy, black licorice, sawdust—and he wondered how they made this, and why. Was it intended to keep people out? He wouldn't be dissuaded that easily. If they had gotten through here, so could he.

Snippets of sounds came to him with the same randomness as everything else. Creaking boards, a small bell, murmured voices, a mourning dove—none lasting more than a second or two but very real for that time. It was all just a distraction, but from what? What reality hid underneath these fantasies?

His leg hit something solid. Inspecting it with his hands he discovered a rough-hewn wooden ladder. Touch. That's what it all covered. He could trust that sense, if nothing else. He began to climb, slowly in case there was a door at the top. What he'd experienced of this place so far didn't encourage him to think he'd passed through all of the defenses. He counted rungs as he climbed. When he reached eight he began to hope the top was near. Twelve. Seventeen. How long was this? Twenty-one. Twenty-eight.

He stopped. Something felt off. Jason reached out to the side. Nothing there. The other direction. Nothing. Above. Only more ladder. He thought for a while as he stood in place. There were a few more directions to try, but he suspected they'd be the same. Maybe they intended for him to give up before reaching the top, or maybe this route led to nowhere—another distraction. Being real didn't make it the correct path. Almost thirty rungs up. That was too high for this underground space, and there weren't other buildings close enough to the house to account for it either. He took a hesitant step back down and found the same soft ground waiting for him below.

He kicked the ladder in frustration, and he felt it give. There was no sound of it landing; it had simply gone. This was preposterous. He'd stuck with this absurd tunnel out of stubbornness, but it now seemed to have been nothing but a distraction. Perhaps there'd been a hidden passage back in the cellar. Concealed entrance, with an intriguing decoy to misdirect searchers, leading them into a sensory maze. Bizarre, yes, but possible with clever building and subtle gasses. Clearly it worked.

He turned, reasonably certain he faced the way he came in, and walked. Barking dogs, salt air, a kaleidoscope of colors and noises and smells buffeted him, and he fought to stay focused. Only his feet existed. What they touched was real. Never mind the ladder. Ignore everything else. He was more sure of himself leaving the tunnel, but it still took a long time to retrace his steps. It seemed that way, but the constant barrage of new input made time stretch so badly that he couldn't be sure. The ground rose and fell beneath him, but he refused to think about it. He couldn't let the illusions get to him.

The door came as a surprise when he found it. He couldn't see it, but his fingers traced over the old wood until they found the knob. He turned it, pulled the door inward, and let out his breath when a different darkness cut through the hovering shapes. When the slice was large enough, he slipped through and pulled the door shut behind himself. He stood reeling, growing accustomed to the stability of everything around him and the continuity of small sounds. Electricity buzzed upstairs in the kitchen. Water moved through pipes. A furnace pushed air to the upper floors of the house.

Once the room settled down, he gave it a cursory glance. It was larger than he remembered, much larger, with a massive furnace dominating the center of the room. Ducts spread out from it, forming a squat metal sculpture of an oak tree. Tucked behind this monstrosity of engineering lurked a wide workbench. Several tools hung from the pegboard fastened above. Jason considered whether he'd looped back to another part of the basement or gone straight through to another building entirely. With everything assailing him in that corridor, his grasp on time and distance had been fuzzy. Wherever he'd wound up, he'd gotten out of there at least. He took a moment to assess his condition. No injuries. Slightly nauseous, but improving. He still had all his gear. A little scouting and he'd be back on mission.

He started by examining the basement more closely. An inflatable pool spilled out of a box beside him. Puzzle boxes and games collected dust on a gray metal set of shelves. A disorganized heap of clothing spread under a chute next to a washer and dryer. The walls were large, painted bricks rather than the rough stones where he'd started. That raised the odds of this being another building, but he couldn't figure out where. This was a residential basement, and everything close to their target had been strip malls and offices.

He peered out of the dirty windows under the joist. It was still dark out, but he couldn't make out details through the grime. There were too many nearby lights to be still in the mansion. Jason located the staircase, still bare planks, but the flashlight revealed old gray paint on them. He turned off the light and crept up the steps, keeping his feet toward the edges. There was a door directly at the top of the stairs, and after a quick check he opened it. Beyond stretched an unlit hallway—to the right a kitchen, a door and staircase to the left. He went to the right.

There was no one in the kitchen, but he took his time heading to the back door. Small table. Sink. No drying rack. Dishwasher concealed or absent. No toaster. No microwave. There was a boxy appliance he took for an oven initially. On closer inspection it had lid flaps in place of the range. Baffled, he lifted the smaller of the flaps. It covered a wide chute that had some food residue on the side. Weird place for a waste bin, but he didn't keep up with home appliance trends. Under the larger flap lay a keypad and monitor. He couldn't read anything in the light that filtered in from the window over the sink, and his curiosity didn't overcome his reluctance to use the flashlight near windows. He closed the top and felt along the slightly protruding sides for a handle, figuring that the facade concealed some way to heat food.

A buzzing started in his ears, and he winced. The blaring alarm that followed was harder for him to misinterpret. Jason spun and leveled his gun at a drone that hovered in the entrance of the room. Red lights flashed from within a dome atop the machine, and he assumed the speaker lay underneath, between the rotors. The sound cut out, replaced by a tinny recorded voice.

"You have been flagged for [UNLAWFUL TRESPASS]. Your image has been sent to the Criminal Activity Database for processing. Please remain still to avoid incurring more charges while officers respond."

In the short silence before the message repeated, he heard movement upstairs. No need for quiet anymore, and he'd rather not wait for the cops to come for him. Whatever the hell this was, he was done spending time and energy on it. He raised the gun, aimed, and shot the center of the drone. The dome shattered, sending shards of clear plastic arcing to the floor. One rotor fell silent and hung loosely from the sphere. Sparks flew from the underside, and the voice was replaced by spurts of static. The remaining rotors struggled to maintain balance for the broken machine. The person above had stopped moving, which Jason thought showed wisdom. The silencer might have reduced the sound enough to prevent the entire neighborhood from being alerted, but anyone in the house knew what had just happened.

He unlocked the back door and slipped outside, leaving the wounded drone moving randomly in short bursts.

CHAPTER FIFTY-TWO

Livinia Monroe

She let Cassie finish off the last of the invaders. The wolf was an enthusiastic assistant in the counterassault, leading Livinia to wonder just how much the spirit comprehended about the threat these intruders represented. Certainly she knew they were a danger to her host, which prompted her uncharacteristic aggression. Was this creature also aware that they were undoing the death of Pia, or was she merely picking up on the tension?

A question for another time. Having personally murdered one of the would-be assailants with a dress dummy in the sewing room, lured one into the library stacks, helped another stumble to his doom in the Passage, sunken a fourth into a void underneath the canopy bed, and assisted Cassie by providing various illusions and distractions, Livinia had to admit that her wrath had been depleted. She could have simply disintegrated them to make her point, but she'd allowed her guests to come to harm. Her fury over this failure had demanded expression. Albert had always found her petulance charmingly aristocratic, but she'd been human then —merely a wealthy young woman with a facility for languages and a curiosity about the work that he and her father did. He'd never seen her with enough power to vent her spleen so malignantly.

Regretting her actions, but not sufficiently to undo them, she cleaned up the traces of her unwelcome company. Bodies broken into raw atoms and weapons stashed. Broken items restored. Blood removed. Door lock repaired. Nothing remained to indicate that anything had happened in here. That accomplished, she returned to the library.

The others were where she'd left them, which pleased her. She hadn't needed Cassie's assistance, but tricking Pia into sleeping had seemed a wise precaution. They were the most impulsive one in the group, and with them under control she'd been confident that Miss Altura could keep the other in place. Finding them chatting on the floor was unexpected but gratifying.

Although the pathway to her memories of the future had been significantly altered, there still remained some routes she could see that led to her guests joining the household. Unfortunately, the disruption had been too great for her to see much beyond a few months along any possibility. The recollections of her initial existence as the library and house were already growing murky, leaving her less grounding for how events *should* play out. The potential new futures expanded so rapidly that navigation of them quickly exploded into too many possibilities. Time would tell if her old certainty would ever return, but whatever had caused the severe fracture happened when the Kuipers' goals had clashed with her own. Perhaps history would heal once they resolved the conflict.

Misses Altura and Alexander looked up at her.

"Hey, boss."

"Everything clear, Mrs. Monroe?"

She allowed herself a smile.

"For a rather specific value of 'everything,' yes. The house is now safe, thanks to Cassie's kind assistance."

Miss Altura remained quiet during the return journey out

of the stacks, which indicated its desire to have a lengthy conversation with her about what had just happened. That was acceptable to her, as they had much to discuss while the others slept.

CHAPTER FIFTY-THREE

Janice Altura

It stood with Livinia in the armory, looking at the small stockpile of weapons that had filled its crumbling Monarch all of those years ago. The vehicle itself was long gone—and in all honesty even the Ion was hardly worth maintaining anymore—but all of that precious gear from the Scientific Investigation Unit had been kept pristine down here. The beautiful thing about living in a magical house was the availability of perfect environmental conditions.

Its last assignment for the SIU had been to retrieve this stolen arsenal in a joint operation with the Shale County Sheriff's Office. While her colleagues still worked to discover who had been behind the theft, it had responded to the tip about where the items had gone. Just before the raid, Janice had lost contact with Madru Harbor. Afterward, it had dropped in on Livinia to see if she'd had any ideas. Once they'd confirmed that the city's dimension was inaccessible, all they could do was hope to one day find the Madru key and use the Passage.

"I'm not seeing it, boss. Those whippersnappers are too green. Sticking fancy pea shooters in their mitts won't make doughboys out of them."

"Cassie is quite capable, and being merely a spirit she has

the advantage of being impervious to harm. Well, any harm Kuipers are likely to 'dish out,' as you might say."

"So we tuck Pia in for a nap and take her doggie for a walk. What do we do with the other chick? She's a great kid, but she's short on spunk."

"You must have something defensive for her. How did you avoid being hit?"

Janice shrugged.

"Didn't, personally."

It thought back to the catalog of missing equipment. Not everything was recovered, but one item of possible interest had been. It viewed the belt as more suited to surveillance than to combat, but the device might be able to keep Dale safe enough to stand upright. A quick rummage through the boxes tucked at the bottom of the cabinets, and it held up the contraption for Livinia to see.

The belt was wide, as though made for lumbar support, and made of rough cloth. There were wires all through it, connected to small lights of varying colors and an attached metal box bearing a large switch. There was a homemade quality to it, as though someone had grabbed whatever they'd had on hand to prove out an idea, and to Janice's understanding that's exactly what had happened. One of Madru Harbor's many researchers had discovered the light-bending properties of an extremely rare mineral and made this prototype invisibility belt. The fact he'd been captured by the SIU for using it to steal resources for further experiments only confirmed its effectiveness.

"Please tell me that's a prototype force barrier."

"I'd be fibbing. The brains call it an invis-o-belt. Name spoils the surprise, really."

"Will she be able to fire while it's on?"

"Let's say 'sure.' "

Livinia took the belt and hung it on a hook.

"It's a start. Do you have any manner of weapon that would be safe for her to use?"

Janice stared up at her from where she crouched.

"Sweetie, why are we loading for bear? You rewound the tape because it went bad, but we're clear now. They won't try that again."

Livinia knelt and took her friend's hands in her own.

"Things have changed. There is a way back to the path of history, but I can only say we would do well to be prepared in case of another intrusion."

"What happened? What did you rewind?"

Her gaze dropped.

"I was distracted and didn't notice them enter. They weren't supposed to. You had killed six of them before... stopping. The seventh found Dale and Pia. By the time I noticed, only Dale remained."

Janice hugged her.

"Oh, Liv. My poor bookworm."

"I couldn't let her die. I couldn't send the spirit back to captivity."

"I know. With all my metaphorical heart, I love how ride or die you are about your pals' futures, but all of us will push daisies eventually. Even if you recite every line the same as your first trip to eternity, we see our dust in your eyes. That's a bad vibe for paving memory lane. We need you here, really here, unafraid to mix things up. Can you do that? Can you swear on your card catalog?"

They held each other in silence briefly.

"I don't use cards. Never have."

Her body shook with a sudden giggle fit, and Janice rasped out a few quiet chuckles of its own. It was going to be a long night, but they'd get each other through it.

CHAPTER FIFTY-FOUR

Annette Kuiper

It was six in the morning, and Annette was anxious. She'd been calling Robinson to no avail and could not shake the suspicion that something had gone horribly wrong in the raid. If that wolf bitch had been captured alive it would be incredibly difficult to get rid of her cleanly, and she clearly wouldn't be able to use Toby's pet mercenary to take care of it.

Lakeland answered, by the second ring no less. The man often bordered on insubordinate behavior but he was reliably available.

"Yes, ma'am."

"Where the fuck is Robinson? His phone says he's not in the service area."

"Good morning. Yeah, we haven't heard from him or his team since they breached the house. Lenny's back though. They threw him out around ten p.m., and we thought he was dead. Checked him as we retreated, and he was breathing, so we carried him out. He woke up a few hours ago but says he can't remember anything after entering the apartment. No idea what they did to him in there. Seems okay, though."

Annette rubbed the back of her neck. She didn't know who Lenny was, and she was too tired to yell at Lakeland about it.

"Fucking terrific," she said coldly. "What's going on in that house?"

"I'm afraid we just don't know. Robinson took three of his people and three of ours in while the rest of us guarded the exits. We never heard a thing, but the storm got pretty wild. Hard rain and thunder boomers. We waited for hours through that before retreating with Lenny."

"Lenny. Lenny! Why should I give a shit?"

"They let him go," Lakeland answered petulantly. "That's important. They took him from the apartment into that damned house, and they let him go. He doesn't know anything, but I've seen where people remember things under hypnosis."

He might have something there, and the thought of it intensified her frustration. She should have thought of that herself.

"Where is this miracle spy?"

"He's sleeping in the van."

"Keep him there. I need to make arrangements."

"Will d—"

She hung up and went to the top floor.

Toby's door didn't respond to her card. Rather, not in the way she expected. The scanner emitted a nasty beep and flashed red when she held her company card to its sensor. She knew he wouldn't answer his phone, so she texted him.

Need to talk now

NOW!!

There was no response, but a few moments later the message statuses updated from "sent" to "received." A lengthy minute after that there was a click as the door unlocked. Annette flung it open and strode through the waiting room into the office. Toby already sat there in his business kimono, laptop open, intent on the screen.

She sat down, not waiting for his attention or an invitation.

"What the fuck, Toby? Your great cleanup man disappeared."

He continued to type furiously. "That he has, little sister. It is most disconcerting."

"Disconcerting? You're disconcerted. How fucking inconvenient you must find that."

"I do, actually. You know how I feel about displays of anger. You may wallow in your base instincts, like our father, but I will remain in control of myself. Because of that, I have realized several things you'd have noticed if you were calmer."

Annette clenched her jaw and snarled through it.

"Such as?"

He stopped typing and looked at her for the first time since she entered.

"Somehow these four women have slain or incapacitated a seven-person team of armed intruders. While our family secret can be a nuisance, the kill order should have made her easy to deal with. The woman who found her is an out-of-shape shut-in with no combat experience. This leaves the two others, about whom we know little. Either or both made the difference, and we have no information as to how.

"That lack of information is disconcerting. We are dealing with individuals of unknown capabilities who we never noticed before now. This raises many questions that I know you don't have the patience for, so I'll skip to the parts that involve your interests.

"If killing her outright is beyond our capabilities, then capturing her is out of the question. Unfortunately that puts us in a worse spot with the other family branches. We will have to let them know that we are too weak to do it ourselves, and they will send in their own people to make sure she's recaptured. Not only will you still be required to breed her with Kevin, but if our father is disgraced, the odds favor our branch being cut off rather than his incompetent heirs being allowed to continue in his place.

"Politically, it's disastrous."

Annette's mind had assessed the information as he'd been speaking. This was bad. They'd be fortunate simply not to lose the limited control they had in the business. Her damage control instincts took over. She needed options.

"Okay, you're ahead of me. What are you thinking?"

"We can still come out ahead, but we'll have to hold off on eliminating the wolf girl."

"Jesus, Toby!"

He waved a hand dismissively.

"If we have to go through with it, we can always use IVF. The donor could be anyone. We both know there's no benefit to remixing our genetics into that line, but we can pretend if needed.

"But we can still remove Father and stay in the good graces of the other branches. The finances of Kuiper Innovations are as shady as you'd expect. In my efforts to apply a veneer of honesty to the books, I uncovered a secret account used to hide funds from the family. Funds shifted there look like debt and count against the points we pay as part of the consortium. It's likely that every business in the families does something similar, but exposing this to the council will ingratiate us to them."

"They wouldn't throw us out with him?"

"Unlikely. We are the current keepers of the blood. If we follow through with that and turn over Father's records about that account, they'll let us stay. Our branch may be on probation of some kind, but we'd still be on acceptable terms with them, and they may help us remove Father from our companies."

Annette mulled that over. She still resented having to keep that horrid creature and raise its bastard child, but removing their father would be a nice consolation prize.

"You yourself pointed out that we'd be considered weak if

we can't retrieve her on our own. How are we going to manage that?"

"One thing at a time, little sister. First we need to get our hands on Father's account registers. I know where he keeps them and who can retrieve them for us. They'll need to be convinced, and I will rely on you for that. You can be quite charming when you care to be. You need to convince them of your earnestness, so tell them anything you need to, even the truth. But get them to do it."

Already exhausted at the prospect, Annette asked simply, "Who?"

"The residents of Aletheia, of course."

The light in his office glinted off his lenses just so.

CHAPTER FIFTY-FIVE

Dale Alexander

I woke up exhausted and headachy. Sun infiltrated the room from the tower windows, adding to the warmth of the covers and the body beside me. I opened my eyes. Pia lay mere inches away, watching me with a peaceful smile. Maybe my brain had decided they could be predatory.

"Hey," I said softly.

"Hi, Dale."

We watched each other's eyes. Theirs were so clear and pale I could believe they were under a powerful spell—not a bane, but something beautiful and amazing.

"I want to lick your nose," Pia said.

Their serious tone made me giggle.

"What?"

"I've been watching you sleep, and I really want to lick your nose."

"That's a little weird," I said, grinning at them. "I've been kissed on the nose but never licked."

"Oh."

Pia looked disappointed, their smile gone. Crap.

"Hey, I didn't say you couldn't."

Pia hesitated, their face full of possibilities. I braced myself, but they moved so quickly that my nose was wet before I could react. The tip, a bit of one side, and most definitely across the nostrils. I crinkled my face involuntarily at the unusual sensation. Pia watched me closely.

"Was it everything you hoped?" I asked.

Pia grinned and looked thoughtful as they smacked their lips.

"Healthy overall, but you need to eat more meat."

Did they have canine senses? I wasn't sure what exactly came with being host to a wolf-spirit.

"You can tell that from the taste of my nose?"

Pia laughed and buried their head in the covers.

"No," they admitted from under the protective layer of bedding.

I fought my sudden frustration at having been fooled. Pia had been playing, not mocking me. My defensiveness wasn't their fault. But the mood had broken. There were problems that needed to be solved, and I absolutely needed my therapy session, if I hadn't missed it already. I reached down and retrieved my laptop from the floor, opening it to check the time. Almost eight o'clock. Enough time to log in but not to make myself presentable.

"Afraid we need to get up. Got a private meeting."

Pia moaned as I got out of bed. I set the laptop on the floor and lay on my stomach in front of it just as my alarm went off. I logged in and joined the video call, quickly adjusting the camera to hide my five o'clock shadow. It was a silly vanity—Bastian knew who I was and kept any judgment to himself—but I didn't want to see myself like that in the inset video.

"Dale, good morning. New workplace?"

He was always frustratingly upbeat, but given how much crap he had to listen to from his clients it was probably a useful trait.

"Yeah. I'm staying with a friend to help them out."

"Oh no! I hope everything's okay."

"I think it will be," I lied. "Just supporting them through some family drama."

Pia chose that moment to trot past in their underwear chanting "bathroom." My cheeks felt warm as I waited for his reaction.

"Are you okay to talk where you're at?" he said instead.

"Uh, hold on. I think there's another room that's out of the way."

"Take your time."

I muted the mic and turned off the camera. There was that other door beside the entrance to this bedroom, and we hadn't opened it yet. My guess was that there was space there for another room nearly the size of this one. I got up and took a look. It was slightly narrower than I'd expected, but that could just be an illusion from the closets along the back wall. There were a makeup dresser right near the door, a few more comfortable-looking chairs, and I swear to God an actual chaise longue with a reading lamp on a table beside it. Three windows let in the morning sun. It would do. I lay down on the floor and turned on the camera again.

"Sorry about that. I'm back."

He continued looking over his notes. I checked the screen and saw I was still muted. Trying not to be too angry with myself, I reactivated the microphone.

"I'm back."

He looked up.

"Ah good. Was that your friend or someone else staying with," he checked his notes, "them?"

I nodded. One of the things I liked about him was that he really tried to be respectful. My previous therapist had turned out to be a TERFy little bitch. I hadn't been happy to draw a male therapist next, but he'd been nothing but supportive since we started together, and if he ever found my existence disgusting he'd never hinted at it. I'm pretty sure he'd read *Welcome to Dorley Hall* because I'd talked about the book, but he never mentioned it.

"That was them. Pia."

"Is this a new friend? I don't think you ever mentioned them before."

"Yeah I just met them..." I thought about it. "I gave them some food Wednesday night, and offered to help them yesterday morning."

"Wow, that was fast."

"I... I guess it was."

"Sometimes life is like that. How are you feeling about this, being outside of your apartment and your routines?"

"It's a lot. I'm not entirely comfortable about any of this, but also it's been kind of exhilarating. Just a whirlwind of thoughts and emotions right now."

He nodded.

"Okay. Well what do you want to focus on today? It sounds like a lot is going on, and you're feeling overwhelmed by it all. Would it be helpful to talk about any of that?"

There was no way that I could tell him about most of what was happening. As much as we'd built up some good trust, I was likely wanted at least for questioning over the death in my apartment, and any talk of an (allegedly) insubstantial wolf or an endless library that was also a woman who was a house might earn me a psychiatric intervention. Despite all of the things I'd been mentally noting I should bring up with Bastian, now that I had him in front of me there wasn't much that I felt safe discussing.

So I talked about Pia, their warmth, their joy, and a sanitized version of their sheltered upbringing. He noted the way I talked about them, and I admitted that I had a huge crush on them and that they seemed to like me too. This led to the real topic—my feeling that this attraction was immoral. Sometimes therapy takes a meandering path like that.

"Why do you say that? Is there a part of you that is telling you this?"

He knew goddamned well, but if I feigned ignorance he'd just ask more pointed questions until I couldn't ignore him anymore.

"Yes," I admitted. "But I don't think this is an attempt to protect myself. They're just so... young."

"Oh, really? How old is she—sorry, are they?"

I didn't know, really.

"Hard to say. Physically, somewhere in their mid-twenties?"

"Well, Dale, you're only thirty—"

"Thirty-one!"

"That's a difference at your ages, for sure, but if they're somewhere around twenty-five, that's certainly not anything harmful or unusual in itself. Have you asked them how old they are?"

"I... I don't think they'd know."

"Why is that?"

I'd made a mistake bringing this up. How could I explain without revealing that their family had been holding them prisoner for some weird incestuous breeding program?

"Their parents were... neglectful. I don't think Pia got to celebrate birthdays."

"If that's the case, then they may well be seeking that deep affection and approval they didn't get as a child. Is there anybody else in their life now?"

"Well, a... an older couple has taken us in. I think Pia may like them more than I do, but they've been good to us."

"That's good! Does this couple expect to stay involved with them?"

"I think so. We're both staying until some things are sorted out, and then I can go back to... to my apartment. I think the expectation is that Pia would continue to stay with them."

"So these two are filling the void left by the parents. How do you feel about leaving Pia with them?"

Damn him.

"Empty. Lonely."

"Is it possible that your attraction is healthy?"

"Not a chance. They're so vulnerable and inexperienced, and I think the power dynamic is off."

"What sort of power do you have over them?"

"Well, I found Pia. So, they imprinted on me."

"Are they a puppy dog?"

Kind of.

"You know what I mean. I helped them when they were huddled on the street!"

"And you think that gives you power?"

I didn't answer.

"Let me ask you, if they're bonding with people who will be giving them shelter, how much control over Pia do you have?"

"Not much," I admitted.

"Not much. Why would you be telling yourself there's a problem?"

I hadn't the foggiest.

"Take your time."

Time wasn't going to help. I had no idea.

"To have an excuse for not getting into a relationship," I guessed.

"There you go. Your protector's afraid you're going to get hurt again, and it doesn't want that for you. Now maybe it's right, and maybe it's wrong, but you need to acknowledge its warning and figure out what you want."

He made sense. He always did, the jerk. I still felt that having named them might give me undue influence, but I also remembered that Janice had suggested "Pia." Shit.

We continued to talk and celebrated how well I'd been handling so much disruption and socializing. I didn't tell him I curled into a ball and pissed myself, but then again I left out all of the stuff about gunmen and multiple home invasions. I promised to talk with Pia about setting appropriate boundaries and start checking in with them about their feelings and needs. And with that, we signed off.

I had a little time before the morning work call. Maybe there'd be food downstairs.

CHAPTER FIFTY-SIX

Elena Arana

She sat in Frank's chair, waiting for him to come in. He still regularly came in early, and she wanted to catch him before her partner's fashionably late arrival. It was petty, but she needed just that little feeling of cooperation before returning to Paris-wrangling. He strolled in with his nasty old plaid thermos of coffee and shook his head slowly when he saw her.

"Elena. I don't bring donuts anymore, so you might as well leave."

"Sorry, not yet. I want to know more about the Alexander case."

He set his thermos down and stole another chair to join her at his desk.

"You mean the Utley case," he said.

"The who now? Is that your body?"

"Yup. Wes Utley. Thirty-four-year-old smalltime loser. Mauled by an unknown animal in Alexander's apartment shortly after parking his truck in the lot and emerging with an unidentified person, whose whereabouts are equally as unknown as the inhabitant's."

"Damn, Frank. That's what I'm talking about! What about the others, and their car?"

"What is this? Are you bored with your massacre?"

She considered and then nodded at his monitor.

"There was a small trailer our victims brought from Massachusetts. The inside walls were covered in fingerprints. Didn't belong to any of the bodies we found, but it did match some in one of the rooms they had. Still looking for a hit in the databases, but I wondered how things were going for processing your scene."

He grimaced and laughed briefly.

"I know you, Elena. You think it's your magical disappearing bald girl, that she somehow got into the Alexander apartment, and that she got into a black car with our missing renter, our unidentified intruder, and a tiny mystery woman dressed like a beatnik."

She smiled crookedly.

"Something like that, yes. I sent you the file, in case you want to have it compared to your case."

"Okay. Sure. I'll let the lab know to check our prints against that first. Since you're so interested, I've got something you or your puppy can run down for me."

"Shit work," she grumbled. "Okay, Frank. What can I have Paris do for you?"

He grinned.

"See? I'm helping you. We have an owner for the car that sped away. Some nonprofit called the Jessup Foundation. The executor or manager or whatever wasn't at her office when we traced her yesterday. I expect she'll say it was stolen or something, but maybe you can secure the vehicle."

"It's a deal. Send me the name and address."

"Good. Now get the fuck outta my chair."

CHAPTER FIFTY-SEVEN

Dale Alexander

When I came downstairs, the scent of sausage and maple syrup drew me directly to the dining room. Pia's plate overflowed with scrambled eggs, sausage links, and pancakes—all smothered in syrup. Platters of breakfast foods held plenty of extra servings, as well as biscuits, Canadian bacon, apple muffins, and hash browns. A coffee urn stood awkwardly on the outskirts of this feast. Pia had chosen to drink straight out of a pitcher of grape juice. They'd also poured syrup into their juice glass and took occasional gulps from that. Everything bore their sticky handprints except for their silverware.

They made an enthusiastic noise that I took for a greeting, although it mostly sounded like a mouth stuffed with sausage. I grinned and waved at them. There were place settings at every seat along the sides of the table, but I suppressed the urge to sit next to Pia and clean them up. We were only in a potential relationship, after all, and I wasn't committed enough to sit in the splash zone. I settled for sitting across from my energetic wolf-spirit-hosting prospective girlfriend.

As I poured myself some coffee, Livinia came in and sat down in the larger chair at the end of the table. She didn't appear to notice Pia's poor table manners, which I took as evidence of an impressive strength of will. Maybe being a house gave her some emotional distance.

"I hope everything is to your liking. Inform me of your food preferences, and the house will accommodate them. This was an attempt to satisfy a standard American palate with what I'm afraid is my somewhat outdated understanding."

"This is amazing," I said. "Better than I've had in years, actually. You really didn't need to go to so much trouble for us."

Livinia smiled, a warmer expression than the calm indulgence I'd become used to. She seemed more present than she had been, and I remembered what Janice had told me about her experiencing the world as memories. Perhaps last night's activity had something to do with the change.

"It's not the slightest bother, Miss Alexander. Food is rarely required here, but it is a simple accommodation that the house can provide."

"Well, thank you. And your house, I guess. I really appreciate it."

Pia made a noise that sounded like pancakes and assent.

"You're both most welcome. It's been quite some time since things have been so lively here. I find it a pleasant change of pace. Making allowance for the circumstances, of course."

I buttered a modest stack of pancakes on my plate.

"Of course. Sure you don't want any?"

"No, dear. Thank you. Tea will suffice for me."

I hadn't noticed a teacup before, yet Livinia sipped from it now. She really did control everything inside of here. Of her. My mind refused to pursue the thought that I was having a breakfast conversation with her inside of her real body.

"Where's Janice?" I asked, seeking to distract myself.

"Miss Altura is gathering information about the condition and accessibility of your apartment. We thought you'd like to retrieve more of your belongings without the risk of apprehension by the police or... other parties."

I swallowed the warm, sugary bread in my mouth and dabbed at my chin with the cloth napkin beside my place setting.

"Thank you! Yeah, there's some stuff I'd like to have if we're staying here. If that's still okay with you after, well, everything that's happened."

"Perfectly all right. I'm here to support and assist you while this affair is sorted out. You are welcome in my house for the duration. I wouldn't dream of turning you out to endure this on your own."

I helped myself to a piece of Canadian bacon, which I set in the syrup pooled alongside the pancakes. Pia had folded three pancakes around a handful of sausage links and was attempting to eat it like a sandwich wrap. Syrup dripped on their plate, the table, their shirt, and down their chin. I wondered if the house had an outside hose.

"Forgive the question, Mrs. Monroe, but why are you helping us, even after your house was invaded last night?"

I very specifically did not want to know what she'd done to the intruders.

"Nothing to forgive; it's a reasonable question in this day and age. If I may be frank, my initial interest lay with Cassiopeia."

I chewed some meat while I thought about that.

"You mean the combination of both?"

"I do, indeed. The classic presentation is for the attached spirit to share the body, which alters to accommodate both. That can be through a permanent alteration or through alternating physical appearance."

"A werewolf."

"Yes. Those are two documented types. They are rare, and they typically don't live for very long. The spirit and the host are merged, each affecting the other, but when they aren't aligned the dissonance causes problems—anger, emotional withdrawal, feelings of shame and guilt, hyperawareness, anxiety, self-destructive behavior, that manner of issues."

Nausea poured over me as I heard the symptoms. They were far too familiar for comfort.

"Sounds awful," I said quietly.

"It is, which is why your photograph of Cassie alarmed me. Her unusual existence outside of Pia's body, as well as their close sympathy, makes them much less susceptible to disintegrating psyches and an early death."

Pia continued to eat with abandon, not demonstrating interest in our discussion about them and the spirit wolf. I could see why the pair would be fascinating, even to people as extraordinary as Livinia and Janice, who definitely weren't normal. Me though, I'll admit that some people would think I was creepy or evil, but I was just an ordinary, traumatized, trans woman, hiding in the safety of my dark apartment. Rather, a guest in a naturally lit, overdecorated mansion, but that was accidental.

"A werewolf piqued your interest, and once you've dealt with their family you'll want to study them. Meaning they stay here, and I go back to the apartment and try to pretend I still feel safe there."

It only made sense that I was merely a secondary concern at best, but I was invested in Pia now and my life had been upended. I was part of whatever this was, and I wanted to be on the inside instead of being shuffled around and set to the side to wait.

Livinia sipped at her tea, not looking at either of us. The sound of Pia slurping at dripping syrup dominated the room. I poked at my own breakfast, but I wasn't as hungry as I'd thought. At last Livinia set down her teacup and stared into it. She raised her head, her face tight with resolve.

"This house and I share many secrets, and I keep them jealously for my protection and that of the future. Your current struggles are a small part of a large threat that looms over several states and Canadian provinces in the best-case scenarios. I plan to recreate the Society for Preternatural Investigations, or an organization akin to it, for the immediate goal of putting an end to this menace as well as resuming investigations of unusual phenomena in order to keep everyone safe, human and otherwise."

She paused as I absorbed this and Pia's pace began to slow.

"I would like you to join us. Join me. Help me remember my humanity. Help me do field research. Help organize specialists. Help me make the world safer for all."

I dropped my fork, and it clattered loudly on the plate before sliding into the leftover pancakes.

"You just met me, and you want me to go chase ghosts with you? That's a little hard to believe."

"I suppose it must be. We've had this discussion many times. I enjoy watching Pia eating with such innocent relish. Forgive me, that was not an answer. You are with us today because of your empathy. You saw an injured animal and wanted to assist it. Feeding it, posting its picture, following it to our friend here, and bringing them to your home. That demonstrates resolve and strength of character. Though you lack wisdom and experience, you have many essential traits that are difficult to teach."

Pia had finally stopped eating and smiled at me, watching as I squirmed through the endorsement. I stared at my messy plate, feeling undeserving of kind words. I'd done nothing but fuck up from the beginning. I'd wrecked my marriage, and in the wake of that I'd let everything slide and let depression have me. For years I'd existed more out of habit than from any desire to be alive. That hardly felt like strength or resolve. It was simple apathy.

"I don't think I'm any of those things, really. I'd only let you down."

Pia's eyes were welling up, and I was afraid they'd give me a very messy hug. Livinia sipped tea again, although there was no pot she could have refilled from.

"The tea leaves suggest otherwise. They speak of a woman that persevered despite of a longing for release; a recluse that reached out from her isolation to offer aid to a stranger; a pensive soul that refused to abandon hope; and a glimmer of promise that kept safe until given a reason to grow."

"You're the best, Dale!" Pia added.

I couldn't look at them, and my face burned from the kind attention, but they did seem to somehow believe this about me. Bastian would be so smug when he heard about this.

"The leaves said all that?" I asked, deflecting from my discomfort.

"I have very sensitive tea," Livinia replied.

For a moment I marveled that this reserved lady had made a joke. Then I doubled over laughing, the corners of my eyes wet. Humor had always worked to release my pent-up anxiety.

There was a sudden clatter from across the table that led to Pia hugging me fiercely. Surprise gave way to more laughter, and I clung to the sticky arms encircling me. There was nothing for it. I'd need a nice shower and some fresh clothes.

"No need to decide this morning. We have enough to consider in dealing with the Kuipers."

"Thanks. Is there a shower in that tub upstairs?"

"There is now, yes."

CHAPTER FIFTY-EIGHT

Janice Altura

Slipping into the apartment had been simple. Janice had been an investigator long enough to know it took one part tools and three parts confidence. Authority helped, but projecting it made up for the absence of any. It had first collected items from the bathroom that seemed personal. Some jewelry, lipstick, and a salmon-colored plushie brain with squiggly lines in a thought balloon. The thing kind of screamed Dale.

The bedroom was even more cluttered than the rest of the apartment, and it had decided that the closet and drawers were probably irrelevant. Checking for valuables or important papers had seemed to be useful, though. It had proceeded to search in as methodical a manner as time allowed, which amounted to a cursory examination of everything.

In quick order, it had nearly filled two duffel bags. It'd found some devices of a personal nature in the night stand, which it packed, and some books, which it didn't. Everything ever written was already in the house. It did think Dale would appreciate the original of her own diary, so it made an exception for that. After placing the journal in the bag, it heard the apartment door open.

Janice moved to the wall next to the bedroom entrance.

"Whoever's in here, you're not allowed! The cops are still investigating! Just drop everything and get out of here, and I won't need to tell them you were in here!"

Not police then. That was good. It could deal with this, with the somnumatic if need be. The voice sounded familiar, and placed in the context of the apartment there was only one possibility. It walked down the short hallway into the living room.

"Hi. Maggie, isn't it? I'm Janice. We met yesterday."

Maggie nodded as Janice came into view.

"Yeah. Dog lady, right? Was Dale able to help?"

"She was, thank you. Rocky's back home, safe and sound. Now I'm lending a hand. She wanted some goodies from the hoard but wasn't ready to get back in the saddle."

Maggie looked at the aftermath of the apartment invasion and subsequent investigation.

"I can see that. Must've been traumatic. Why you? No offense, but you didn't even know her yesterday morning."

"No, I didn't ha ha. I was still on the spot when it all popped off. She freaked, and I owed her one, so I pulled her out of the fire."

Maybe Maggie would need to be knocked out after all. Janice hoped not; it didn't like to think of doing that to such a helpful person.

"Dale left with two other women who were carrying a man."

Janice shrugged.

"She was flying solo, but my ride's the sweet black coupe with big kitty spots."

Maggie still looked skeptical. Casting about for a nonviolent resolution, it decided against the policy of self-reliance. It was Dale's apartment, and she knew Maggie, so let her smooth things over.

"Hold on, let me get Dale on the phone."

Maggie watched while Janice pulled out its phone, looked

up the entry it'd made for Dale after setting her up on the network, and hit dial. After several rings, during which Maggie's glare deepened, the call went to voicemail.

"Hi, Dale. I'm at your pad with Maggie, and she'd like to chew the fat with you. Make sure everything's cool. She's been keeping eyes on the joint for you. Seems like a swell pal. Anyway, it would be peachy if you could shoot me a line back as soon as you get this. Thanks, kid. Talk soon."

It attempted an embarrassed smile but was met with a fixed glare and pursed lips. That seemed bad.

"Okay, 'Janice.' Out. Now."

The somnumatic would work, but the dosage was iffy on shorter people. Maggie stood only a few inches above it, about Livinia's height, and might have weighed roughly the same, but she had more muscles. Two shots was the recommendation for putting someone to sleep, but on someone that size that could be enough to cause a fatal overdose. A blow to the head was a reliable standby, except sometimes there needed to be a few hits before it worked, and there was always the danger of blood clots or brain injury. Janice might reach the woman in time to cover her mouth, but then what? The gun was beginning to look more viable. What if it shot as it lunged, to keep Maggie quiet while the sedative took effect?

"Not joking, lady."

"I know, I know. Would've been keen if she'd picked up. We're both watching out for her, but I get why you'd think I'm sketchy. Hats off, by the by. It's cool you have her back. She'd seemed—"

Janice's phone rang, playing a snippet of an old vampire song by Concrete Blonde. It answered before the guitar kicked in.

CHAPTER FIFTY-NINE

Dale Alexander

I heard my phone ring from the shower. It was "Juicebox Baby," the song I'd set for people I actually wanted to talk to. I'd forgotten about it over the last few years, and as I shut off the water I wondered who I'd used that for that would want to contact me now. I dried off hastily, wrapped the towel around myself, and trotted back to the bedroom we'd been given.

The song stopped before I got to the dresser where I'd set the phone. There wasn't any message, but the caller ID read "Janice Altura." I hadn't entered any contact information for Janice. Never had any thought of asking, either. It was irritating to have had that pushed to my phone without my consent, but it bothered me more to not know how it had been accomplished. How advanced was Janice's tech? Or was this part of Livinia's strange powers? All of my devices stayed fully charged here, even the ones I hadn't plugged in. Could she alter the data in them as well?

A chime sounded and an alert popped up to announce a new voicemail message. I read the transcript. Janice needed help dealing with Maggie? It seemed laughable, but for Maggie's sake I'd better call back. No telling what that weirdo might do to her.

I hit the callback on the message, and Janice answered right away.

"Dale. I'm glad you called back ha ha."

It sounded strained. After only a day, I knew that fake cheer was a bad sign.

"Sorry I didn't answer. I was in the shower. Let me talk to Maggie."

"Right-o. Here she is."

After a moment of fumbling sounds, Maggie came on the line.

"Dale?"

"Yeah. Hi, Maggie. Thanks for looking out for me."

"No trouble. You're one of my favorites around here. Always thanking me and never complaining."

It seemed to be the day for weird compliments.

"Well, I appreciate what you do for us. Listen, I know my place is a crime scene, but I really need to get some things. Could you let Janice grab some stuff for me?"

"I'd like to help and all, but if the cops find out I had anything to do with this—"

"Don't worry. Neither Janice or I would rat you out."

"Ah, thanks. But... just what the hell is going on? The cops have been looking for you. They think you were involved in something bad, at least as a witness. What went down yesterday?"

"All I know is that these guys forced their way into my apartment and terrorized me and, uh, a visitor. I didn't even see how the shooting started. I was on the floor and kind of in shock."

"Okay. I'll leave the apartment and pretend I didn't see your new friend here, but I think you need to talk to a lawyer."

"Thanks, Maggie. You're probably right."

"I'm guessing you're not coming for Blueberry Nipples tonight."

I'd forgotten all about the show. So much had happened

that my mind had thrown it over a wall of discarded thoughts.

"Oh, shit. I'm sorry. Thank you so much for inviting me, but things have gotten completely out of hand. I'll try."

"Would it help if I brought your car to you?"

Shit, maybe.

"That would be amazing, but I'd hate to get you involved in this. Lemme ask Janice if it's safe. We're sort of... in a situation."

"Sure."

Another pause while the phone changed hands.

"Thanks. You're a pal."

"Sure. You're doing me a solid. Couple things."

"Shoot."

"I'd appreciate it if you could bring back my razor and stuffed GIR."

"What's a grr?"

"Looks like a goofy green dog. He should be on my bed. Maybe nearby. Sorry, I'm a restless sleeper."

"Think I peeped that. What else."

"Maggie mentioned bringing the car over. Would that be dangerous?"

"On a scale of going concern to instant worm food, I'd say playing on a side street. Sure you want her wrapped up in this?"

"No, but she's the only one I ever talked to before yesterday. I'm not gonna shut her out if she wants to help, but I want her to understand the risks before she decides."

"Roger that."

"One more thing, when you get back we need to talk about you fucking with my phone."

CHAPTER SIXTY

Elena Arana

Paris had been furious over getting more work in return for what she felt was basically nothing. So Arana had gone to interview the lawyer on her own. The office hadn't been hard to find, but parking had been a challenge. Old Downtown only had street parking, and it was surprisingly busy for how few businesses were still open. There was a blood donation center in the area, and a cash advance place. Lots of things dedicated to leeching off the working poor, including a low-rent attorney or two. She pulled in next to a shuttered furniture boutique and walked the two blocks back to the small office building.

A directory hung in the foyer, beside an elevator that bore an old sign reading "OUT OF SERVCE" in marker with the missing *I* inserted with a red pen. She found a row for the Jessup Foundation's financial manager, Nichole Cousin, but the room number had fallen off. There was nothing for it but to climb the stairs and search every floor. At least there were only four of them.

She found the office on the second floor, which she took as a good sign, and entered. The room was small, crowded with a modest desk, two folding chairs for clients, a single filing cabinet, and a rather short, faded plastic ficus plant. A young woman sat behind the desk with a laptop set up in front of her. She looked too respectable to work in this building. Her hair was styled in a tapered pixie cut, which let her gold clasp earrings really draw attention. The burnt orange of her suit worked well with the darkness of her skin. Elena dared to hope that at least she wouldn't have to deal with more white people nonsense here.

Cousin looked up at Elena with cautious expectancy.

"May I help you? The debt consolidator is up one floor."

Elena entered and closed the door.

"I think I'm in the right office, as long as you're Nichole Cousin."

"I am. Pull up a chair."

Elena settled uncomfortably into a metal seat.

"I've opened a new document for notes, so let's start. What's your name?"

"Detective Elena Arana."

Cousin looked up from the computer and appraised her.

"Is this police business?" she asked.

"I just have some questions about the Jessup Foundation."

Cousin tapped a few more keys and sat back.

"Why are you interested in the Jessup Foundation, Detective Arana?"

"A black Saturn Ion registered to the foundation was seen leaving an incident, and we're hoping the driver might have seen something."

The lawyer studied her a little more, grimaced, then seemed to reach a conclusion.

"The Foundation's staff is small and a matter of public record. The only one you'll find with a driver's license is Janice Russell, the network administrator. Pronouns it/its. Take a slang dictionary."

"Thank you, Miss Cousin."

"Mrs." She raised her hand to show the wedding ring. "Now what do you really want? You should have been able to find that information from your desk."

"It's a serious matter, Mrs. Cousin, and I was hoping you could give me some context on what foundation business would require a visit to the Fuller Apartments."

"Use of the car is not restricted to business purposes, so long as it remains within the city. Janice and the caretaker live at Aletheia, and it's the foundation's policy that reasonable usage of the car is part of their compensation."

"Free rent in a mansion is an unusual package, isn't it?"

"The Jessup Foundation is a very generous donor and investor in the area, Detective Arana, and its charter stipulates that all of this is contingent on maintaining the mansion as a livable space for the direct employees. Whatever you're imagining, they receive very little pay outside of room and board for all they do."

"And what is it they do, counselor?"

Cousin smiled tightly.

"I believe I've answered your questions about the car."

Elena had no reason to push further just now, so she dropped it. At least she'd confirmed that there should be only one driver.

"I'll need to speak with Janice Russell."

"I can let her know to make herself available."

They exchanged stiffly cordial goodbyes, and Elena pondered the nature of Jessup Foundation on her way back to the office.

CHAPTER SIXTY-ONE

Cassie

The wolf had checked in on Dale, who'd gotten dressed, begged off of work for the day, and stayed on her computer anyway. Upstairs, Pia was exploring the old furniture and boxes. That had been fascinating at first, since much of what hid up there smelled real. Most of the rest of what she'd encountered had that same lack of substance that the home's owner did. It might all be present enough to touch, but it was just the house playing pretend. Even the food that her host and friend had eaten had been nothing more than the house's thoughts.

These material goods had been abandoned, and after enjoying their refreshing solidity she'd lost interest in them. They didn't matter, not as much as the fantasies that surrounded them. The creatures that lived here were capable and provided a safe place to rest, but she suspected that they would be less effective outside the house. There were other firm objects in the basement, tools for war, and those would be necessary soon, but what intrigued her was in the library.

She walked softly to the locked room and passed through the door. This was a dangerous place for those anchored to this dimension, but in her current state she was safe. The possibilities unfolded in her vision to a map that would lead to the thing she sensed. She saw the owner perched at one of the many versions of the writing desk along the path, but she paid the creature no mind. Trotting through the looping stacks, she shortly reached her destination.

It was a human, one of the many that had entered the house last night. She'd thought they'd all been killed. The mansion had added their armaments to the collection in the basement and recycled their bodies and clothes for future use. This one had apparently been left to wander through the library. There didn't seem to be a point in letting the man continue like this, and she considered putting him out of his misery. Her host would need to be asleep for her to do that, though, and while she could always return later it felt unlikely that she would. He had come in to capture or kill Pia, after all, and she didn't actually care about his suffering. Besides, maybe the house was keeping him for something. She decided that it wasn't any of her business what happened to him.

The house's owner stopped what she'd been doing and left the room. The wolf followed, hoping that the woman had finally learned something helpful. She collapsed her perspective to the room's origin dimension and seconds later walked down the stairs to the main hall.

The outside door swung open on its own, and Janice walked in carrying a duffel bag. She still didn't trust it, but she accepted its presence. Another woman entered behind it, also carrying a bag, and she recognized her as the one she'd met at the apartment building. She was a much more welcome figure.

"You must be Maggie," the house said through its human guise. "Welcome to Aletheia."

"Thanks..."

"She's Liv."

"Mrs. Monroe, if you please."

"Thanks, Mrs. Monroe. Where can we drop these?"

Footsteps thundered from the third floor down to the hall.

Pia rounded the stairs and threw themself at the newcomer, who hugged them back in self-defense.

"Maggie!" they shouted.

"Hi... you!" Maggie stammered.

Dale came down with less enthusiasm but nearly matching energy. She walked over to Maggie, grinning broadly, and stood awkwardly beside her.

"Thanks for coming. That's... that's Pia attached to you. They seem to remember you."

"From where?"

"Here, let me take that bag for you. I'll try to explain in our room."

" 'Our room'?"

"You three gals go have a chinwag. I need to give the boss the new headline."

It removed Pia from their victim and handed them the bag.

"Good pup. Now bounce."

Dale led the other humans upstairs. Despite her interest in the new arrival, the wolf lingered in the hall. The two remaining women walked into the parlor.

"They're gonna spill the beans about us to her."

Livinia settled onto a chair.

"I wasn't aware that they had any beans of yours, Miss Altura."

"An eensie one, maybe. You sure you're cool going public?"

"If we don't make it through the narrow band of possibilities, it won't matter who knows anything. Besides, this girl may be helpful to center Dale's thoughts. She's been blushing at Pia ever since her therapy session."

"Aw, puppy love's so cute."

"I assumed that you had something of importance to share."

Janice stood at the tower windows, peering out with a more-than-casual interest.

"Nichole called. The fuzz is onto my wheels. Gonna be coming to check me out. Check us out."

"That would be distressing if we had anything to hide."

Janice turned from the window.

"Sure, I'm a mushroom and you're a house. No need to keep that under wraps."

"I doubt they'll ask that. Admit to helping and bringing our guests here. Nothing more."

"And when they dig for more?"

"I'll offer them tea."

CHAPTER SIXTY-TWO

Maggie Star

She'd only intended to drop off the car and make sure that her favorite tenant and prospective project was dealing well with everything. A home invasion would freak out anybody, and Dale had always been nervous and cagey. Maggie'd been afraid of finding her huddled in a dark room. Instead, she'd met a happier and more vibrant version of the woman, sharing a sunny bedroom with a lanky butch enby. It was an unexpected transformation but a joy to see. After hearing a rushed story about confusing events, she wasn't sure whether it was any less credible than this sudden change in demeanor.

"So, you're a wolf?"

Dale started to answer, but Pia beat her to it.

"Wolf-touched. I'm a host for the family's wolf spirit."

"And your family got that from... a bane?"

"That's what Mrs. Monroe thinks. We still don't know why."

"I like the wolf. I wouldn't mind if it wasn't for the cell." Pia snarled a little on the last word, screwing their face up with resentment and anger. Dale touched their arm lightly.

Maggie shook her head. "Your own family. Any idea why?"

Pia shook her head. Maggie frowned.

"From what Pia and Mrs. Monroe have said, I get the sense that the wolf-touched are seen as unclean. Like the family sins made flesh."

Maggie nodded.

"The scapegoats. That's awful. I'm so glad you escaped, Pia!"

Pia smiled.

"It was scary, but the man who killed my guard ordered me to run. I was more scared of him than of going to the new cell!"

"Fuck," Dale said, wrapping her arms around them. "You never said how you got out. You're really fucking brave, you know that?"

"Honestly, I'm in awe. You've been through so much, and you were forced to leave what you knew, what, yesterday?"

Pia counted their fingers, mumbling to themself. Dale saved her.

"I found them Wednesday night, well, Thursday morning. Cassie was the night before. So, two days."

Maggie looked around the room.

"The wolf, right? Where is she, anyway?"

"She's only visible when Pia's asleep."

Pia tilted their head to the side, focusing elsewhere.

"She's downstairs with the others. Livinia is calm, but she can't figure out Janice."

"Who can? I think it means well, though."

"You and the wolf really are psychically linked."

Pia furrowed their brow and turned to Dale.

"You share thoughts."

"Not really. She started talking to me a little yester— two days ago, I think. But I dream about what she does, and if I focus hard I can do that while I'm awake."

"So you really did recognize me?"

"Yeah! You wanted to take Dale somewhere."

Maggie nodded.

"Yeah, there's a concert tonight at The Lez. Ten dollar cover. I was hoping to get her to go out and meet people."

Dale turned red.

"Why did... how did you know I like girls?"

Maggie grinned, gradually retracting it to smile as she realized Dale was genuinely puzzled.

"Uh, for the first year all you talked about was your ex-wife. Plus, y'know, the piles of yuri in your apartment."

"What's yuri?"

"Comics about girls who like girls," Maggie said.

"Oh. What's a comic?"

"Mind if I pick one up from your apartment for her? I need to head back there anyway to pack some things."

Dale had been hiding her head, no longer following the conversation. She looked up warily.

"What?"

"Can I grab some manga from your room while I'm packing?"

"Packing what? If Janice got me what I asked for, I should be set."

"Packing a few sets of my clothes so I can stay here with you for a few days."

"You can't! It's dangerous! We were attacked here last night!"

Maggie studied the two of them, noting their lack of injuries, then looked pointedly around the room, pristine aside from the clutter around their bags.

"Yeah. Looks like it was a fierce struggle."

"I slept in the library while Cassie and Livinia took care of the guards."

"Thanks, Pia," Dale groaned.

"Yeah, thanks. So, you mind if I pick up a book or two for them to look at?"

CHAPTER SIXTY-THREE

Livinia Monroe

Livinia waited a minute after the doorbell rang to simulate needing to hear it and react. Then she walked to the door and opened it. A woman stood there, in nice but not dressy clothes. She was barely taller with short dark hair and a police badge.

"May I help you with something?"

"I wasn't sure anyone was even here. I'm Detective Arana. I'd like to ask you some questions."

Livinia feigned confusion.

"Whatever could bring you to Aletheia, Detective?"

"Could we discuss this inside, please?"

"Certainly. You're welcome, of course."

She let the detective in and guided her into the parlor, creating a tea set with a freshly steeped pot along the way.

"I was just about to have some tea. Would you care to join me?"

"No, thank you," Arana said, waving her hand. She sat uncomfortably on the loveseat.

Livinia poured herself a cup and perched on a chair. She still found tea soothing, and it made an excellent prop for social situations. Unfortunately, now she'd have to find another way to make the detective drowsy.

"Ma'am," Arana said. "You haven't told me who you are."

Livinia smiled. She considered replying that she'd never been asked, but her goal was to pacify, not to test limits. Fortunately, Janice had long ago created an identity that would pass limited inspection.

"I'm the caretaker, Miss Elizabeth Chevrier."

The detective wrote in a little notebook.

"Do you live here, Miss Chevrier?"

"Yes. I reside here full time as part of my duties."

"And how long have you been living here?"

She knew the exact amount of time that the paperwork would show, but precision might attract undue interest.

"About a decade, I should think, although it feels like much longer than that."

"Don't like it much?"

"On the contrary, Detective. I love it. It feels like I've spent my entire life within these walls."

"Have you been out at all in the last few days? Appointments, shopping, anything?"

"No. I haven't left the house in at least a week."

"So if anyone entered the mansion, you'd know."

"I'd like to think so. I keep the doors locked, and only a few other people associated with the foundation have keys. However, I often spend hours in the library, so it's possible that someone could enter without my noticing."

Arana took out her phone and showed it to Livinia, who set down her teacup to lean in closer. It was an old picture of Dale, with a short masculine haircut and a lifeless expression. She looked thinner, younger, and utterly miserable.

"Have you seen this person?"

Livinia reached out to stabilize the phone while peering closer at the image. One of her fingers brushed against the detective's, allowing her to invade the woman's nervous system. She spurred the release of brain chemicals to induce sleepiness. Then she nodded and let go.

"Yes. I've seen her."

"Her name came up in an investigation, and we're looking for her to answer some questions. A tip led us here. If you have any information as to her whereabouts—"

Footsteps on the main stairs distracted the detective. Livinia had been fully aware of Dale's movements upstairs, but she looked toward the sound as well out of politeness.

"I believe that's her now," she said.

Dale, who had been listening intently from the top of the stairs, wandered carelessly into the parlor.

"Hey," she said, gazing from Livinia to the detective. "What's going on?"

"I thought you said nobody entered the house," Arana said, looking at Livinia with suspicion.

Livinia shrugged slightly.

"My apologies, Detective. I tend to be rather literal, and hadn't realized you were asking whether Miss Alexander was here."

Detective Arana let it go, but she didn't appear to have been mollified.

"Dale," Livinia said. "This is Detective Arana. She wanted to ask you some questions."

Dale examined the detective.

"Is this about my apartment? I don't think I can go back there, the whole thing just..."

Dale struggled with her emotions. Livinia reached up and touched her arm. She and the others in the Society had never become accustomed to the horrors they uncovered. By that scale, what Dale had experienced was nothing more than a slight annoyance, but it was real and powerful to her.

"I'm sorry. We're trying to put together what happened yesterday."

Dale nodded and wiped the wetness from her eyes.

"Okay," she said and sat in the chair near the other end of the loveseat.

"Shoot," she said.

Arana addressed Livinia.

"Could we speak alone, please?"

Livinia shifted to rise, but Dale objected.

"I'd like her to stay, please. If it's okay."

The detective frowned but nodded her head.

"Since Miss Alexander is not currently under suspicion and is understandably shaken, I'll allow it. Just remember that I'm here for Miss Alexander's observations, not yours."

Livinia nodded. Arana watched her for a few moments more before shaking her head quickly and returning her attention to Dale.

"Miss Alexander, the people who entered your apartment... can you tell me why they were there?"

Dale shook her head.

"No idea. They claimed they were looking for a dog, and then they just charged in."

"Was there a dog?" Arana asked.

Dale frowned pensively.

"No," she said. "There was not."

"You seem hesitant. Are you sure?"

Dale nodded.

"No dog. I... posted a picture on the county chat. It was a bad fake. Phantom dog by shrubs. I thought it was funny. Never thought anyone would believe it."

"So, you posted a gag photo, and someone came looking for the dog?"

Dale nodded again.

"I mentioned an area near my apartment, but they figured out who I was and where I lived."

"How many were there?"

Dale closed her eyes and took a deep breath.

"Two of them. Two men. I told them it was a stupid joke, but they wouldn't go away."

"Can you tell me what happened after they entered?" Arana asked quietly.

Dale said nothing at first. Her face fell slack, and her eyes unfocused. Livinia suppressed the urge to comfort her guest, opting instead to turn a judgmental glare on the detective, who was focused on Dale.

"It's okay," Arana continued gently, struggling to contain a yawn. "Anything you can remember is helpful."

"I didn't see much. I was on the floor, terrified. I think I... I peed myself." She looked down at nothing, ashamed.

"It's okay. Did they hurt you?"

"No. They left me alone."

"What were they doing?"

"Searching, I think."

"For the dog?"

"I'm not sure."

"Okay," Arana said. "Then what happened?"

Dale shook her head in bewilderment.

"There was shooting."

"Shooting? Who was shooting?"

Dale looked between the detective and Livinia.

"It must have been them."

"Sorry," Arana asked, having temporarily lost focus. "Who did what now?"

"I don't know who was shooting."

The detective looked at her notes and shook her head before jotting something down.

"Was anyone else there?"

Dale frowned.

"No. Maybe."

"What makes you say maybe?"

"Just... why would they shoot each other?"

"So you're guessing?"

"Yeah," Dale admitted. "It's weird, though."

"Weird? How so?"

"Just... I think there was an animal."

The detective became visibly more alert.

"What makes you think that?"

Livinia tensed. She didn't believe that Dale would do anything to compromise Pia—who remained upstairs, pouting—but she would need to give them enough to explain the injuries to the gunman.

"I heard growling. I wasn't sure if it was a person or a dog. But then the shooting stopped, and... the screams... It was awful." She looked vaguely toward the detective, clearly seeing something else. "It sounded like an animal attack, like from a nature show."

"Did you see it?"

Dale blinked and focused on her.

"No. I was trying to hide." She made a self-deprecating exhalation. "In the middle of the room."

"What happened after that?"

"It's a blur, really. Someone got me up and led me away. I was too out of it to notice."

"Was there anyone else with you?"

"I... don't know, sorry. There was one person for sure. Maybe one of the guys who broke in. I just don't know."

"That's okay. Where were you taken?"

Dale shook her head again.

"I was dropped off. Not sure where."

"Alone?"

She nodded.

"Yes."

The detective yawned.

"Excuse me. How did you get here?"

"Someone found me, I think. I'm not sure of anything before I woke up today."

"And you're here of your own free will?"

Dale nodded.

"Miss Chevrier has been very kind."

Livinia felt relieved both that Dale had been listening and that she had answered so vaguely. The young woman was more prepared to handle herself than she knew.

"Okay. Can you tell me anything else about yesterday?"

"Just that I'm sorry. It was just supposed to be a joke about all the dog sightings."

Her eyes filled again.

"That's it for now," Arana said. She stood up abruptly, fighting to keep her eyes open. "I may have more questions later. Let me know if you're going to leave this place."

Dale nodded.

The detective turned to Livinia.

"Is it okay for her to stay here?"

Livinia rose.

"Of course. I've already cleared it with the foundation."

"Mrs. Cousin knew nothing about this when I talked to her."

"I called just after you left her office. Miss Alexander is a talented programmer. The foundation funds more than just the upkeep of this mansion. They're considering this a recruitment operation."

Arana looked back at Dale.

"Good luck on the job."

Dale gazed back distractedly.

"What? Oh. Thanks. I haven't interviewed yet."

The detective produced a card and handed it to Dale, who took it absently.

"Let me know if you remember anything else," Arana said. Then she turned to Livinia.

"And have Janice Russell give me a call. Your car was seen at the apartment complex, and we'd like to know if she saw anything."

Livinia led her to the door.

"It only mentioned finding Miss Alexander in a panicked state, but I'll pass your message to it."

" 'It,' right. Thanks for your help."

"Don't mention it."

CHAPTER SIXTY-FOUR

Janice Altura

They were all in the sitting room now, slightly more comfortable and a lot less public than the parlor. Liv had even lit a fire, which added to the cozy feel. Janice was certain that the temperature of the room had been adjusted for the sake of the guests. It watched Pia gnaw on a stick of jerky and laughed internally, adding that image to the delight of seeing Dale stoically clutching her ridiculous green dog toy. The pair had been a lively addition to the house, and it hoped Liv's plan to keep them around would work. The jury was still out on the third young woman, who'd only just returned with her overnight bag. Maggie appeared friendly enough, but her motives were unclear as yet.

"It's been difficult," Livinia was saying, "but I've uncovered records from the eighteenth century of an aristocratic family in the Netherlands that kept a wolf child locked away. Examination of letters and diaries indicate that this practice has twisted around their descendants through the generations to the Kuiper family of today. There are several branches of the family; Tobias, a local industrialist, is second cousin to the current patriarch, Matthew, and the last keeper appears to have been Nathaniel, a nephew. It's likely that he is the one who transferred our Mx. Kuiper to Shale, although we do not yet know the motivation for this."

Dale touched Pia's arm with her free hand, and they squeezed it. To Janice, it appeared as though Dale was the one that needed reassurance.

"Up until yesterday evening, the response of the Kuipers to their escape had been to recapture them and complete the transfer. Last night the dynamic shifted. Seven armed intruders broke into our house intent on slaying them. They succeeded, and gravely wounded Miss Altura in the process."

Janice watched the reactions of the others. Livinia didn't interact with people often—not real people—and she sometimes forgot that she hadn't already explained some of the stranger things about herself and the house. Pia seemed not to have understood, Dale glanced conspiratorially at Janice, and Maggie looked around the room as though hoping to find sense somewhere. Good time to intercede.

"The boss lives in a singular moment," it explained, forcing itself to use words deliberately. "All time is one to her. When she saw us get wrecked, she chose to drop in earlier to make sure it never happened."

"Like time travel?" Maggie asked.

"That is close enough for the purpose of our discussion," Livinia replied.

"So you can just make this all turn out," Maggie declared. "Tell us what we need to do to counter their every move. That's great!"

"I fear it's more complicated than that, dear. Within this house I am capable of a great many things, such as foiling a small number of intruders when prepared. I can visit particular times, but only until I alter them. If I indicate what I wish to prevent, it ensures that it occurs, which makes it difficult to effectively communicate the need for action."

"Like an oracle," Dale said.

Livinia considered.

"Insofar as I must remain cryptic about the future,

perhaps. A large distinction is that I do not receive a vision of divinely foreordained destiny. Rather, I live in the constantly shifting recollection of history. Last night's assault had not been meant to occur. Another being has begun to make alterations, requiring me to take corrective actions to steer events back on course."

"Hold on," Dale said. "You only saved us because we didn't die in your memories of this time?"

"Naturally. I couldn't let that stand."

Janice sighed deeply in her mind.

"Dale," it said sympathetically. "Remember she has millions of years crammed into her noggin. However much she's wild about us, we are just a tiny smidge of her memory. Plus, she did whack those creeps. They probably hadn't died before either."

"One of them normally died tonight in a heated argument," Livinia informed them. "But to Janice's point, most lived for many more years. Two of them had children yet to father. I hate to think about the chaos this incident has introduced into the flow of time."

"Thanks, boss," Janice said ungraciously.

Livinia looked at them all and took a deep breath.

"My apologies. I'm unused to active participation in my memories. Most typically, I simply revisit and don't need to take an active hand. When required to act, I tend to reveal my removal from humanity. This is a happy period that I have visited over and again. The three of you are precious to me, and that is what I meant to convey by saying that I couldn't let your untimely deaths stand."

She looked at Maggie curiously.

"You're new, brought into this because of the changes. My memories of you aren't established as yet, but I hope you'll be a positive addition to the group."

Having lost interest, Pia laid her head to the side to gaze sleepily at Dale, who looked cautiously mollified. Maggie, meanwhile, frowned in apprehension.

"This morning, police detectives came to question Dale about the activity in her apartment. That never happened at this stage before. The deviations are occurring at an accelerating rate, and I can no longer tell which are caused directly by this other intelligence and which are incidental fallout. Our one potential advantage is that the alterations are occurring in a linear manner, moving forward in time. My reactions to counter them are not themselves countered. Whoever is carving a new path for the future appears to be living fully within the timeline, as you do. They may not even be cognizant of my actions or that they are changing history. They may in fact have no unusual ability at all but have been set down another series of actions by a small fluctuation."

"Where does that leave us?" Dale asked. "What do we do?"

"For now, we rest, so that we may react when the time comes," Livinia answered.

"When will that happen?"

"When it does," Livinia said simply.

Janice stood abruptly.

"Why don't you three come to the basement and let me show you how to use my gear. Might come in handy."

Dale looked uncertain but got up, pulling Pia with her. After a moment, Maggie followed.

CHAPTER SIXTY-FIVE

Maggie Star

She hadn't expected a survivalist's arsenal in the basement, but having found herself in one, she would not have anticipated so many devices that resembled props in an old science fiction movie. There were handguns and rifles, of course, and even a rocket launcher, but there were also lights on spinners, what appeared to be a knockoff Nerf gun, big glasses attached by wires to strange boxes, wide belts covered in doodads, and assorted flavors of discs and orbs.

Janice worked through them, explaining how they functioned and making recommendations. When it discovered she was on an engineering path at school, it directed Maggie to the analytical devices: binocular glasses, X-ray earphones, and radio cameras. Dale learned the use of an invisibility belt and several varieties of grenades. As backup they were all taught how to fire shock pellets from tiny yellow guns. Pia was handed a small bottle of knockout drops.

Through it all, Maggie tried to figure out what was going on with their tutor. She'd thought it was odd from the moment it had called her over to ask after Dale's apartment. Under the strip of fluorescent light, its paleness appeared less like an affected look created with makeup than its actual skin.

The texture was off, as well. The smoothness that she'd ascribed to a thick foundation seemed almost rubbery.

"Miss Altura?" she asked.

Janice turned to her, its lack of expression not helping her manage a growing unease.

" 'Janice' is okey-dokey."

"Janice... we know something about Mrs. Monroe's situation, and Pia's whole wolf-touched deal, but... if it's not too intrusive... and we know what all this stuff does..."

"Chill," it said. "I dig it. You chicks want old Janice to give up the secret sauce."

"Phrasing," Dale muttered.

Everyone looked to her for an explanation, but she just shook her head and studied her feet.

"A test tube jockey kitbashed me together out of a dead woman, his special chemical cocktail, and a fungus he'd scraped up from some ice cave. A jolt of juice and some ancient hocus pocus, and there I was, with no clue who or what I was. He dubbed me Janus, because I was the first, but there were a handful before me. I was just the only one that made it."

Dale and Maggie stared at it.

"Bullshit."

"No fibbing. I was rescued by Dr. Madru himself, running with the squad that became the Madru Harbor Science Investigation Unit, charged with keeping the lid on the labcoats."

"There's no such place," Maggie objected.

"Not around these parts. It was a place that butted into this world, but wasn't of it. Sort of an extra-dimensional closet. I guess Dr. Madru whipped it up before Michigan became a state. It broke loose in the 1980s, and I was on the wrong side of the door when it closed."

"Ridiculous," Maggie said.

"More so than a house that eats people?" Dale asked gently.

Maggie grimaced.

"Magic, I can accept. Who knows how that works? But mad science is just fiction. Science guides us to practical rules about how things work. You can't just shove mushrooms inside a corpse and create a new form of life."

"It said there was a ritual of some kind. Maybe it's just a form of magic that has a laboratory vibe?"

"Okay," Maggie relented. "Sure. Why not?"

"Only trad mads use incantations. The mods prefer nukes."

Dale held a finger to her lips, glancing worriedly at Maggie.

"Yeah, no. Still magic. Just sprinkling cesium chloride instead of pixie dust."

She glared at the construct, daring it to continue, wishing that it would change its expression to acknowledge her victory on this point. Instead it just continued staring blankly at her. That had to be good enough.

"Anyway, I'm sorry you went through all that, Janice. Glad you came through it."

"Water under the bridge, Maggie. Now, let's go upstairs so you can get some grub."

CHAPTER SIXTY-SIX

Annette Kuiper

Annette stood alone before Aletheia. Technically she had a diminished squad of contractors waiting at the edges of the property as support, but her faith in them was undermined by the continued absence of Robinson and his strike team. Toby had not even theorized what could have happened, but his plan depended on the people inside being capable, deadly, and hopefully more desperate than she was.

She summoned the confidence that she felt at the office. This was just another human resource issue, and controlling humans was what she did best. She walked up onto the porch and knocked. After a short delay the door opened to reveal a smartly dressed woman in her fifties. From the reports, this was the mysterious resident of the mansion.

"I'm Annette Kuiper. I think we should talk about our mutual interests. May I come in?"

The woman sized her up and smiled stiffly.

"Of course. I'm Miss Chevrier. Do come in and have some tea."

"I'd be delighted," Annette lied.

She followed Miss Chevrier into a cluttered old parlor furnished in tacky Victorian chairs and floral arrangements. After a morning spent in Toby's spartan office, it was a vast overcorrection. She didn't trust people who couldn't be normal about their decor. She sat on the seat offered to her. Well used to uncomfortable chairs, she acted as though this was a delightful accommodation.

While Miss Chevrier poured the tea, Annette casually looked around the old place. There was no sign of any disturbance in this part of the house, and while the clutter could hide a lot, it would also have created an enormous mess in a struggle. She decided that whatever had occurred hadn't happened in this particular room.

Annette accepted her cup of tea and tasted it politely.

"Mmm," she said before setting it down. It was warm water and little else. Tasteless, like everything about this so-called mansion.

Miss Chevrier had seated herself and looked preposterously comfortable sipping her lightly colored water. It was clear that she was in no hurry.

"Miss Chevrier, it's unclear to me what your involvement is in this matter."

"What matter would that be, specifically?"

It would be like that. Annette scanned the room, but there were too many places to hide a microphone. She cursed Toby again for sending her into this tacky den of wolves, but he'd correctly observed that her actions had caused this whole mess.

"I need to know who the leader is inside the house in order to come to an accord. Is that you, Miss Chevrier?"

The infuriating woman smiled over her tea with false modesty.

"I am the caretaker. As such, I am merely responsible for the upkeep of this historic mansion. Perhaps I should summon my guests. I believe that your primary business is with them."

Annette suppressed her anger with a polite smile.

"Please do, if it's no bother."

"None at all."

Miss Chevrier set her tea down and reached toward the table beside her chair. She delicately picked up a little porcelain bell that had escaped Annette's notice and rang it gently. A small tinkling sound escaped from the fragile trinket, and there seemed little chance that it could be heard outside of the room. Nonetheless, within moments there were footsteps coming from the back of the house.

Four women entered from the next room. Annette recognized the wolf girl immediately, and the one next to her was likely the one who'd found her. They both wore the shabby, ill-fitting clothes of a shut-in. Following behind them was a small, more fashion-conscious woman with an extremely pale complexion. That must be the other mystery woman, who'd rescued the others from David's men. She moved to stand behind the loveseat while the other two sat in it together. Another rather short woman came last, a tomboy with a curly bob and shapeless overalls. She hung back, leaning against the door frame.

"Which of you is in charge?" Annette asked.

They all looked at each other.

"Of what?" asked the one that sat beside the wolf.

"Of negotiating a peaceful outcome," Annette explained with patience that she did not feel. Her smile struggled to look natural.

They all looked over to Miss Chevrier, who shook her head slightly.

"I'm merely providing shelter," she said. "I'm willing to offer advice, but this is not my affair."

The two on the couch then looked hopefully to the one standing behind them, who held her hands up defensively.

"Don't look at me. I'll back you two up, whatever you decide."

The one by the door was already shaking her head before they turned to her. At that, the final pair looked to each other, and it wasn't long before the question was resolved. The one who'd found the infernal creature slumped, rallied, and turned back to Annette unhappily.

"I guess that's me," she said.

"And who are you, exactly?"

Anger flashed in the woman's eyes.

"You sent goons to break into my apartment, and you don't even know who I am?"

Annette maintained her composure.

"You assume a great many things, but for now—no, I do not know who you are. But forgive me, I haven't introduced myself. I'm Annette Kuiper."

"Dale Alexander."

"Dale, I would like to discuss keeping your new friend out of my family's custody."

CHAPTER SIXTY-SEVEN

Dale Alexander

My mind rebooted while I stared at the Kuiper woman. We outnumbered her five to one—technically six, functionally five because of how Pia and Cassie worked—and one of us was actually the house, but somehow she dominated the room.

"What?" I asked.

"I don't want my family to succeed in reclaiming the wolf girl. Assuming that aligns with the outcomes you desire, we should be working together."

"Your people came in last night to kill Pia," I pointed out. "Why would we trust anything you say?"

"She has a name now? Adorable. Before you can understand why I'd turn against my family, you need to know her history."

"We're listening."

"My... our ancestor, Lord Edmond Doherty, was arrested in 1649 for being a witch. He was stripped of his titles and lands and sent to the gallows. His son Richard had already fled to the Netherlands seeking refuge in business ventures. Richard Doherty was the first occurrence of a wolf-touched in our family. Family lore is that Lord Edmond dabbled in magic, and he had bound the wolf to his son to ensure success and prosperity. It is well documented that he had a fascination with paganism and collected occult artifacts, from Europe and Western Asia in particular. This obsession was entered as evidence against him at his trial, with an accounting of every unsavory item.

"However Richard came by his affliction, he passed it on to his firstborn. This is not to say that another wolf came into being. At the birth of a descendant, the spirit leaves its current host and enters the new one. The previous host's body does not survive this transfer."

She paused, and I realized the implication. If Pia had a child, they'd die. That friendly wolf would cast them aside for a fresher body to inhabit. Annette Kuiper continued.

"A few generations turned suspicion to fact, and ever since the family has isolated the wolf-touched so that nobody becomes attached. I am sorry for that much, Pia. I can't imagine what it must have been like to be hidden away.

"The responsibility for care and breeding of the wolf-touched is rotated through the widening branches of the family for many reasons. The least important reason is to promote genetic diversity. This is mostly lip service and runs counter to the prevailing attitude of preserving our heritage, but that's what is claimed.

"Next least is that it keeps us from fighting each other over the wolf-touched. Most believe that good fortune comes to the immediate family of the latest, ah, genetic donor. This is nonsense, refuted through independent studies by both myself and my older brother."

I've always had difficulties in conversations because odd things would stick out and snare my attention. Meds had helped, but really I'd had to learn how to wrap those things in mental tissue and throw them away. This, though, was intriguing. Annette Kuiper and her brother had looked into the family legend separately at first and suddenly they'd shared results. They weren't always in alignment with each other or with the larger family. I wasn't ready to trust this woman, but I started believing that her motives weren't in lockstep with the rest of the Kuipers. Rather than tissue, I wrapped this one in foil to save for later.

"The single most important thing, the part of the family legacy that keeps us preserving this line despite all the pain, trouble, and verifiable lack of influence on our fortunes, is that the wolf doesn't die. You can kill the host, but the wolf survives, moving on to the next closest family member. It's happened a few times over the last three and a half centuries, when a wolf-touched has died before successfully mating. The pattern isn't clear, but the surviving parent, half-siblings, and an aunt of the bloodline have been chosen in this manner. It's in the interest of each generation's keeper of the wolf-touched to see that their charge is passed along safely to another branch of the family, preferably one that is less closely related."

I guessed where this was going.

"They were being brought to you. You were the new keeper."

Annette Kuiper nodded.

"Our branch's turn came up. My father wanted to protect himself, so rather than being the keeper and using one of my brothers he chose me to have the honor. I was expected to breed her with my son, Kevin. He wouldn't give me a meaningful role in the organization, but he'd use me and my child to shield himself from the family secret. I could not allow it.

"The transport arrived in Shale late in the evening, and I told them that we needed another day to finalize the wolf-touched's quarters. They checked into a motel and placed guards around her, but they were lax. There'd been no difficulties on the journey. They didn't expect anyone to attack, and my men had little trouble releasing your friend from their care.

"I'd expected that to be the end of it, but I had underestimated my father's reaction. He ordered my younger brother to find and return her, and then he warned me that I'd better do it first. David's people conducted the attacks on your apartment and this house, led by Toby's top operative."

I scrutinized her face but couldn't tell what, if any, of that might be true or truth-adjacent.

"And you had nothing to do with any of it?"

"I've played a part. My people followed you here, but David's followed them. I urged Toby to tell his man to fail at extracting the girl from the house, but I never imagined they'd try to kill her. The three of us are at cross purposes, and it's only going to get worse when the prior keeper gets involved. He will, too. Your Pia is his daughter, and her safety is of the utmost importance to him."

"So what can you offer, if there are two or three of your family still trying to get her back?"

"Or kill me," Pia said, glaring at her distant relative.

"It would cause difficulties with the larger family, but a branch can decline custody of the wolf-touched, especially if the branch head who accepted the offer retires. If we wrest control from my father, we will have such an opportunity. Toby is in agreement that I would become head, allowing me to refuse the wolf-touched. Even if he betrays me, he doesn't want any part of this business either. It's a waste of resources in his view.

"My offer is this: you do me a favor that will help us wrest control of the branch from my father, and in return I'll remove my branch from the picture."

"We're not hired killers," I stated, aware that some of us had indeed murdered people for free.

"I'm not hiring you or asking you to kill anyone. I am offering you the protection of my branch of the family in return for minor larceny."

I glanced at the others to gauge their feelings about this. Livinia maintained a polite disinterest, while Pia glared unrelentingly and Maggie studied a landscape painting. Janice was as unreadable as ever but seemed attentive. They really were just putting this all on me.

I thought about what would be best for Pia, telling myself that I was just the broker and would not make the decision for them.

"Before we get to what you're asking of us, what would that protection look like? Aside from your branch not bothering us?"

"We wouldn't simply not bother you. You all would be considered friends of the family. If necessary, we would hide you from the other branches."

"Sounds like mob shit."

"I confess that it seems that way from how I've been talking. This is the only time I will ever ask you to do something illegal, and you can refuse. We are here to help, if you request, and I won't say we'd never ask anything in return. You are under no obligation at any time to come to us or to do as we ask. Given your obvious skills, it would be akin to being favored specialists. If wolf-touched exist, what else is out there? You seem capable of assisting should something along similar lines come up again."

"Your personal paranormal investigators."

"Preferred investigators, but yes."

"What if there's nothing to investigate?"

Annette gave a pinched shrug of a smile.

"Then there'd be no investigation to offer you."

I turned again to the others.

"Before we continue the conversation, what do we all think about their side of the offer?"

"Could be worse," Janice said. "Could be better. From the sounds of it, the last keeper isn't gonna take it lying down."

"If I may ask a question of Mrs. Kuiper," Livinia said.

"Ms.," Annette corrected her. "If I had married into the family I wouldn't be made a keeper. But please, ask your question."

"It seems in all of our interests to address the motive behind the family's practice. If the legacy of the wolf-touched were to be separated from your lineage, there would be no need to fear or control Pia. As you observed, we have among us some affinity for circumstances beyond the ordinary. I, myself, am a researcher in occult matters. It is possible that I could modify the spell that initially bound the wolf, had I access to the references and notes used by Lord Doherty. Will you turn over those materials and other documentation of the ritual?"

"I'm afraid that most of it is gone. Toby is a collector of occult items, and I think he has obtained a few of Lord Edmond's effects. There may be something in them."

"Anything would be useful. Good copies would suffice, if your brother is amenable."

"I'll ask him. As you say, the entire affair could be resolved if you managed to split my family from the curse."

Pia bristled at being called a curse, and I squeezed their hand.

"How about you, Pia? How are you feeling about this so far? If you're not comfortable, we don't need to continue."

Their eyes watered as they smiled at me. God, that lovely face.

"I trust you," they said.

I swallowed. That was so incredible to hear, but I needed them to speak their mind.

"That's great. I appreciate it. But this whole discussion revolves around you, so if there's anything you want or need that we haven't covered, please say so."

Pia thought, frowning adorably. I forcibly pulled my thoughts back to the choice they needed to make. I liked to think I was a good person, but would I even be in the middle of this weirdness if I wasn't attracted to Pia? If I didn't see in them a chance to be happy again? I needed to concentrate on being certain that Pia's needs were centered.

"I want to meet your son," they said. "Kevin, right? And your brothers. I want to be a part of the family, even if we don't become friends. I want to come to dinner with my girlfriend and send birthday cards. I know we're not closely related, but we're all here in this city, and we are family."

We were all shocked, none more so than Ms. Kuiper, who was so taken aback that she needed to close her mouth and recover her poise.

"I... I'm not sure how well that will work out for you. We're not very close-knit. Father raised us to compete with each other."

"That's what I want. No deal unless you promise."

Annette looked for support from me, and finding none she eventually nodded.

"Very well, cousin," she said in a strangled tone. "I will introduce you to Kevin and maintain a cordial family relationship with you. I can't promise that my brothers will cooperate, but I will advise them of your wishes."

Pia grinned.

"Thank you, cousin Annette."

I felt so happy for them, despite thinking that spending holidays with Annette Kuiper sounded distinctly unpleasant. But if I was the girlfriend they had in mind, I'd willingly endure it. Now it was time to get to the downside of the deal.

"Okay," I said. "That's us; what are you asking in return?"

Annette rallied considerably.

"My ability to deliver on my side of the bargain depends entirely on my father relinquishing control of the branch. The best way to do that is to secure the evidence that he's been cheating the family consortium out of funds. With those records in our hands, he would have to step down to avoid the wrath of the greater family. If he refused..."

She shrugged.

"What Toby and I would like you to do is steal those records for us."

"Why us?"

"The best people we could find entered your house last night. Apparently, you are better. Besides, it wouldn't be a peace agreement if you didn't do something for us; it would just be surrender."

I stared at her. She really was awful.

"It adds up, in an icky kind of way," Janice said.

"Okay," I relented. "Where are the records, and how are we supposed to get them?"

"David keeps them at home. He's not very clever, so Father trusts him for such matters. We have the plans to his house, where he's likely storing them, and a window tonight during which he will be attending an emergency meeting at Kuiper Innovations headquarters. We also know the security service he uses, so you can disable it."

"Just like that," I said. "We walk in tonight, pick the shit up, and walk out? It can't be that easy."

Annette made a noise with her tongue, and I realized that I'd just heard an actual tsk.

"Of course not. You may not be professional thieves, but you are clearly skilled and resilient. If complications arise, I trust that you'll deal with them. It is, after all, in your best interest to succeed."

Annette produced a thumb drive and set it on the low table between us. It was bulky and red, bearing a severe logo built around a *K* and an *I*.

"Now, do I leave this here, or do we go back to our stalemate?"

I stared at the drive. If we accepted the deal, we'd be criminals, and the police were already interested in us. The Kuipers would always have that to hang over us, and promises about rights to refuse would mean nothing with that secret in their pocket. Accepting this meant working for Annette for the rest of our lives. Well, mine and Pia's. Maggie's, if they helped. The question was whether that would be worth it for Pia. Feasibility first. If we couldn't do it, the decision would be simple.

"Thoughts?" I asked.

"I don't like the timeline," Janice said. "It's too fast. But it sounds like we need to step on it before the whole hive's abuzz. If the tidbits she brought us are as legit as she claims, we should be able to swing something tonight. Might not be swanky."

Janice addressed Annette.

"How will we ID these receipts? Are they bound ledgers? Excel files? What?"

"Toby has the electronic data, but it was entered only a few years ago. Without the proof of the original books, it's difficult to assert that the copies were accurate or that Father knew anything. Those ledgers were created by the former CFO, who Toby worked under. He's included a description of them in the documents we're giving you."

"Not going to be a snap to cover our pilfering," Janice continued.

"Don't bother. It will be evident soon enough. As you've said, we need to act quickly."

"And where's the drop-off?"

"Come to the top floor of Kuiper Innovations as soon as you have them. My brother and I will be there, and he can find what he needs as soon as possible. I'll leave passes with the night guard."

Janice nodded, and I wished yet again that its expression revealed anything.

"Miss Chevrier?"

"I trust Miss Altura to assess an endeavor such as this. I shall verify the house schematics and search for other pertinent information, should you elect to proceed."

"Maggie? You can sit this out. No hard feelings."

She ran a hand through her hair and sought counsel from the hardwood flooring before looking at me and nodding.

"Might not be much use in there. Maybe I can drive or something?"

That just left Pia. I looked into their eyes and clutched their hands protectively.

"I know you've been held in a cell all your life. You don't

have any experience doing shady shit. So if you want us to do this, there's no need for you to come."

I caught Janice shrugging in my peripheral vision. Pia gazed back at me with concern.

"Do you, Dale? Do you have experience doing shady shit?"

I couldn't look away, nor could I lie to Pia's face.

"No," I admitted. "I don't."

Pia smiled bravely, shaking their hands for emphasis.

"Then I'm coming with you."

"Is it worth it, Pia?"

Pia leaned in and rested their forehead on mine.

"You are," they said.

My doubts melted. Since this had started yesterday, I'd felt like my life had been derailed. But really it had been jolted into motion after sitting abandoned for years. Maybe I could choose where to take it from here.

"You are," I agreed.

I pulled back, just enough to turn my head, and faced Annette.

"We have a deal, Ms. Kuiper."

Annette smiled, and at least some part of it seemed genuine.

"Please, call me Annette. It appears we're to be related soon."

I blushed as Pia wrapped me in a hug.

"I expect we all have a lot to do, so I'll leave you to it," Annette said. "Together, we will prevail. I'll expect you later tonight."

Livinia saw her to the door. When she was gone, Janice flopped onto the chair Annette had sat in. I could feel myself grinning like a fool, but I didn't care. Pia and I held each other, and for the moment I felt better than I had in years.

"Is she jake, do you think?" Janice asked.

"I don't know," I admitted. "I think she would like to force her father out. This robbery could actually be part of a plan to do that. Whether she'll follow through on her promises afterward..."

"She has to," Pia said. "Family supports each other."

I wanted to remind her that everything Annette talked about was defying her family, but instead I tried to find the faith that they had.

"I think Pia is correct," Livinia said as she re-entered the room. "She will honor our requests after you three talk to her brother Toby tonight."

Janice and Livinia shared a look, communing through their long familiarity. Having known them for only a single day, I resorted to words.

"Did we die again?" I asked. "Are you correcting another bad outcome?"

Livinia looked at us sitting on the couch together.

"I speak only from the vantage of the original flow of events. I dare not allow further divergence. Now, Janice, if you would please assist me with Ms. Kuiper's device, we may let these turtledoves enjoy a quiet moment to themselves."

Janice hauled itself out of the chair and grabbed the thumb drive. Maggie had already vanished.

"You got it, boss. Don't break the loveseat, you two."

The furniture suffered no damage, but we enjoyed a nice cuddle ahead of tonight's adventure.

CHAPTER SIXTY-EIGHT

Annette Kuiper

Annette smirked from her driver's seat. She called Toby.

"Speak," he commanded.

She ignored his tone. After Father was dealt with, she'd get rid of him next.

"They took the bait. How are the preparations going?"

"I've informed Father of Robinson's demands. That should be enough for him to call the meeting tonight, but I'm prepared to do it myself if he doesn't respond quickly."

"I'll wait for the call, then."

He hung up on her, but that was okay. It wouldn't be long before she'd be above him in the family's eyes.

At least she'd had the pleasure of dismissing Lakeland. After tonight she'd have much more capable contractors in her pocket.

CHAPTER SIXTY-NINE

David Kuiper

"Are they there yet?!"

Talking to the old man over the phone was like being forced into speaker mode. David angled the phone away from his ear as much as possible. He stood in the corner of his basement, watching as Nathaniel's men settled in and checked their gear.

"Yeah, dad. They arrived about a half an hour ago and are already turning my basement into a makeshift barracks."

"Why the fuck didn't you call me?! Your brother told me his fucking mercenary has our asset and demands a ransom!"

"What? Toby told me nobody came out of the house!"

"You've mishandled this from the beginning, David! Robinson wants a fucking meeting, we're gonna meet! Your house! Nine thirty tonight! I'm bringing Nathaniel straight from the airport! Get his boys ready! We'll show that son of a bitch how we negotiate with thieves!"

The line went dead, and David put the phone back in his pocket.

"Good talk," he said.

He informed his guests of the change in plans and went upstairs to try to get some work done while the security operatives turned his basement into a kill zone.

CHAPTER SEVENTY

Janice Altura

David Kuiper's house was nearly indistinguishable from those around it in the subdivision. It was a mansion in the modern style, large but cheaply made, and packed in closely with its neighbors, all with identical boxy footprints and drab siding. What most set it apart was the lack of playsets in the backyard. Of course, the GPS had helped to find it as well.

Janice led the way through the wet leaves and grass behind the houses, crouching low and watching the windows for possible witnesses. Behind it followed the other two: Dale, attempting to copy its movements, and Cassie, loping along excitedly beside her and looking nearly solid in the darkness. Pia herself slept in the back of Dale's car under Maggie's care. They'd decided that since the wolf was essentially immortal and had already proven her capabilities, she could take the risk instead of Pia. The wolf seemed to agree.

A dog barked from inside a house they passed, and they hurried along before anyone came to look. Other dogs in the area picked up the call, and before anyone could stop her Cassie howled in response. They hid behind a large grill outside a dark house, Dale hugging Cassie to calm her. Janice thought again that it should have come alone, but Livinia had made it clear that all of them needed to go.

She had specifically said that the three of them needed to speak with Tobias Kuiper Jr. She didn't seem concerned that they were taking Cassie instead of Pia, but no mention had been made of Maggie. That didn't mean they needed to all actually come here, did it? Perhaps it was the most direct way to meet him, but were they going to pull off this theft? Would it succeed? Would they be caught? Livinia had never made a pronouncement about the future in all the long years of their acquaintance. Janice had to assume that things were dire if she had done it now. Replaying events, declaring an outcome—it hoped Livinia wasn't spinning out of control. They'd had theoretical discussions about what Livinia's experience of and interaction with time meant about free will and predestination, and they'd always agreed that allowing time to pass without intervention seemed best.

Janice had to assume that its actions tonight mattered, and it meant to get its two charges through this intact. They weren't ready to look after themselves yet, not in a situation like this. It noticed Dale peeking around the grill and pulled her back further. Just because she'd had five minutes of training with the belt and grenades didn't mean she was at all ready to use them.

The dogs finally settled down. Two lights had come on, and there'd been the sound of a back door opening, but mercifully no one had noticed them. Time to go.

They swiftly passed the last two houses and settled against the back wall of Kuiper's residence. There was a light on inside, which could just be a safeguard while David was away. If everything had gone to plan, he should be at a meeting. Janice pulled out a tool it called its spy stethoscope, a pair of chunky headphones attached to a speaker cone through a small box with dials for frequency and volume. It gathered more sophisticated devices were now available, but the great thing about Mad City technology was that nobody thought to defend against it.

It set the bell against the house's siding and adjusted the knobs. Static, with regular patterns in it. If anyone was in there, they were holding very still or were out of range. It was a big house, after all. Mildly satisfied, it put the gear away and motioned for Dale to follow.

They went to the sliding door, and after looking inside, Janice pulled out two pieces of petrified wood, separated them, and handed one to Dale. They hadn't covered this one in their impromptu training session, but its use was simple. Janice bent over by the door handle and pressed its piece against the bottom of the glass. It nodded at Dale, who followed suit at the other end of the sliding door. Janice slid its chunk up the glass and flicked its free hand up a couple times to encourage imitation. Dale did the same, and she jerked in surprise when the wooden rod followed their chunks of petrified wood.

Wood magnets were mostly a toy, but when you needed them they were brilliant. Not so much an invention as a discovery, the pieces were taken from the single known petrified forest that produced xylite, a hard substance that reacted to the magnetic fields of plant matter. Efforts had been underway to create the material in a lab, but when the dimensions had separated there had not yet been any positive results.

Janice had Dale lift her end of the rod while it pulled its own along the bottom. They set the bar into place along the side and carefully removed the magnets. That accomplished, Janice made short work of the basic lock and slid the door open. It raised a finger to its lips and ushered the other two inside.

Cassie's nails clacked on the wood flooring of the family room, and Janice wished it'd thought about that when they'd decided that bringing the wolf would be the better choice. Lessons. There were always more lessons but only one first time for taking a canine along on a job. It slid the door closed behind them all and held a hand up to Cassie. The wolf sniffed her hand curiously. Janice started building a training program in the part of its mind that wasn't laughing in frustration. It crouched down and whispered in Cassie's ear.

"Stay here. Alert us if anyone approaches the house." It thought for a second and continued. "Good girl."

There'd been no sign of the alarm, which indicated that its hack of the system had worked. There was no need to tinker with the local installation when you had access to the company servers. It wasn't that their network security was bad, but it couldn't stop someone who had access to everything ever written. With Janice's guidance, Livinia had needed only an hour and a half to turn up all of the information needed to log in and flag David Kuiper's account as inactive.

Livinia had also confirmed the house schematics they'd been given. In the basement there was indeed a safe room, which was where the data from the thumb drive suggested they'd find the ledgers. Janice led Dale to the basement door and down the steps. Dale wasn't skilled at sneaking around, and her footfalls on the wooden planks sounded like stomps to Janice. Additional material for the training course was being generated all the time.

It was dark in the basement. The light that came in through the high windows provided a thin outline of some of the taller items stored down here but that wasn't enough to show trip hazards or many other obstacles. Janice pulled out its cat's-eye glasses. Another staple technology of the Scientific Investigation Unit, these lenses bounced incoming light between their layers in order to amplify night vision. There were downsides, the largest of which was high reflectivity. They also created a certain fuzziness, as each incoming image had an extended duration. The overall effect was of multiple film exposures of the same scene, with current and past motion overlapping. Small prices to pay for such useful fashion.

Unfortunately it only had the single pair, fitted nicely to a deep purple cat eye frame that had been custom fit for it. They'd need to get special goggles of this dimension's technology for Dale if she stayed on.

Taking Dale's hand, Janice carefully guided her across the floor to the entrance of the safe room. It was about to enter the door code—also courtesy of Liv—when light overloaded the lenses. It turned its head away and reached hastily for the glasses.

"Uh-uh," warned a voice from behind the brightness. "Hands where I can see them. You're not getting out of this one."

CHAPTER SEVENTY-ONE

Dale Alexander

I toggled the invis-o-belt, squeezing my eyes shut against the lights, hoping I'd been fast enough to avoid being spotted. I hadn't been able to count them all in that initial moment of partial sight, but there were at least three large light sources along the side walls of the basement. I hoped that Janice had a backup plan for this, because it was all I could do not to throw myself on the floor again. I focused on being invisible and not peeing.

Janice stood impassively as ever, but I didn't blame it. There were a lot of weapons aimed its way. There seemed to be six well-armed people down here with us, dressed in dark clothes and balaclavas. The only things I knew about guns were from playing video games—and that brief introduction by Janice this morning—but I thought that assault rifles and shotguns were a bit much for two women and a dog.

Where was Cassie? I hoped she'd escaped. The wolf might be an immortal spirit, but she seemed to share damage with her host. I wasn't sure which of them had hurt their ankle, but they'd both limped when I'd met them. If injury passed from wolf to host, Pia could be killed.

I slipped away into the back of the basement in case my presence had been noted. Janice had been moved to the wall beside the safe room door, where it stood with its hands up, cat's-eye glasses still in place. Two guns were trained on it from a safe distance. I had to admit their caution was warranted.

One of the armed people pressed a button outside the door.

"Situation is contained, sir," he said.

The door slid open. An older man dressed in an ill-fitting suit walked out. His red face looked like bad rouge applied to a corpse. He strode into the basement with the confidence of an end boss, and I hoped the cutscene would give me time to find a way out of this. I ran a mental inventory of what I had at my disposal. There was a tracker in my pocket, but Janice already knew where I was. I had an empty backpack on for stashing the ledgers we weren't likely to get. I had a penlight in my pocket. Then there was the sampler of mad science grenades: one to muffle sound, one to negate gravity, and one to bounce incessantly, each of which effects would last a minute. I didn't think any of them were useful, and I hesitated to use one.

Another man slipped out of the safe room, a younger version of the one in charge. This one tried to emulate the swagger of the older man, but he seemed too unsure of himself. He kept glancing at his elder nervously. These must be Tobias Kuiper Sr. and his son David, the owner of this house.

"Which one is this?" Tobias barked, looking around at the room for an answer.

Yet another man stepped into view, although he remained in the safe room. The light from the powerful lamps glinted off his glasses.

"I believe that's the one known as Janus. We think she's a contractor of some kind. She's proven quite capable up until now."

Tobias looked it up and down, a process that didn't take long. He laughed.

"She's four feet nothing! A fucking midget." He hit David's arm. "Your guys got beat up by a midget? No wonder you needed Toby to set this up for you, you fucking loser."

Dale stared as best she was able at the man in the glasses. The rotten old bastard had said that Toby had set this up. Toby had either betrayed Annette, or he'd enlisted her to lure them into the trap. Either way, they were fucked. She wondered if that was Toby himself, smirking in the darkness at the result of his gambit. What was it Livinia had said? Annette would keep her word, but the three of them had to talk to Toby. That suddenly felt very conditional and extremely unlikely.

Incredulously, she watched one more man emerge from the safe room, pushing his way past maybe-Toby and peering around the room. He was somewhere in age between Tobias and his sons and bore the unmistakable glower of a Kuiper.

"You know what I don't see? I don't see our goddamn property! You said they'd bring her, Tobias!"

One of the armed men spoke up.

"Our agent watching the outside reported that two women and a large dog were making their way here. She must be in the area, sir."

Tobias walked over to Janice and glared down at it.

"Where is it, you fuck? Did you leave it upstairs?"

Janice stood quietly, and it was no surprise to Dale that it out-waited the blustering patriarch. However, the other older man broke the silence before either of them.

"You two! Go find it!"

The two men closest to the stairs hastened up them. Everyone waited quietly, if not patiently, so the loud crash and sound of glass hitting the floor above caught all of their attention. The men upstairs yelled and started shooting, but after two horrible screams, silence fell. Those below held their breath as they heard heavy, clacking footsteps. Then Tobias went into motion, grabbing David and racing for the safe room.

The door slid shut before they could reach it, and I fought to contain my sudden laughter. One man moved to the bottom of the stairs, while the pair guarding Janice looked hesitant but stayed where they were. That left one guard who took position in front of the Kuipers and their guest, who were all yelling at Toby to open the door. The intercom crackled for one short message.

"Enjoy your own petard, my dear family," Toby said. "Annette and I have come to an equitable arrangement, and I'm afraid we'll need your shares. Bad luck, uncle Nathaniel, but you really should have let us handle this internally. At least you'll be clear of the curse this way."

Tobias hammered on the impregnable door, screaming epithets that implied horrible things about Toby's parentage and nature. David sank to the ground, crying and mumbling prayers. The remaining one, Nathaniel, turned to face whatever was coming, taking a pistol from one of the armed men.

There was a burst of gunfire from the base of the stairs. A moment later the shots stopped as a massive creature landed on the man and bit down hard over his head. It was a giant wolf, much larger than any I'd known existed, absurdly bulky, and it was wreathed in dark purplish phantasmal tendrils that sprouted from its nape like a tattered, living cloak. And it was a soft yellowish brown.

She looked different, but I knew that Cassie had come for me

CHAPTER SEVENTY-TWO

Maggie Star

Time spent waiting in Dale's car stretched. After they'd parked along the side of the curving street of the upscale development, she'd remained behind to watch Pia and be ready to drive them away hurriedly. They snored contentedly in the back seat, having taken something to ensure drowsiness. Cassie had appeared outside on the sidewalk, sitting patiently while the others had climbed out and checked over their supplies one last time. Maggie herself had brought one of the tiny pellet guns, but she planned to peel out before needing to use it.

She wanted to check her phone, but Janice had made them leave their devices at Aletheia. That had probably been smart, but that made the car's clock the only way to see how long they'd been gone. She wasn't going to call attention to the vehicle by turning on the electronics, so she just had to hope for the best. Janice had left her a glass plate attached to a suspicious box of switches and a small dish antenna, supposedly a remote television screen, but she didn't want to use it. She was not willing to give in to accepting mad science.

Cassie had almost reached the car before Maggie noticed that the wolf was racing back. She looked for the others, but they were nowhere in sight. The wolf scratched frantically at the back door. Feeling foolish and not a little scared, Maggie grabbed the pellet gun and slipped out. She crouched low and made her way around to the passenger side as quickly as she could manage, continually checking for anyone coming out from behind the nearby houses. The wolf looked at her directly and touched the back door handle with clear deliberateness.

"Okay," she said. "But what the hell's going on? Is Dale in trouble?"

The doors had been left unlocked to speed access in a potential escape, so she just had to reach out and pull on the handle. As soon as the door cracked open, Cassie forced her way inside, crawling over Pia. The door closed softly behind her, not latching, but not allowing Maggie a vantage to see what the wolf was doing. Moments later, the door burst open again, and Pia hurled themself out of the car, landing on their chest, feet still inside on the back seat.

"Pia," Maggie whispered urgently. "Are you all right? Where are the others?"

Pia groaned and turned away from her, curling around their belly. They rocked, muscles spasming, and Maggie carefully approached them. She knelt over their trembling body and touched their shoulder gingerly.

"What's going on? How can I help you? Do you need something to bite down on?"

The shaking stopped, and she wasn't sure whether that was good or bad. She thought to call an ambulance, but again —no phone. There were plenty of houses around. Maybe someone would answer and agree to help.

Pia grew explosively, their clothes shredding as their body transformed into something much larger, with a long torso and elongated face, and Maggie retreated quickly. It was a smooth change and very rapid, every part of them moving at once from woman to massive wolf. The end result was a grotesque parody of Cassie, impossible to mistake for a dog, barrel-chested and thick-legged to support its weight. The fur looked thick and coarse, and the wide length of the tail resembled a giant wool feather duster made of bristles.

It scrambled to its feet and immediately ran back the way Cassie had come. Maggie stared after it, reconsidering her position vis-à-vis mad science. Whatever was about to go down was going to be indescribable, and if that radar glass could help her see it, then she'd embrace the madness.

CHAPTER SEVENTY-THREE

Cassiopeia

We lay on the grass, the cool dampness of the night soothing us after the effort of the transformation. We'd never blended our selves before, although the wolf spirit had known that her alignment with her host had been sufficient for the merger. Being our first attempt, there were some points of poorer integration. Our vision was doubled, making it more difficult to focus. The human's sense of body and balance fought with that of the wolf, and the conflict left us clumsy on our feet. Fortunately our ears and nose were functioning properly, and our mind had one clear goal: save Dale. We needed to get into that basement.

Sore all over, we ran for David Kuiper's house. Our legs were awkward at first, but as they worked and stretched we found our balance and rhythm. The wolf's experience took the lead, and we learned to adapt our motion from that basis. We were faster than either of us had ever been alone, and we closed in on our target rapidly. The dogs that had challenged the wolf earlier slunk away silently, afraid to attract our notice. Our goal in sight, we picked up a smell. It belonged to the house but was out here in the open. Oil and steel, and sweat under heavy clothing. The odor that had come from the basement.

We veered toward the scent. Had they brought Dale outside? Were we too late? Our speed increased again, and we felt our shroud's tendrils whipping behind us. There was a guard in front of us, surprised and fumbling for his large gun. He was the source, and he was alone.

We leapt before he could aim at us, and our weight and speed knocked him to the ground. He gasped for air, but we walked over his body and sat on his stomach, glaring into his face. Saliva dripped from our mouth as we asked him what had happened to Dale. After demanding that he answer us, we realized that he couldn't understand our growls. He was useless. We needed to go, but we were also filled with hatred for this man and his weapon. We placed our jaws around his neck and shook our head until his spine cracked in our teeth.

Freed of our distraction, we ran once more toward where we'd last seen Dale. Unwilling to slow down to open the sliding door further, we crashed through it. It barely slowed us down and didn't hurt at all.

Two more guards stood between us and the basement, and they shouted as we shook glass out of our coat. We sensed that Dale was still down there, along with that other woman, the walking fungus. We growled, but the men did not move out of our way. Already holding their weapons up, they started firing at us. Our tendrils shot forward and blocked most of their bullets. The few that got through felt like sharp pinches, annoying but not dangerous. Between bursts from their guns, our tendrils grabbed one of the men and dragged him to our jaws. We clamped down on his leg and whipped him around the room until he stopped moving on his own. We threw his limp body into the other man. Their bodies fell separately as they collided, and we pounced to land with all our weight on the chest of the one that still lived. All of the air inside of him came out in one explosive breath as his heart and lungs collapsed beneath us.

We stalked to the basement door. There was another guard at the bottom of the stairs. He shot up at us, and our shroud protected us. We walked down a few steps and pounced, landing on the man before biting off his head. More shots came from behind, and our tendrils couldn't reach them. We whirled around and faced two more guards, with more people hiding behind them.

One of them dropped after a few soft zipping sounds. A glance to the right revealed Janice crouching along the wall, holding a small, odd gun. We remembered it from Dale's cell. It put people to sleep. We also remembered the pleasure of mauling the man beside the couch. Janice engaged another guard right beside her, leaving only one to protect the three others. Keepers.

The guard stopped being defensive, aiming his shotgun at me. Something came from behind us and hit the cement floor. It bounced up, striking the barrels of the gun before ricocheting off into the back of the room. His blast made a hole in the ceiling above us.

We grinned at him. He made a good club to use on the keeper that held his own tiny gun. The two cowering behind him were worse than mere guards; they told the guards who to keep. We had no mercy on them and continued to toss them around and rip into them, taking our years of helplessness out on their broken bodies. The shouts of the dying stopped, and we kept going as new shouts rose. Pleading not for our targets, which had begun to fall apart, but for our own sake.

We paused. Blood dripped from our mouth and covered our fur. One voice had gotten past our rage, that of our chosen, the one we were fighting to protect. We saw Dale standing in the harsh light beside us, tears running down her face. She approached us, smiling but afraid.

"It's okay," Dale said soothingly. "It's over. You got them. We're safe now."

She leaned against us and buried her head in our gory fur. We gently held her in place, wrapping her in tendrils.

"We love you," we said, but it came out as an anguished whine.

"I know," Dale replied. "It's okay."

Dale was safe. She was here, pressed against our side. Everything was going to be fine. We began to calm. Our breathing slowed. Our pulse came down. Coolness washed over us as my vision changed. The world became colorful. The scents grew muted. I stumbled a little as my weight shifted, but remained standing, my arms around Dale.

"I love you," I said again.

Dale cradled her head against my bare shoulder.

"I'm starting to believe you do," she answered.

I hugged her tighter.

"Trust me," I whispered.

Dale pulled back and looked up at me. Blood from my coat and skin were smeared across her face, but she had never looked more lovely. I knew I must be truly disgusting. I could feel the gore drying around my mouth and chin. There were bits of fabric and hair in my teeth. But Dale smiled at me with obvious affection.

"I do," Dale said. "I trust you."

The bouncing grenade came back our way, having smashed a lot of the boxes and old furniture stored down here. I snatched it out of the air and held it firmly to the side as it wound down. As we enjoyed each other's gaze for a few moments, Janice went over to press the intercom to the safe room.

"It's over, Mr. Kuiper. You can come out now."

We turned to greet the man who'd betrayed everybody.

CHAPTER SEVENTY-FOUR

Janice Altura

The door slid open, and Toby Kuiper stepped out into his brother's basement. He made no effort to avoid the blood, but Janice noticed that he'd put on shoe covers. He also carried the ledgers.

"Good work," he said. "Who's taking these to my little sister?"

Pia unzipped Dale's backpack, which had managed to stay comparatively blood-free.

"You set us up," Janice said.

Toby walked over to pack his prizes for transport.

"I set them up. I outright lied to Annette. You would never have consented to murder, so I needed to feed her a story she'd be willing to take to you."

He stepped away from Dale and Pia.

"Zip that. I don't want to get blood on me."

Pia sealed the backpack, watching him carefully.

"You set us up," Janice repeated.

Toby spread his hands in gracious acceptance.

"If you prefer."

"I don't. We could have been croaked."

He shrugged.

"I doubt it. You disposed of my top problem solver and his

personnel so thoroughly that I may never discover what you did with them."

He held up a finger and shook it dramatically for emphasis.

"Very useful, by the way. This will all be blamed on a dispute between him and poor David. It seems that the nefarious Mr. Robinson had collected your furry friend over there but demanded a ransom for turning her over to my brother. Alas, Father decided to set a trap for him instead. I was fortunate enough to reach the safe room when Robinson set the beast on us. When it was all over, I dared to open the door, only to find my family and staff massacred with Robinson and his creature in the wind."

"That's not what happened!" Pia yelled. "That's all a lie!"

He nodded readily.

"It is. It's a lie that I will tell the family representatives when they arrive to look for you. A few more clues will send them on a multinational tour. I've committed myself and my resources to laying a false trail for you for as long as it takes the family to lose interest. For what I've gained, I consider it to be a fair price."

He reached into a box behind the lights and pulled out two pairs of rubber shoes. He handed one to Janice and the other to Dale.

"Those have partial shoe print patterns on the bottom for survivalist boots. Please put them on and walk around where you've been standing down here. The wolf girl is fine; she was supposed to be here anyway. Leave by the back and get out of here before the police arrive. With all the gunfire, I imagine they've already been called, but they won't be anxious to arrive at an active shooting. When you leave, I'll report coming out of the safe room to find this."

The rubber shoe covers weren't easy to put on, but they managed. After walking around a little and crossing their old prints, Janice motioned for the younger women to head upstairs. It turned to face Toby.

"In case you ever think of snitching on us, you should know that Livinia mopped up your Robinson and his pals all on her own. The rest of us chilled with some classics."

It showed him the largest, most horrifying grin in its repertoire.

CHAPTER SEVENTY-FIVE

Annette Kuiper

Miss Altura arrived at Toby's office alone, a tiny figure carrying a large bag of heavy books. It also had some patches of blood on it. Annette stood and went quickly to assist with the books. Once the bag was on the table, she went to the small tray of glasses and drinks.

"You look like you could use a drink. What can I get you?"

Miss Altura sat carefully in a chair and checked its hands and forearms before putting them on the table.

"Water's fine, Ms. Kuiper."

Annette poured whiskey for herself and took a bottle of water to the table for her guest. This meeting needed a delicate touch, so she sat next to Miss Altura in order to convey assurance and understanding. She considered placing a comforting hand on its arm, but decided against that for now. If the situation required more sympathy later, it would be a good gesture to have in reserve.

"What happened?" she asked quietly. "Are the others okay?"

"They're upset, but they weren't injured. As to what happened—" It turned icily toward Annette. "Make me believe you didn't know."

Annette endured the stare, but she sat up straighter and slid her hand off the table. She did not pick up her glass.

"I don't know what I'm supposed to deny. I told you everything you needed to know at your mansion. There were details that were for the other part of the plan, but that shouldn't have involved you."

"Let's say it did. What did you know? Keep in mind that Toby has already spun his tale."

Annette was lost, and she knew her furrowed brow showed it. What had her sneaky fuck of a brother done? She needed a little more context to even begin getting an idea of the mess he'd made.

"You already saw Toby? You were supposed to come directly here."

"We did. The others are in the car with Maggie because we zoomed straight here instead of hosing all the blood off of them."

"So... he was at David's house?"

Miss Altura remained silent.

"I don't know what happened tonight anywhere but here. Toby had arranged for messages to come from Robinson claiming to have the— to have Pia. Demanding money to return them. They were sent to both Toby and David, and if David didn't take the bait, Toby was going to bring in Father and broker a meeting to discuss terms. Robinson worked for Toby, so it would make sense that he'd be involved."

"Where was that meeting?"

"It was supposed to be in the boardroom. Robinson wouldn't show up, of course." Annette looked at Miss Altura conspiratorially. "More texts were scheduled to delay and eventually call off the meeting. The whole thing was a distraction to get David away from his house."

"You have someone who knows how to spoof phones?"

Annette shrugged.

"Maybe. Not something I ever needed done. Irrelevant though, as everyone who went into Aletheia that night left their phones outside. Toby does have someone to bypass security."

Miss Altura continued to watch her, and Annette finally let herself drink the whiskey. Just what the hell had happened at David's house tonight?

"Why did David try to whack us, and why would this Robinson do it against Toby's wishes?"

Annette shook her head and took another pull of whiskey, hoping she could maintain this particular lie.

"I don't know. It may be that Robinson himself decided it would be easier. Toby told me it had been David's order, and I believed him. I didn't question further because it wasn't worth it. The attempt had been made, and it had failed. We had to deal with the situation as it stood."

"It's okay to tell me," Miss Altura said. "You stood the most to gain by killing Pia, and David followed Pop Kuiper like a whipped puppy. I don't think he'd have risked going against orders. No. I think you went to Toby with a proposal to help him get dear old dad out of the way in return for killing the wolf-touched. It was a win-win deal, except you thought you were getting the better end of it because you'd get rid of the wolf-touched on top of getting control of the company. Quite the deal from your point of view.

"What does big brother get for his trouble? I'm guessing shares? You gave him something else, I'd bet a nickel on it. And then he presents you with a clever ruse to solve all your problems by wasting your dad and kid brother's time laying a false trail for Pia's kidnapper while we steal the incriminating books. It's perfect! Dad's forced out, you get everything scot-free. And what does Toby get again?

"I'll tell you what he got. When we were shuffling the ledgers to a clean bag in your parking lot, I flipped through a few of them. I'm not a bean counter, but I've handled ledgers in my time. These may implicate your dad, but do you know whose initials are all over them? We just stole the evidence of Toby's own bean juggling."

It stood up, picking up its water bottle.

"They had that meetup. It was in the basement of David's pad. We were dead on arrival. The only reason that we came out of it is that Pia reached deep inside of themself to protect Dale. It was... juicy. Expect a call from Toby offering you his condolences for the loss of your dad and younger brother.

"You've won, Ms. Kuiper. Congratulations. I won't tell the others you issued the kill order. As you said, it's spilt milk. Going forward, I hope you remember which of your buddies kept their end of the deal."

It strode out of the room whistling an old, jaunty tune. Annette stared sidelong at the bag and finished her drink.

CHAPTER SEVENTY-SIX

Dale Alexander

Maggie had kept the scraps of Pia's clothes, but there was nothing usable. They had to make do with the hoodie I'd given them in the basement, but didn't complain. We got into the back seat of my car together and held each other while driving quietly to Kuiper Innovations. No one told Maggie what had happened, but she seemed to understand not to ask us.

I helped Janice transfer the books to the bag we'd brought in the trunk. We'd be leaving it with Annette, so I'd insisted on using something other than my own backpack. Good thing, since she probably wouldn't want to see the blood. Pia curled up in my lap when I got back in the car. I half-expected to see Cassie appear, but no such luck. She hadn't been seen since we left her upstairs in David Kuiper's house. Just Pia and the exaggerated wolf form they'd assumed. Wherever she'd gone, I hoped that she was well.

Janice returned, and we continued back to Aletheia. It handled explaining everything to Livinia while the rest of us dragged ourselves upstairs. While Pia showered, I helped Maggie get settled in the bedroom next to ours. From the goth and electronica posters plastered over the antique wallpaper, we assumed this was Janice's room. It didn't need to sleep, it seemed, so we were only imposing slightly.

When Pia came out of the bathroom, I took my turn. Magical plumbing had the benefit of never running out of hot water, and I stood under it for a long time. We were free from our pursuers, although the police were still sniffing around. We'd prepared in case of violence, but I didn't think even Janice had expected it would be that bad. The shooting had been terrifying, and I didn't know how I was going to deal with that feeling; I certainly couldn't tell Bastian about any of this. What Pia had done, though, that had been so much worse.

The absolute fury with which they'd attacked the Kuipers scared me. Killing the others had been ugly, but they'd done it efficiently and through need. It's not like they had anything but claws and fangs to use. And... the things I didn't want to remember. But I could accept that as unfortunate necessity. The Kuipers though, their own relatives, they'd attacked mercilessly and with no need. Nathaniel could have been easily subdued, and the other two had clearly been no threat.

I thought about everything that Pia had been through. They had been treated as an animal for around twenty-five years, caged and nameless, alone except for the negligent care of guards. I'd only known them for a few days, and they'd seemed so happy and cheerful for someone who'd been subjected to that. Of course it was going to be awful and violent when that all came out. Hadn't I always been super-aggressive when something poked at my trauma? I hadn't had a body made for rampaging, but I'd been outright abusive in defending myself against nothing. Therapy had helped me keep in touch with my feelings so I could act with more thought nowadays, but no one had ever helped Pia with their pain.

They needed help, and they needed support, and they needed love. I could give them those last two, and I'd tell them about the first. We'd ask Livinia and Janice for one last favor, to help us find someone who could provide the counseling Pia needed without reigniting drama with their family. They themself wanted to move forward and connect with the Kuipers, and I thought I saw now where they were coming from.

Abandonment must be an even bigger issue for them than it was for me, and with that I realized why I'd been trying to avoid our relationship. Yes, I had issues that made me fear losing them, but my focus on their inexperience hadn't been a deflection to protect myself. On some level I'd felt their desperate need, and I knew that casual dating or a fling would leave them devastated. If I stayed with them, I'd eventually have to commit fully or break their heart.

I turned off the water. What we'd lived through tonight had been far worse than a breakup, even than Liz calling me foul names and threatening to sue me for fraud over our marriage certificate. No, not worse than that, but horrid in a different way. The point was that we'd both been through some shit, and if it ever came to that we could survive without each other.

It's just that I wanted to be with them.

CHAPTER SEVENTY-SEVEN

Cassiopeia

I sat on the edge of the bed, wearing one of her shirts so my nudity wouldn't bother her like Pia's had last night. A lot of things made sense now that my mind was integrated. No longer a human and a spirit, I was something new that partook of both. I loved Dale, because we had both loved her, but I was the one who'd seen her fear. It wasn't just the way I'd lost control. That could be explained, although I'd never attempt to do so. I owed her so much better than playing to her emotions.

She'd been afraid of us all along. I mean to say of becoming close to me, or them. Reviewing our memories of Dale, she'd seemed to have overcome her initial hesitancy and started to return our affection this morning, but by afternoon she had withdrawn again. It might have just been how she'd dealt with the preparations for breaking into a house, but it had felt like a step backward. In the aftermath she'd been comforting, but it had been with the sense of friendship, not romantic interest. My wolf spirit half saw no problem—we were physically attracted to each other, what more was required?—yet it had never experienced love of this nature. As for my human side, it knew more about Detective Buster Grimes than it ever had about relationships.

I wanted to talk with Dale, to explain who I was now and allow her the opportunity to pull away, and if she stayed anyway I wanted her to help me try to break this bed. She came in, her tee and shorts sticking to her. She dropped her clothes in the corner and looked at me. Hope and misery warped her face, and she struggled to open her mouth.

"Dale, I love you."

I tried to sound reassuring, but she heard the qualifier coming.

"But?" she asked, defeat unifying her expression in sorrow.

"I'm not trying to leave you. I want us to be together... but I can't let you think I'm Pia."

She froze.

"You..."

I shook my head.

"I'm the two of them combined, Pia and Cassie. They both loved you so much, and when they thought you were in danger they decided to strengthen their bond. It was Cassie's idea, but Pia immediately agreed."

Dale sank to the ground.

"Pia's... gone."

I lowered myself to face her.

"Hey, no. No, I'm still here! They're here. It's just their thoughts, my thoughts, are Cassie's too. I'm not dead, just... more than before."

She watched me vacantly.

"You're not Pia, but you are. They're not gone, but they'll never come back. How am I supposed to feel? Who the fuck are you?"

That hurt, but I understood. If she couldn't accept me, I'd have to let her go, despite the heartache. But she hadn't left yet, and I wasn't ready to give up.

"Dale, I can't tell you how to feel. All I can do is remind you of what Janice said. Human and wolf spirit were always just parts of a whole. They're whole now. I'm... I'm Cassiopeia."

Her eyes flicked over me, possibly confirming that my body hadn't changed.

"You were always meant to be one?"

I nodded.

"With such a high degree of alignment, it was always going to happen."

She thought about that.

"Are you... are you happy?"

I shook my head.

"Honestly, I'm too scared of losing you."

I felt the tears welling and turned away. I didn't want to cry in front of her. Out of the corner of my eye, I saw her crawl over toward me. She sat down next me, not touching, but so close I could feel her warmth.

"I'm not going anywhere," she said. "You've finally discovered who you are, and that's incredible. I'm proud of you. I'm happy for you. And I'm excited to get to know the new you."

I let myself peek at her, searching her eyes. In them I saw earnestness and perhaps a touch of distress.

"You mean that?"

She reached out and squeezed my hand, leaning in closer.

"I do. I'm sorry. I only just realized what I was doing to you. Liz, my ex, she... didn't respond well to me becoming who I needed to be. I really liked both of you apart, but you need to be who you are now. You're Cassiopeia, and I'm here with you. For you."

Relief slackened my tense muscles, and I pressed my forehead against hers. We gazed into each other, and for my part I saw only tenderness.

"What do we do now?" I asked.

She flicked her tongue over the tip of my nose and grinned at me.

"I think we continue getting to know each other."

I swallowed down the excitement that started to build.

"Like, a date or something?"

"Or something," she purred.

She stood up and held out a hand to me. I took it and stood alongside her. We kissed, briefly at first, softly, as we worked out how to connect.

"Something consensual," she murmured into my lips. "We can slow down... or stop... whenever you want... and I'll never... stop... wanting you… Cassiopeia."

We stayed like that for a long time, consuming each other beside the bed, our hands desperately seeking sufficient purchase to hang on forever. One of hers pressed against my front thigh and stayed, and it was a while before I noticed that she had two hands feverishly occupied elsewhere. I pulled my head back, not far, and we panted hungrily as we locked eyes.

Slowly, I slid a hand down her body, squeezing and pinching everything I touched along the journey. Fear touched her eyes as I reached under her belly, and I kissed her as gently as we had at first. My fingers traced her lightly, fluttering, and she gasped, staggering against me. I held her tighter with my other hand and pressed more firmly.

"I'd like to continue this in the bed," I told her.

She agreed readily and sat quickly on the covers. I walked up and leaned over her, my arms supporting me as I pressed closer.

"We can slow down, if you want," I told her.

She lay back and pulled at my shirt.

"I'll try to keep up."

CHAPTER SEVENTY-EIGHT

Maggie Star

She could have gone to the show anyway and left Dale's weirdness alone. It would have been fun, with a lot less slaughter, and right now she'd be making out with one or more of her polycule, or even with someone completely new. That's not who she was though. She was helpful and inserted herself into people's drama, as though she could repair them like an AC unit on the fritz.

So now she got to lie awake, her mind filled with awful images seen through that ridiculous contraption, listening to what sounded like very enthusiastic sex in the next room. Good for them, really, but it was a little hard to take.

She rolled over and put the extra pillow over her head.

CHAPTER SEVENTY-NINE

Livinia Monroe

The immediate crisis had passed, and though the resolution had been bloodier than before the divergences, they'd been left on better terms with Annette Kuiper than in the previous aftermath. She remained motivated by greed and her son's well-being, but as long as those needs were met and unthreatened, she could be relied on to behave professionally to people not under her control. That had possibilities, and since Janice had encouraged her to take a more active role in the present, Livinia decided to act on one of them. A call to Nichole had set things in motion, and a week later they were now ready to announce the result.

Maggie had returned to the apartment complex, dropped off by Dale after a hearty breakfast the morning after their deadly encounter with the Kuipers. Toby had spun a tale to the police that approached implausibility without quite tipping into it. It involved a 160-pound wolf illegally imported from Russia, an attempted theft during transfer from Nathaniel to Tobias, and an ex-military contractor who took advantage of the situation. Perhaps he had been behind the botched initial attack. The police had seized on the explanation and sent out alerts for Derek Robinson and a giant wolf.

They'd learned all of this when Detective Arana returned with Detective Horst, who had been working the break-in and murder at Dale's place. The case remained open while they tried to identify Utley's accomplice, but it seemed the men had been hired by David Kuiper to find the missing cargo and had mistaken Dale's prank for a lead. Ironically, the wolf they'd been seeking had entered and attacked them. The new detective had asked again if Dale had seen the animal, and she hadn't ruled it out. That had satisfied them enough, and they'd told her that it was now safe to return to her apartment.

Cassiopeia, after revealing her new state, had accepted the offer to stay while Livinia searched for more about Lord Edmond Doherty's spell. Their successful union, combined with the images of the remaining artifacts—delivered by Annette, as promised—had given her more leads, and she'd begun to suspect that it had actually been an attempt at a boon. It would've had to have gone spectacularly wrong to have caused such lingering pain.

With her girlfriend staying on at Aletheia, Dale had given the Fuller Apartments notice that she'd be moving out. Livinia had turned the dressing room into a space for her to store her belongings. Another carload of books and clothes migrated every evening after dinner. Dale had even brought over her bedside picture of her ex-wife so that she could ritually burn it in the cellar with Cassiopeia.

Livinia had enjoyed being a participant during that time, watching her guests settle in and grow comfortable with themselves and each other. Cassiopeia especially fascinated her, because they'd always remained separate entities in the first history. They were very similar to how Pia would have become on their own in another decade, but their self-assurance coming so early in the relationship was changing the dynamic in interesting ways. They had always been a good couple, but now they were on their way to becoming a strong one as well.

That was a blessing not only for their own sake but for the troubles on the horizon. Recent events had been unexpectedly difficult, but the worst remained in the very near future. The potential histories still converged toward a cataclysmic event, ranging from a few months to a year away. It would come, and they had very few opportunities to pass through intact with a world they recognized.

Today would be the first step toward that outcome. Maggie had arrived and was talking animatedly with Dale and Cassiopeia in the sitting room. Janice sat with them, simply observing. There were two more invited, but she only expected one of them. Eager to get on with it, Livinia moved forward in time to the start of the meeting.

She stood in front of the fireplace, addressing the four assembled in the seats around it.

"I'd like to introduce the manager of the Jessup Foundation, my friend Nichole Cousin. She's going to explain the new venture that will be managed by the foundation with the help of an outside commercial interest. Please give her your full attention, and please hold your comments and questions for the end."

Nichole thanked her and began to lay out the business case. She shared the vision of researching strange events and helping people handle encounters with the unknown. They sat quietly while she explained how the corporate partnership would give them access to equipment and facilities they would not have otherwise and would allow consultations with professionals. She stressed that as a not-for-profit company there was no need for commercial concerns, and that the assistance of external grants and donations meant that salaries and benefits would be competitive. Offers would be forthcoming for all of them, as well as discussions about what their roles would entail. All contingent, of course, on their interest and acceptance. With that, she opened the floor to questions.

"Who's our corporate sugar daddy?" Janice asked.

Nichole had dealt with it before and answered without pause.

"Interim CEO Annette Kuiper of Kuiper Innovations is a member of the board and has pledged facilities, donations, and equipment to the company."

"And how often do we need to scratch her back?"

"There are protections in place to ensure the division between Kuiper Innovations and Societas Aenigmatum remains intact. The corporation may submit a request at any time, as may any legal entity, but its requests do not take any priority over other investigations."

"I don't understand why Annette didn't tell me about this at Kevin's game," Cassiopeia commented.

"Ms. Kuiper understands that it's best to not speak of legal arrangements until they're finalized, even to family."

"Can we talk about the name?" Maggie asked.

"No," Livinia answered.

Nichole smiled.

"The paperwork has already been filed. If you sign on to work for Societas Aenigmatum, you may of course petition upper management with suggestions."

"Which will not be approved," Livinia cautioned.

"What's it even mean?" Dale asked.

" 'Enigma Society,' " Janice said. "Or maybe 'Society of Enigmas.' My Latin's rusty."

Everyone turned toward it, some showing more curiosity than others.

"I got bored wrangling phone lines for a hundred years," it said.

Dale broke the silence that followed.

"I'm interested. I'd like to know more when you're ready to present the offers."

"Thank you, Miss Alexander."

As the arguments, and questions, and side conversations

continued, a consensus formed that they would all at least see what came next. Livinia took strength from their willingness to greet the uncertain future. She'd have to learn from their example as her past continued to fall away before her.

Epilogue: Jason Henderson

He lay in his cell, staring at the monitor above him. There was nothing else he could do. It was more of a cabinet than a room, a morgue drawer for a captive. He could wiggle, he could scoot up and down the one foot of extra length, and he could stare at the monitor encased behind protective plastic.

It came to life, and though it hadn't made any difference so far, Jason began to scream at it. He demanded his rights, he threatened his unknown captors, he pleaded, and the drab functionary on the screen continued its monotonous announcement.

"Jason Henderson, your deviant thoughts and behaviors have been determined to be beyond correction. Therefore you will receive a control module to monitor and override your executive functions. With that, you will be allowed limited reintegration as a productive member of society."

The encased monitor receded into the ceiling, and slim robotic arms wielding blades emerged from the darkness beyond. His screams became less coherent.

ALETHEIA - FIRST FLOOR

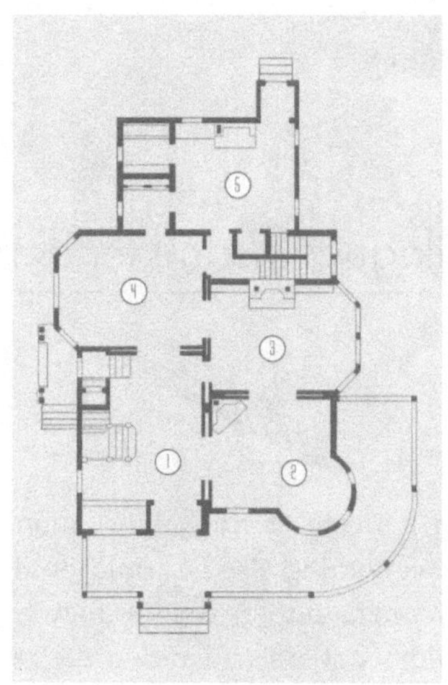

ALETHEIA - SECOND FLOOR

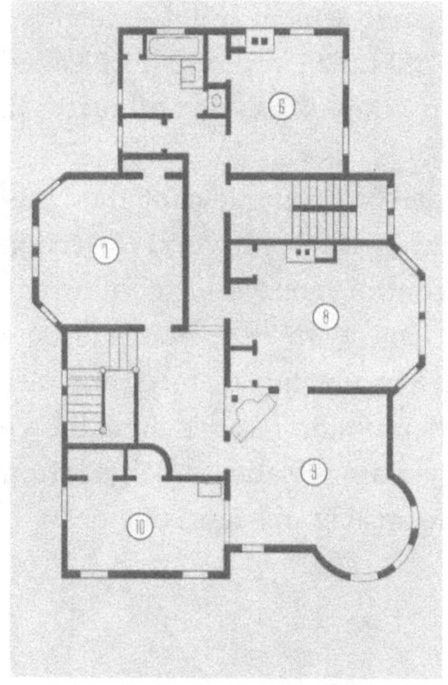

Aletheia Map Key

1. Main Entrance Hall
2. Parlor
3. Sitting Room
4. Dining Room
5. Kitchen
6. Computer Center
7. Library
8. Janice's Bedroom
9. Dale and Cassiopeia's Bedroom
10. Entertainment Center

Cast By Faction

GLOOMY APARTMENT FACTION

Dale Alexander
Cassiopeia
Maggie Star

ALETHEIA FACTION

Livinia Monroe
Janice Altura
Nichole Cousin

KUIPER FACTION

Tobias Kuiper
Tobias "Toby" Kuiper, Jr.
Annette Kuiper
David Kuiper
Kevin Kuiper
Nathaniel Kuiper

POLICE FACTION

Elena Arana
Charlotte Paris
Frank Horst

Faction Agents

TOBY KUIPER'S AGENTS

Derek Robinson

Briana Katt

Christopher Gordon

Jason Henderson

ANNETTE KUIPER'S AGENTS

Mike Lakeland

Patricia Markham

Gregory Tallman

Paul Fielding

Steve Campbell

Rick Chalmers

DAVID KUIPER'S AGENTS

Wes Utley

Lenny Tremain

Acknowledgments

This book exists because of the support and assistance of many people.

First and foremost to my wife, Wendi, who not only made the beautiful cover but created the floor maps of Althea from a page image of a 19th century issue of *Scientific American*. She also kept me supplied with coffee while I poked at the digital keyboard every morning.

Marcus Arena was invaluable as my alpha reader, giving me an audience to keep me writing and valuable feedback about what wasn't making sense and how worried he was about my imagination. I also relied on him to let me know when my ignorance of guns was showing.

This cleaned-up release was made possible by Chris Zable of CZ Edits, who I brought in to proofread after the limited release last year. Thank you, Chris!

A lot of people contributed very specific but important tidbits, even if they've forgotten. I'd like to thank Chris Piuma for help with Latin; C.M. Rosens for a discussion about narrative perspective; and L.A. Guettler for the use of the band name Strawberry Headache, which she dropped on us during a meme game. I'm afraid that Blueberry Nipple was my own contribution.

I'd also like to thank L.A. Guettler and Vivian Moira Valentine for being my beta readers. I'm extremely honored that such amazing talents agreed to provide feedback on my debut novel!

A hearty shoutout to the indie writing community on Bluesky, who accepted me as one of their own without question and have encouraged and supported me every step of the way. Abra, Dani, Ever, Helen, Lea, Quill, Soph, Sylver, Vivian, and many more that I'm getting to know as my network grows—thank you so much for giving me courage and cheering me on!

Lastly, thank you so much to my Patreon supporters, who joined before I had anything to show as a writer. I appreciate your faith in me, and I hope to continue fulfilling my promise to you as an author.

About the Author

Sadhbh Frost is a consulting programmer based in southeast Michigan, where she lives with her wife and cats—all of whom put up with an extraordinary amount of her nonsense. Her debut novel *The Wolf Bane* is informed by her dedicated viewing of horror and science fiction films of varying quality and coherency, which may explain her refusal to stay politely within genre lanes.

Her first name sounds like Jason Statham saying *scythe* to rhyme with *five*.

You can find Sadhbh on Bluesky to keep up with her every stray thought or on Patreon for news about her writing.

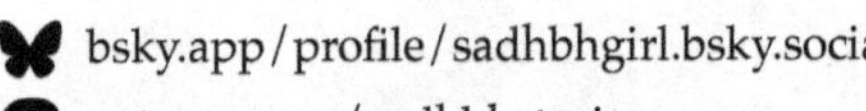

www.ingramcontent.com/pod-product-compliance
Lightning Source LLC
LaVergne TN
LVHW100512110826
845146LV00002B/612
* 9 7 9 8 9 9 5 8 1 8 6 2 5 *